J.T. [illegible]ARPER

UTOPIA'S EDGE

A WORLD DIVIDED

ISBN(s)
Paperback: 978-1-7365960-2-9
EBook: 978-1-7365960-3-6

Daugherty Press LLC

Daugherty
PUBLICATIONS

Special thanks to EV, LoriB,Sue, and Håkan. You know who you are and how much you have meant to me.

Contents

Chapter One

Wallyce stood between the Heaven of her Presidential Inauguration and the Hell, knowing she might make a fool of herself in front of the world. The entire world!

She could smell the snow in the air, her sharp instinct telling her that the world would soon be covered in the blanket of the angels, what her dad called it when she was a kid on a weekend ski trip. Then, the heaven of her childish joy was layered between the thick clouds of Hell that came with being General Tilton's daughter. There was no room for average. She'd either glide down the mountain with grace or stand for the at-attention lecture about mediocrity that was sure to be her punishment when she stopped at the lodge.

Today felt like that; terror mixed with a heaping layer of mile-high jubilation. Even though most people believed in her enough to vote for her, her deep-rooted sense of inadequacy gave her nightmares about the lecture, with a dose of failure added, her father would always give when she faltered. She would never allow herself to falter again.

"I, Wallyce E. Tilton, do solemnly swear that I will faithfully execute the Office President of the United States and will to the best of my ability, preserve, protect, and defend the Constitution of the United States, so help me God." As she spoke those words, repeated by every incoming President, she thought, I mean this with all my heart. Wallyce was convinced she believed in America.

Chief Justice Amira Langford reached out her hand to congratulate the newly sworn-in President. "Congratulations, Madam President."

Wallyce turned to face the crowd stretching beyond the reflecting pool's end. This crowd was only a fraction of the millions who applied but had to be turned away for safety.

There wasn't any room for them to stand anywhere in the visual range of the Capitol Building anyway. Wallyce Tilton was the most popular President ever elected.

The roar of the crowd was deafening. Wallyce bathed in love from the people she would now serve with everything she had in her. Finally, her promise to serve as the President of the People would be fulfilled. She intended to guide America through the most complex, significant restructuring the United States had ever seen. She raised her hands and signaled to the crowd to allow her to speak. "Please," she smiled, "please . . . thank you . . . I'm humbled. Thank you."

It took a full minute for the crowd to settle. As the roar softened to a whisper, Wallyce became aware of another sound—the humming, buzzing stream of dozens of Secret Service drones well above the crowd. Their ultra-high-density laser-focused cameras fed a steady upload of images and sound to the centralized Homeland Ident Secure Server

(HISS). Hundreds of thousands of pictures would be processed and matched against the database of known bad characters and potential threats to the country's security. Wallyce had been briefed only last week about this particular threat-prevention system. She knew that even with close scrutiny, many criminals and terrorists could sneak into the gathering today. It comforted her that most criminals would be apprehended long before the event began this morning. Any creeps who might have somehow avoided detection in the first round would be easy marks for the system now. Scanning would be fast and perfect because the people all sat with their faces pointed in the same direction. Wallyce also knew these "ate catches" would be grabbed for verification and escorted off the mall to the waiting vans. Following a long pause, she began to speak to the people who elected her.

"I am proud to be your President. I'm also overwhelmed. Please forgive me if I pause occasionally to figure out what to say to many great people as you sit here waiting for me to say something smart." Ironically, this was a smart thing to say. It established that she would speak from the heart, not from any polished script. The crowd laughed and clapped at the same time. "All I can think is that I'm humbled to be the one you chose to lead America into a new world order in which we make decisions based on science, technology, and our desperate need to save this planet for future generations. My fellow Americans, I'm ready to accept that challenge immediately." She stepped back while the crowd let loose with their shouts and applause. She knew they loved her. She wanted them to believe that she loved them right back. A trickle of tears was visible to the first few rows of guests, and the cameras soon picked them up for all to see on the giant screens. She tried to explain why she, the most powerful leader in the world, would allow such a show of weakness, as her father would say.

"Please forgive my emotions. Today I remember one of the most outstanding leaders I have known, my dad, General Elliott Tilton. Dad was the former Chairman of the Joint Chiefs and one of the nicest people I ever knew. He taught me to be strong in the face of chaos. And with Mom, they gave me the gift of love of nature. Every day is an opportunity to do all I can to be like them. They would be thrilled to see that their two daughters, myself and Morrígan, were elected as your President and Vice President. I speak for the two of us when I say we promise to lead this country in a way that would make our parents proud."

"As announced, I've decided to break with tradition and forego any inaugural balls. Instead, I will donate the amount it would have cost to put on the traditional parties to build a new village right here in neighboring Virginia. That community will be called New Hope City. It will be a fully functioning community with all services and homes given freely to the next cohort waiting in line for Homeless Relief Housing. One of my primary missions is to provide for those less fortunate and to place the needs of our fellow life travelers ahead of our own.

"Now, I'd like to share some of our current thinking. As you know, we're far too invested in tradition, formalities and ceremonies that are a mark of bureaucracy. We must bring the United States to a position where we can act and react to opportunities. We can no longer be handicapped by the restrictions of outdated tradition kept in place by our current bloated government—a government designed to enrich the few and take away from the many. We listen to a history that speaks of a strong middle class in America. This original democracy allowed the masses to live comfortably as a reward for their hard work and ingenuity. We listen and dream of returning to that way of life. We long for it, but we've never experienced that world. We destroyed the middle class long ago. Our society came to a screeching halt due to massive corporate greed. Business Gods became Government Devils who enacted laws that favored the rich and cursed all unfortunate enough to be part of the lower-class masses. Soon, there was no more middle class. It became impossible for hard-working people to earn enough to live on without the handouts of a government that forced them to beg for the necessities of life. The rich got richer, and the rest were damned to live at the mercy of government aid, a life of barely enough."

She let her words hang out in the deafening silence. She knew what they must have been thinking, and she wanted that to sink in. "Yes . . . you're right. I'm wealthy. I'm the richest person you'll ever see up close. Left to that, I'm part of the problem—a huge problem. To most people, I represent the abuse of wealth. But I don't apologize for my success. I celebrate my opportunity. And I'm here to tell you that my tax dollars alone could feed well over the population of a small state. But my plans call for so much more. I have dedicated myself to providing opportunities for those without any, providing food and housing for our employees and their families, and a future they can depend on. That's why I ran for office in the first place.

"Oh, I know I could just give all my money to the poor and homeless. I could donate to medical research, fund education, and much more. But that would be a dead-end path. Once my money was gone, someone else would have to fill the gap. Without that, the process would just continue—handouts and control. But, as President, I'll be able to drive legislation to change the rules, to force commerce back to a time when we all had a chance at life. Then, each of us can make a living and be proud we saved the American Dream for one and for all. The rebirth of the successful middle-class is my vision for America. Please help us get there. Thank you, and may God Bless America."

Morrígan stood next to Wallyce as the crowd stood as one. The applause continued until they left the podium and were rushed to the White House for a meeting Wallyce had called for with important government officials. Her plan was to set the tone for her Administration, and that tone would not sit well with many of them.

Once in the Presidential Limo, the Beast, Wallyce called for an instant update on the press reaction to her inaugural speech.

"Breaking News," she joked to the communication system built into the vehicle. The divider window between the Beast's front and rear sections turned opaque, then displayed the Presidential Seal. A voice asked, "Number of sources, please." Wallyce replied, "Four." Immediately, four news source windows lit up the screen. She pointed her finger at the second news window. The other three windows shrunk to thumbnail size in the lower corner of the active screen.

An interview was taking place. It was a reporter named Audrey Shen interviewing a couple who had just left the mall from the inauguration. "We are here with the Roseman family at the inauguration today. Hi, folks. What's your impression of President Tilton's speech?"

"Hi, Audrey," Mrs Roseman replied. "I loved her speech.

She's such a great lady. She reminds me of my younger sister. She also wants to help everyone else."

Audrey turned toward the camera. "Thank you for your insight, Mrs. Roseman." Now fully into the camera, "And there you have it. No matter how many people I have asked, everyone now supports our new President, Wallyce Elliott Tilton. Her promises to restructure our government, secure living wages for all, and bring back the strong middle class truly resonate with this crowd. I'm Audrey Shen. Back to you."

Wallyce called for her Virtual Assistant. "Goh, activate."

"Yes, Madam President, Goh is active," came the reply as the screen reflected the Presidential Seal again.

"Poll on the results of the Inaugural Speech," she ordered.

Goh displayed several charts onscreen. "In favor, 87% of early polling results."

"Goh, deactivate and standby." The screens faded, and the divider returned to see-through status as the Beast passed through the rear gates to the White House. Wallyce nudged Morrígan, who announced, "Welcome home, Madam President." It was a private joke they had agreed on last night. "And I will say, you also remind me of Mrs Roseman's younger sister." They had a laugh at Mrs Roseman's expense.

It hardly felt like a welcome home. Dozens of reporters and camera operators formed a wall that the Secret Service skillfully moved aside to allow Wallace and Morrígan to pass through into the rear Portico entrance to the White House. Shouted questions made a sound that would soon become a familiar backdrop to both women as they ventured into public areas.

Wallyce noticed that Morrígan maneuvered skillfully through the crowd, barely missing a step, as she moved directly with her two Secret Service agents. She envied her sister for her ease and grace in public. For Wallyce, things weren't so coordinated. Her stumbling hesitancy resulted from the lingering trauma of a previous attempt on her life at the kickoff event for her candidacy. Now, she hoped no one could see her body tremble as the memory of that horrible day flashed through her mind. She was starting to lose her composure—about to look like the scared little girl she felt inside. Finally, a strong arm pulled her in. It guided her toward the staircase that led into the South Portico of the White House, where she could compose herself before meeting with the selection of Senators, Representatives, and certain lobbyists handpicked by Wallyce for this initial gathering. She looked to her savior, a Secret Service Agent. She was beginning to appreciate the Secret Service.

Patrick Lemieux, Chief Usher, met them at the staircase. "Welcome, Madam President, Madam Vice President. Your guests have begun to arrive, mostly through holographic images, as you have instructed. The hologram platform is in the East Room, where your Press Secretary has introduced them to your meeting agenda. Please, allow the aide to lead you to where you may freshen up if desired. Otherwise, we can go directly to the East Room." He bowed to President Tilton.

Still shaken, Wallyce wasn't ready to face the government power brokers. "Yes, I'd like to freshen up." She turned to an aide, a young woman dressed in a simple business suit. "Please lead on." The aide crossed the hallway and started up the stairs. Wallyce waited to see her turn back and motion for them to come forward. "Good," thought Wallyce.

They told her. I hope all staff know to check before leading me into a blind area. No sense in taking chances, is there? She nodded to Morrígan, and they headed up the stairs to a dressing room where the aide had placed fresh coffee and water on the side table for them. "Thanks," she waved to the aide, who left on cue. She couldn't wave off the Secret Service agents. They were never more than a few steps away, and no power in the world would come between them and the President—not even the President herself.

"Morrígan, this is just so weird to me. I mean, I'm the President now, but the White House? Holy crap." They giggled like they used to when they were teens.

Vice President Morrígan Meath Tilton, surname bestowed by her adoptive parents, was in awe of her sister Wallyce. Over the past few years, she understood the near-magical combination of business instinct and charisma Wallyce used to grow her business and financial domains to unimaginable proportions. Industry, business, and technology leaders would fall in line with her army of devout supporters, like cult members. This magic enabled Wallyce to become the wealthiest and most respected business leader the world had ever seen.

"Wally," I'm so proud of you. Nothing scares you, not just because of what you've done, but for the person you are." I'm looking at being the Vice President and wondering if I'm up to the job. I've no idea how I got this job. Well, that's not true—I know, it's President's sister syndrome. If I wasn't your sister, I'd never think of running, much less winning." She waited for Wallyce to agree.

Wallyce knew Morrígan was right. Morrígan was a great leader, charming and well-regarded—a sweetheart to all who knew her. But Vice President? For her reasons, Wallyce's selection of Morrígan as her running mate was bold. Morrígan's warm and calculated way of speaking and genuine warmth balanced with Wallyce's abrupt decision-making style, intuitive and quick to act, firing off decisions like a string of firecrackers, leaving the people around her trying to figure out if they heard her correctly. The team of Morrígan-to-Wallyce gave conservatives comfort, while the progressives liked Wallyce's snap decisions and radical insights.

"Morrí, let's take a reality check here." Hoping to show her sister support, she felt it was time to drop the formal Morrígan in favor of the familiar Morrí. "You have two doctorate degrees and success as the founding CEO of Tilton Fund. In addition, you've spent ten years as the Founder of The Daylight Project, which has enabled tens of thousands of low-income kids to graduate from college and become successful employees and employers. So, I think you have more than the profile for the Vice Presidency. I'm lucky you didn't run against me. You're the perfect choice as Vice President." She watched her sister. The slight blush on Morrígan's cheeks told Wallyce that Morrí knew she was great at her businesses but needed support more frequently as the campaign wore on. It was a result of being second in command, Wallyce guessed. And she liked that positioning. She knew Morrígan would be easier to control when the org chart placed her second in order. There'd be less chance that Morrígan would keep questioning her decisions.

"Morrí," Wallyce said. "I never dreamed we'd end up at the top of the world. Oh, I know. When we were kids, we'd talk about what it must be like to be grownups? And we pretended we were princesses and had everyone bow to us when we entered the room? We never thought for real we'd become like American Royalty." Right?"

Morrígan thought hard about that. Yeah, she thought, I remember. But I recall that you made me curtsy to you, and then there was the time you made up that you would become the Queen. You made me call you Your Majesty for a whole week. You told me you'd tell the General I was being mean to you if I didn't comply. But she didn't say it out loud. She wasn't the type to hurt someone's feelings so casually. Instead, she said, "Yeah. I remember."

Wallyce's wristband vibrated, alerting her that the Meet and Greet with the invited powerbrokers had started in the East Room. The details were announced softly into her ear implants. The initial meeting of guests begins in two minutes. Please go to the Meeting Communication Center in the East Room of the White House. A second vibration let her know the message had ended.

"Morrígan, we need to head to the meeting." She tapped the "Guide" button on her wristband to display the positioning markers leading her to the East room meeting. A series of laser-drawn guide markers came to life on the floor of her room, lighting a path to follow to the East Room. Only she could see these marker lines. Her optical technologist tuned them to the same spectrum bandwidth as the lens implants in her eyes. Wallyce had been so impressed with this technology that she acquired the patent rights several years earlier. This technology's explosive success proved to be the platform she used to build her financial empire. To this day, it remains one of her most vital successes ".

As they walked the main hall from the dressing room to the East Room, Secret Service agents scanned the area to ensure nothing was out of place and there were only people there who should be. Two agents opened the doors as they approached the East Room, visually scanned it, and stepped back to allow the President to enter. Formerly a banquet and concert hall, the East Room had since been converted into an elaborate Official Communications Center. In the center of the room stood an oval desk with a half dozen oversized leather chairs, each bearing the person's plaque whose seat it was, gathered around it.

The most formal chair, positioned closest to the doors and facing the rest of the room, was marked 'President Wallyce E. Tilton.' To her side was a chair for Vice President Morrígan M. Tilton. The rest of the chairs at that table were for the Press Secretary, The White House Chief of Staff, and the Presidential Assistants.

There was a striking absence of any other chairs or tables. Instead, the facility team fitted the room with several larger raised platforms. This enabled the President and Vice President to see anyone who might be present in a virtual sense. The Secret Service briefed Wallyce on the process. These platforms were VR projection areas where participants would be represented virtually through holographic projection.

Wallyce and Morrígan joined the others at the desk. A nod from Wallyce to the Press Secretary was the signal to open the room to all participants. Images began to fill the space as the projection systems displayed all participants, first from the Senate. The House of Representatives, and select cabinet members. Finally, guests from the financial world and large businesses filled the room's balance.

This event wasn't the first time Wallyce or Morrígan participated in such a virtual gathering. Wallyce used them frequently in her business dealings. The Senate, Pentagon, and Supreme Court had transitioned from in-person meetings to this preferred virtual style. It just made sense and was the safest way to gather. Radical groups would no longer be able to attack specific governmental groups since these large groups rarely met in person. The Virtual Assembly Act allowed the government to operate at an efficiency level never before possible. At first, thought to be risky and too informal, technology soon became the preferred method of high-level operations.

Throughout the hall, ghostly images became increasingly visible—not quite opaque but no longer transparent. For the newcomer to this technology, the process could be somewhat strange. Still, after things started and discussions continued, you could almost forget you were speaking to a projected image. When all attendees were in place, a voice announced, "Ladies and Gentlemen, the President and Vice President of the United States, Wallyce Tilton, and Morrígan Tilton." The participants rose to their virtual feet and gave welcoming applause to the new Administration. To Wallyce, it was a kind of royal bow.

Wallyce took control. She told them she was here to launch a fast start to her administration, and although it was nice that the participants paid their respects, she was all business. "Thank you, and now please be seated," she announced over the applause. "We need to make some announcements, and I have much to do before I leave for California tomorrow morning." A low rumbling sound came from all corners as everyone took their seats, asking each other if they heard her right. Was she leaving Washington, D.C., the day after her inauguration?

"Yes, I'm heading to California tomorrow. We're in the final stages of constructing my new headquarters, and I must be there. But, as you all know, there is no reason I can't be here, just as you are here now. I would guess that fewer than ten percent of you are anywhere near Washington in the flesh right now. Do any of you think your virtual participation is in any way limiting? Anyone? No? Then why would it be limiting for me to operate in virtual mode?"

Senator Bill Argen's name imprinted on the wall above him, a sign that he would like to be recognized. Wallyce looked at the Senate Majority Leader, pressing a button on her desk to allow him to take the floor. "Go ahead, Leader Argen."

"Thank you, Madam President, and let me offer my congratulations. My caucus and I rise in support of your plan to work remotely. We agree that there is no compelling reason for you to lock yourself into any one location. I would also support a buildup of the Secret Service on a more permanent basis in the San Francisco Bay Area to fully protect you when you are there. I will pose that for discussion when the Senate reconvenes." He took his seat.

"Thank you, Leader. Does anyone else wish to speak?" Names were lit up all over the board from all groups. Wallyce decided to go right to the top for the first question. She called on the Senate Minority Leader to speak.

"Senator Sizemore, please feel free to speak," Wallyce said.

The Senator's image was highlighted as he stood. "First, Madam President, I welcome you to Washington. I offer my heartfelt congratulations to you and your sister on your inauguration. I regret that I must stand against both your proposed move to California and your continued stance against the divestiture of your business holdings.

"About the proposed relocation, your position disregards hundreds of years of American tradition that places the heart of our government, the Executive Branch, in the most widely recognized building in the world, the American White House. We might wonder why, except you so easily give us the answer. You intend to relocate to the heart, not of the American Government, but of your massive and complicated business empire, Barca Holdings Corporation.

"Next, concerning the potential for your business holdings interests, it's clear to most of us that your refusal to divest your businesses or at least place them into a blind trust during your term of office poses a genuine potential that you might be persuaded to make decisions that would favor your business bottom line even when such decision could be in opposition to the best interests of the American people. There's no doubt that the references to Emoluments in several clauses of our Constitution were explicitly written to prevent that from happening.

"Many of my associates and I reject the notion that you can simply uproot the Executive branch to move it to California, where you can spend much of your time running Barca Holdings without placing the companies in a blind trust. We would like to hear your response before you hop aboard Air Force One and abandon the heart of this government." The Senator took his virtual seat.

Wallyce remained seated as she absorbed this direct frontal assault from the opposition. Then, still sitting, she began.

"Thank you, Senator Sizemore. I'll be happy to update you," she said. "You are referring to the constitutional clauses that specify detailed requirements of officials to avoid taking or holding any gifts, payments, etc., from foreign governments or domestic entities. The clauses outline that high-level elected officials must place the people's interests before theirs. Many in history have tried to profess that the ownership of multi-national companies such as Barca Holdings poses an enormous risk for the President. The theory, I suppose, is that I might be swayed to make business decisions that would further enrich Barca Holdings but might be against the best interests of our country.

"If we had time, I might be tempted to give you a history lesson, Senator and all who agree with this sentiment. But unfortunately, that lesson would cover more than two centuries of American Presidencies, in which case after case has been brought before the courts in an attempt to force the President to divest into blind trusts.

"Two significant truths came out of this. One that the Constitution only suggests how we should proceed in the case of emoluments or gifts—bribery of any type; it does not require any such restriction – anywhere. The law did not subject the President to its divestiture requirements, even back to the Ethics in Government Act of 1978. Many through the ages have voluntarily divested into such trusts, but they were not legally required to do so.

"Second, please think it through, Senator. Here's the scene: I divest Barca Holdings into a blind trust. Now, I'm powerless to decide how to run the company for a time, even though I still own it. Next, a foreign government proposes that I look the other way on a bill that might be detrimental to that foreign country. Finally, if I comply, there is a promise of a significant purchase of Barca's products. Remember, I can't make decisions for Barca, but I still own Barca, and will benefit from such a sale. Any blind trust management team might take such a large deal just for the financial benefit. It happens all the time in government. Many of your associates practice this every day. Look at the lobbying system. How many Senators leave to take high-level jobs with the companies that lobbied them for years? Your best recourse, then, is to accept that I will act in America's best interests. You can and should prosecute me to the full extent of the law if I relinquish that duty to add to my corporate bottom line.

"So here we are, stuck back in the thinking of the early 2000s, trying to handcuff a President who might just be the best thing that happened to this country. To that proposal, I say no. Please feel free to use the courts to try to stop my plan. Are there any other questions?" No one was willing to touch their "Question" button, so no names were lit as if asking to speak. Wallyce proceeded.

"I'm in the process of vetting my final cabinet selections. I thank Congress in advance for its support in confirming my nominations, and I look forward to hitting the ground running. My communication channels are always open to you. At Barca City, we have created a channel for our efficiency, through advanced technology. This can be used to contact me through the channel with the code name of Goh, a fully capable Artificial Intelligence that can be used for nearly any application I or the Vice President may have. In the recent past, as I'm sure you are all painfully aware, the Executive Office was required to have a staff of hundreds, on call night and day, to perform thousands of functions, great or small ranging from simple communications to complex research, from the minutiae of scheduling to the wide-ranging need for decision-based negotiations. Although Goh is dedicated to the needs of the President and Vice President, he is a valuable addition to our Administration Staff. You will each be receiving an introductory contact from Goh, with instructions to let you know how to access him, and a list of basic requests he can handle on my behalf. Feel free to introduce yourself and become familiar with this new staffing miracle.

"And now, please let us know how we can best serve you and the American public. Again, thank you for your welcome and your support. Sorry to be abrupt, but there is much to do. I will let you all leave with my thanks and highest regards."

Wallyce cut off the projections suddenly. Press Secretary Caton Arana, let out an audible gasp. "You'll get used to it, Caton. I like to avoid predictability when possible. It keeps people from getting too comfortable and forces them to listen to everything I need them to hear. Plus, I'm not a fan of explaining myself too often. It's a waste of time." To prove her point, Wallyce smiled, turned, and walked away. Morrígan followed.

Chapter Two

Wallyce tended toward privacy—rather odd for such a public figure. Maybe private wasn't the best descriptor. It was more like she only let people know what she wanted them to know. Driven by her sense of inadequacy, Wallyce was sure that if the public could see her for what she was—the fraud she had become, they would see the real Wallyce Tilton. But, of course, they wouldn't like what they saw. Imposter syndrome. At least, that's what Dr. Sebastian diagnosed. How else to explain how the most powerful, most successful woman could feel the least bit inadequate?

Wallyce projected confidence, but it was a mask she often hid behind. She feared that if anyone knew the real Wallyce Tilton, they'd see she could not lead a country back to its former greatness. But, at last, her years of therapy were having a positive effect. More frequently, she could venture out of her self-imposed shell and have at least a private moment with another human. Usually, the target of her "outings" was Morrígan, her sister. She felt she could talk to

Morrígan despite her resentment toward her. She believed Morrígan somehow stole her parent's affection from her, but she saw Morrígan as one she could "come out" to in terms of her fears.

Her mind flashed to Dr. Sebastian, her other sounding board. She remembered her appointment to sit with him for a session before they headed to California. "Morrígan," she said, "I have a few things to do before we leave in the morning. You know, papers to sign, briefings to read . . . I'll try to get them done this afternoon, then we should grab a quick dinner before our first night in the White House. You can use the Lincoln Bedroom, and I'll sleep in the Presidential residence. Let's try to meet for dinner at about seven. Meet me in the Family Dining Room. The Aide can point the way. In the meantime, why not have a tour?"

Wallyce noticed the hair on Morrígan's arms bristle. She knew Morrígan resented being given instructions and even orders from her. She watched as Morrígan moved her arms under the table in front of her. "Good idea, Madam President."

"Please, don't call me that. I'm Wallyce to you in private and maybe President Tilton in public."

"Okay, Wallyce. See you at dinner." Morrígan turned and walked to the entrance hall to summon the Aide. Wallyce called for Todd Lyman, her personal secretary.

"Todd, please have the Oval Office Dining Room set coffee and snacks for me. I'll be meeting virtually with my personal adviser. I don't wish to be disturbed. And have all recording devices in the room silenced. This is a private meeting. Please have it ready in fifteen minutes."

"Yes, Madam President." He left immediately.

Wallyce tapped the comm button on her wristband. She

heard the familiar greeting of her old friend, Dr. Sebastian. "Good Day, Madam President."

"Sebastian, you know better than that."

"Sorry, Wallyce. I was being cautious in case you were with other people."

"You needn't ever fear that. I'll only call you when I'm in private. I'll call in a few minutes when I can focus on our meeting." She tapped to end the call. She noticed her Secret Service members were attentive. She forgot they were always nearby.

"What you just heard was confidential. You will not repeat any of it to anyone."

"Yes, Madam President," Agent Nguyen gave a slight bow of his head. "You'll come to know that we will never repeat anything we see or hear unless it poses a grave danger to you."

"That's fine, Agent Nguyen. By the way, I need to set some rather personal and specific instructions. I understand that you and the team have a long-standing and exact protocol for protecting the President. I'm pleased. I'll read your manual on my flight to the west coast, and if I have any questions, I'll ask you for clarification. I understand that you're scheduled to travel with me, correct?"

"Yes, Ma'am."

"Good. Perhaps you can just brief me instead of me reading the whole document. But, for now, I need to establish my own protocol for private meetings."

"Ma'am?"

"Yes. There will be personal meetings not directly connected to my service as President. You understand I serve as a business person and investor in many other capacities?"

"I am aware," Nguyen nodded.

"These personal meetings are to be just that—personal. I will meet in private, sometimes online, sometimes in person. None of the Secret Service are in the room during these meetings. I understand you might have a problem with that, but that's how it will be. Understood?"

"Yes, President Tilton. Understood. But, not agreed."

"I beg your pardon?"

"The President does not have the authority to give orders to the Secret Service, especially when the safety of the President might be at risk. We can develop a plan whereby you feel secure that you are in private and that your words and actions are protected. But, you may not order how we are to protect you. Forgive my abruptness, but I need to be certain that you understand. This is not negotiable."

Wallyce thought for a while, smiled, then nodded softly. "Thanks, Agent Nguyen. I suspect it will take a while to familiarize myself with the protocol. However, I do have a pressing appointment now. I will meet a gentleman virtually in the Oval Office Dining room for about a half hour. This meeting is online but of a very private nature. Would it be okay if you stayed outside the door and I went in and met with him? Is this plan going to work for you?"

"I'm sorry. There will be at least one agent in the room. And, in the future, all such meetings must be scheduled through me."

"Thank you. Future meetings will be part of my schedule, which Todd Lyman will maintain when I am here, and Goh, my virtual assistant, will when I'm in California. Now, I must meet with my counsel on a private channel." She headed toward the West Wing. Nguyen and his team followed, a respectable distance behind her. As she approached the entrance to the dining room, Nguyen breezed past her, silently slipped into the room, returned, and stepped aside to let her enter.

"The room is unoccupied, President Tilton, except for the food server. I'll be happy to show your guest in when he arrives."

"Thank you, Agent Nguyen. He will only be here in virtual form, so you don't need to show him in." Wallyce entered the room, and the door closed behind her. She smiled at the food server. "Might I have a coffee, black and very hot?"

"Of course, Madam President." He pulled a chair away and helped her be seated. He prepared her coffee, set it on the table, added a plate of cookies, gave her a bow, and backed up to stand next to the serving table.

"I'm sorry, I didn't catch your name," she said.

"I'm usually just called Smith. It's my last name."

"Well, Smith, I'd rather call you by your first name. No need for us to be so formal."

"Yes, ma'am. I am William Smith."

"Then I'll call you William. So, William, you may leave the rest to me. I can pour a coffee if needed, and the cookies are perfect should I wish to eat. I will let you know when we've finished." She noticed one member of the Secret Service team had entered through the service entrance. She had taken position just inside the door, listening yet being as unobtrusive as possible. "Thank you, William."

"Yes, ma'am." He looked around to be sure all was in place, then, smiling, he left.

He wasn't gone a minute when Wallyce's comm screen lit up.

Wallyce watched as a man appeared on the screen. He was what might be considered a short, average build, with a complexion that seemed to suffer from perpetual sunburn. He sat in front of the camera and began to fidget with the pen he would use to take notes. As soon as he spotted President Tilton, his demeanor softened, and he smiled broadly.

"Ah, Wallyce. So good to see you. I watched the inauguration from the cheap seats. I wanted to watch the people's reactions. You didn't disappoint one bit."

"Hello, Dr. Sebastian," she said in a low voice. She thought it best to keep their conversation as private as possible. She was comforted that his voice would only be heard by her, in her ear implants. They gave each other a slight bow of the head—their traditional greeting. Wallyce opened. "Of all the times I needed you, this one tops the list. You might not see him, but a gentleman is standing in the far corner of the room, not looking at us directly; however, you should know he is there for my protection. It's one of the burdens of office, I'm told. However, they assure me that I may speak in perfect confidence, and they will never repeat what we say. You okay with this, Sebastian?" The agent glanced up with a puzzled look on his face.

"Whatever you are comfortable with, it's okay with me. But why not just use text instead of voice?"

"That's a good question, Sebastian, but it won't work. There are more cameras in this and every other room than you might imagine. No doubt, they can easily see every keystroke. So, we'll just keep the voice level low. But thanks for the question."

"My pleasure," he replied. "I wondered if the pressure of today would rattle you or not. So, as usual, what was the worst and best of the day?"

Taking a sip from her coffee, she thought of his question. "Well, the worst was the meeting I just had with the power brokers here in D.C. Mostly, it was the Senators. What a stuffy bunch of arrogant jerks. So, when I sprung it on them that I'd be centralizing my administration in Barca City, I felt like my hands were shaking so much, they might have noticed."

"And, how did you cope with it?"

"I didn't. I closed the meeting abruptly and shut down the holograms before they knew I was doing it. I know it was a dumb move, and I probably came off as an arrogant ass, but it just happened, and I couldn't stop it." She looked down into her coffee as if she could hide inside the cup.

"Okay. Now tell me. What was the best of the day?"

"Oh, Sebastian, there were so many great things. My head is spinning. First, When I announced the building of New Hope City for the unfortunate poor and homeless, the crowd loved it. Then, on the way here, the polls closed in on an eighty-seven percent approval rating. Can you imagine eighty-seven percent? But finally, standing up there on the Capitol Steps, next to Morrígan, took the award. Morrígan Tilton, Vice President. Too much."

"Proud of her, aren't you?"

"Huh? Oh. Sure, I'm proud. But it's not that. It means I don't have to worry about some pain-in-the-ass V.P. always trying to prove they're smarter, better, stronger than I am. It means I can streamline the processes of government. It means I gave my father what he made me promise to give—that I would always protect and support Morrígan after he was no longer around to do it himself. So, now, I've made good on that. She's on her own from here on."

Sebastian looked worried. His brow tightened so his eyebrows met in the middle, and he tapped his nose. "I sense a great deal of anger. Would you like to explain?"

"What's to explain? You and I have chatted about this so often that it gets boring. I don't like her. In fact, I dislike her as much as my parents loved her. Who could love someone who was your playmate one day and your sort-of-sister the next? Someone who just flat-out invades your family and makes it her family? Someone who had no business taking your father's affection for you and making it her own." At this point, she could feel the old anger rising.

Wallyce, you're right. We've talked about your anxiety over this. I know you blamed her for a loss of affection from your father. But do you believe that? Isn't there a part of you that unfairly blames an orphan girl for your shortcomings? Sorry, Wallyce. I've promised you to always be truthful and to pull no punches. You know damn well that you must put this pain in the past. It's not as terrible as you paint it to be. Some may even say that you were driven by it. Perhaps this jealousy even drove you as far and as high as you've come. But you need to let it go now. It's becoming an obsession, and we know where that leads. Drop the rock, friend, or it will crush you."

"I have, Sebastian. I dropped it when I nominated her as V.P. Now everyone will see how powerful I am and how much of a fraud she is."

"Are you setting her up for failure?

"No. Morrígan will do that all by herself. Like all Vice Presidents before her, she'll be given specific projects to manage independently. I'll give her a few softballs—already completed projects that she can take credit for. Then, when she feels confident, I'll drop the heavyweight project on her. I'm not sure what it will be yet, but she's certain to come out on the losing end of it. Then the world will know how incompetent she is." She looked up at the screen and scowled at Sebastian. Then, Wallyce stood. "Sebastian, when do you arrive back in the Bay Area?'"

"I leave here in two days. Should I call you when I arrive?

"No. I'll call if I need you. I'll meet with my sister for my first Presidential Dinner. This should be fun."

They repeated the head-bows. "I am so glad you came, Sebastian. I feel better already. See you next week, friend."

Dr. Sebastian faded from Wallyce's screen.

The Secret Service agent knew he must put this into his report. It was going to be a different report, for sure.

Chapter Three

Wallyce tripped backward—the sort of running-falling trip you know can't end well. But still, you try; arms flailing, emergency-level groan pushed out of the lungs, head-turning, trying to see where the crash landing will happen. But at the final drop, an angel swooped in to lift her back to her feet, truly a miracle. Or maybe, not so much. Wallyce came to rest in the beat-up old chair that Morrígan had guided her into at the last possible second. The chair must have been put there by one of the construction managers.

"Guess I got here just in time," Morrígan said as she looked around at the construction-style minefield her sister had been tripping around. "It's probably a bad idea to walk backward dozens of stories above the Bay in a mess like this, and there's nothing to keep you from falling over the edge into the water below." She faked a formal bow. "But, who am I to tell you what to do, Madam President?"

"Again, dear sister, don't call me that unless we're in

public," Wallyce said. And I don't want to keep reminding you, Madam Vice President," she said sarcastically.

"Okay, I'll try to remember, but it's pretty cool to think of you as the President of the U.S., even with all the other superhero titles you carry around inside that inflated ego. So, the question burns my unworthy brain. What makes you want to take such a chance to walk around up here before the outer shell's installed?"

Ignoring the question, Wallyce reached out to shake Morrígan's hand. "So, I'm talking to the actual Vice President. Should I call you Madam Vice President?"

"No," Morrígan replied. "Okay, I get it."

Wallyce took a beat. She didn't want to brush her sister off too quickly. She had to admit that she'd been letting her self-image get out of hand lately. Not too hard to imagine, given who she was and what she had accomplished. At thirty-seven, Wallyce Tilton had taken the Presidential race by the horns, wrestled it to the ground, and won by the widest margin in history. That might not be altogether amazing, given the last four elections had also been won by women—even a couple of young ones, but Wallyce wasn't a politician. She was all about business and technology. Her election would have been a stunning victory for anyone, but she wasn't just a mere mortal. In her brief run at life, she was now the wealthiest, most powerful person alive. And she was going to use that power for the good of all. At least that's what she kept telling anyone who would listen. At the same time, she was fighting to keep a demanding ego, and fragile self-image, from taking control of her.

She thought about the next steps. Her plan was to centralize her business operations with her government functions. She was about to fulfill her goal by completing the core buildings of Barca City, the new home of Barca Corporation, and the Western White House. Barca Corp. would reside in Barca, a city/state in which Barca Business Ops would co-exist with Barca City. All citizens and employees would live, work and enjoy life without ever needing to venture into the impure world that Earth had become. Barca City would be pure. Barca City would be the first wholly enclosed, self-sufficient biodome-sealed environment ever brought to life. And Wallyce was its creator. She felt the tingling in her fingertips that often accompanied such excitement.

All of the buildings of Barca City were completed and connected. The interiors had all been installed and equipped. Now, the final stages involved finishing her private offices and residential suite, testing all systems in order, then finishing the shell were underway. This shell would be a revolutionary combination of on-demand projection/hologram sandwiched in solar-collecting glass that wrapped the entire colony, sealed under a grid-like bio-enclosure designed to keep everything harmful on the outside and healthy inside. Barca City included a perfectly scrubbed environment that provided everything humans needed to continue to live: clean water, perfect air, no viral or chemical invasions, and a pseudo-weather system that always offered bright, sunny days and cool, moonlit nights. This would be the Barcan version of a new world.

Wallyce also planned changes to the government. The time would soon be suitable for a severe rethinking of government functions. Over the last hundred years, nearly everyone worked from home. Technology made it possible for remote collaboration and instant communication with peers. You wouldn't need to leave home unless you were a service or manufacturing employee. These same changes also had a profound effect on the government. Meetings never required participants to gather together physically. Both Halls of Congress now met via electronic means, including video conferencing. The participants sometimes forgot they were hundreds of miles away from the Senator who appeared on their video screen. Wallyce suddenly realized she had lost her focus.

She had drifted into a daydream, forgetting for a moment that Morrígan was waiting for an answer. Wallyce tapped her shoulder.

"Wallyce? You okay?"

"Huh" Oh, yeah. I'm fine. Just a bunch on my mind."

"So," Morrígan asked again, "Any reason you take chances like walking around so far off the Bay with nothing to keep you from falling?"

"I guess it's just that when I'm here, in the place I've dreamed about for so long, I get a little lost in thought at times, you know? Plus, these Secret Service folks are here to catch me, and anyway, the walls will be up by morning."

Morrígan put her hand on Wallyce's shoulder. "Yeah, I think I get it. Although I must say, the Secret Service was pretty far away when you fell. It would suck if you tripped again and your dream ended with you slamming into the water below. So now, my dream is to get you ready for the speech. We set everything up, and you go on in twenty minutes. You don't want to keep the world waiting." Wallyce stood and turned to face Morrígan.

"I'm comforted I have you to save me from myself," she said with a wry smile.

Morrígan paid no attention to the joke. Instead, she walked to the transport, punched the button, and waited for Wallyce and the Secret Service detachment to join her.

Dozens of floors down, Secret Service agents raced each other to open doors for the new President of the United States. They carefully guided her and her entourage into the Beast transport that sped them off to Crissy Field. Cameras and reporters waited for the first glimpse of President Wallyce Tilton as she took the stand that fronted a dramatic view of the Golden Gate Bridge.

It surprised Wallyce that her heart pounded as she approached the podium and faced the twin microphones. She checked the prompter for the carefully crafted notes for her speech. She could read them, although no one else could see them. As she rose to the podium, a deafening silence arrived, to be replaced momentarily by thunderous applause. Everyone loved their new President so much that there was probably no need for the protective shield surrounding her. The love warmed her heart. Gently waving her hands, she tried to calm the crowd enough to begin speaking.

"Thank you," she said, although she couldn't hear her voice. "Thank you," she repeated, waving as if to ask them to slow it down. Soon the rumble shifted to a soft clapping. "Thank you all. Oh, I am so touched. Please . . ." as the noise softened.

Catching her breath and gathering her composure, she began. "First, I want to express my heartfelt thanks to all Americans, even those who voted for the opposition. You are what makes this the greatest country in the world." She held for the applause. "I want you all to know that I selected this spot to give my first public speech as President for a reason. The Golden Gate Bridge that fills the scene behind me is breathtaking and an icon for the California Bay Area—home of the technology cradle where it all started for me. I was born only a short ride from here in Fremont, and most of my businesses are founded and headquartered here.

"But, more than this, the San Francisco Bay is the perfect place to live and work. Judging by the number of visitors yearly, it's the best place to go on vacation. This is my home." She turned to face the bridge and opened her arms as if to take it all into her. She waited like that for as long as the applause lasted. It was a calculated move. It somehow aligned her with this place—this slice of heaven. She turned back to face the crowd. More than a few tears ran down her face.

"I'm happy to tell you that Barca Corporation and my Administration are in the final stages of completing the construction of a significant piece of architecture here — Barca City. I'm sure most of you have seen what we've been doing over the past two years and wondered what in the world we were building. So, let's take a look. "Giant screens in strategic locations around the field came to life with the projected image of how Barca City would eventually look. It was impressive. It spanned the entire South Bay and was as deep as it was wide. The footprint of Barca, including the seaport and airport, was seven miles east to west and stretched from just south of the San Francisco Airport down to the Bay's lower reaches. It was dozens of stories tall and dwarfed anything anyone had ever seen before. Wallyce gave only passing reference to the "fixed-flotation" footing under the entire city that made it possible for Barca City to rise and fall with the tide, which Barcan engineers had limited to mere inches through the construction of a dam system that also served to minimize any potential earthquake movement at the surface. In a sense, Barca City could be called a floating city, except for the airport, which was at a fixed elevation for aircraft takeoff and landing purposes.

"My friends, this is Barca City—the future home to Barca Technologies, housing all employees in luxurious homes, accommodating all manufacturing and development of our vast products, and providing a complete lifestyle for all Barcans. All services, entertainment, food, and jobs will be under a single roof in a series of interconnected villages within the City-Structure. In addition, Barca City will be wrapped in a biodome that will provide the best weather and complete safety. We will capture solar energy to generate electricity to operate all systems at no cost. My dream is to reduce our companies' impact on the environment, and we believe Barca City will do just that. She paused again for applause, which didn't disappoint.

"And now, more exciting news," she continued. "Effective today, my Administration will relocate from Washington D.C. to be here in a unique village within Barca City. Centralizing here does a few things for us. First, it enables me to remain focused on the tremendous responsibility you graciously gave me with your votes. Second, this will allow the American Government to be national in scope and location. Congress will remain in D.C., while the Executive Branch will be on the other side of our glorious country. Third, we will be fully engaged with the American people this way. And finally, I want to ease any concerns you might have about our ability to continue to be responsive in the face of any crises. We have begun to conduct all government meetings virtually for some time, so we are comfortable transitioning to an entirely virtual government.

"Dear friends, I am so excited about this new path, and I pray you are as excited as we are. Although I'm happy to be home in San Francisco Bay, I want you to know that this is not all about me. It is about you, and it is about our country. I hope the example we set today will help us lead the world to a new commitment to our planet to preserve her for generations to come." Again, the people rose to their feet.

President Wallyce Tilton had arrived, and she let everyone know it. The Secret Service detachment was already in action as she stepped down from the podium. First, they cleared a path to hurry her into the Presidential limousine. Next, they quickly surrounded her, guided her into the rear seat, closed the nearly foot-thick door, and secured her into a fortress on wheels. A few seconds later, the Presidential vehicle was rolling away, surrounded by similar cars on all four sides.

Once they were alone, Wallyce turned to Morrígan in anticipation. "How was it?"

"Are you kidding? They loved you and everything you had to say to them. There's none better, she said."

Without warning, the partition between the rear seating and the driver turned opaque and soon displayed the presidential seal. A male voice spoke. "Madam President, the Senate Majority Leader wishes to speak to you. What are your instructions?"

"Put him through, Goh," President Tilton replied. The screen refreshed to the image of a smartly-dressed man, ageless, seated in a well-appointed office that must have cost the taxpayers a small fortune. "Leader Argen," she greeted him.

"Madam President, so good to see you again." He paused in case Wallyce wished to speak first. She was silent. Madam President, are we secure?"

"Yes, Bill, we are. Speak freely." She looked at Morrígan.

"That's correct, Morrígan, isn't it?" Morrígan nodded. "Go ahead, Bill."

Senator Argen smiled. "Well, Wallyce, it went as you predicted. Right down party lines. Your supporters loved relocating the Executive Branch out west, and the opposition did what oppositions do."

"They opposed it?" Wallyce laughed.

"They did. For all the noise those old farts made, you might think there was hope in hell to keep you from what you're planning. The opposition is freaking out over the fact that you'll have divided loyalties—between your businesses and the country. But, we've pointed to the precedent in the last century and that it supports what you want to do. Besides, they don't have enough votes to stop us." There was a hint of irony in the word "us" that warned Wallyce. She made a mental note to bring it up later to Morrígan when they were alone.

"That's good news, Leader Argen," Wallyce returned. She was perhaps extra formal with his title, hoping he understood that he should respond in kind, calling her President Tilton. Although she had more power than anyone alive, Wallyce was not cut out for confrontation—preferring the diplomatic route. She'd remember to add this to the discussion with Morrígan when they could speak candidly. "Now, Leader, I'm curious. How many senators are entirely on our side?"

"Well, Madam President, that's a tough number to pin down. I could only give a rough guesstimate at twenty-five to thirty if you ask for a guarantee. It's pretty early in the game, to be more definite."

"So then, tell me, Leader . . . how can you be so sure they

don't have the votes to stop our plan?" She had to ask the question.

"That's fair, and I'll try to help you understand. Our party caucus meetings have had lengthy discussions on the possibility of further separation of powers than we already enjoy. It's well-known that we'd all be able to get more done if we separate your Administration and the Congress by about twenty-five hundred miles or so." He chuckled.

"Morrígan interrupted. "Mr. Leader, I am certain you didn't mean to insult the President by telling her you would try to help her understand something. Am I correct?"

Bill Argen knew right away he'd screwed up in a big way. "Oh, Madam President, I'm sorry if I . . ."

"Drop it," Wallyce cut him off. "I get the point. Now, I'm concerned. I need to have more assurance in the future. Please meet with your party leaders and reply with the results. And I want names. For now, I'm going forward. That won't change. How I'll negotiate with those not supporting my plan will change. And it will be a tense time in D.C. if and when that happens. Any questions?"

Senator Argen told her there were none, and she ordered Goh to terminate the call.

Morrígan waited for Wallyce to indicate it was safe to talk.

"Goh, close all channels." Wallyce trusted that her virtual assistant would do what she asked. She looked at Morrígan. "Well, what are your thoughts?"

"I don't trust him as far as that goes," Morrígan began. "We might need better intel on him, something we can use if needed."

Wallyce thought to herself for a minute. "Morrígan, you

know how much I dislike being direct and pushy with people. But I think Argen needed a little wind out of his sails. He's just a bit too familiar for my tastes. I'll let him think he's important to my needs now. He believes it to be the case. The fact is, I've already secured more than half the Senate's commitment. I own businesses in just about every one of their states. That packs a lot of power with the Senators." She smiled. "It's already a done deal. Barca City will be the new location of the People's White House. Washington, D.C., will now function as the eastern satellite office for the administration of my Presidency. When I am no longer the President, my successor will have the right to relocate back to the eastern White House. She would not, in any case, be able to remain in the Barca City headquarters. That is unless you are my successor."

The last part stunned Morrígan. "That will never happen, Wally. It's crazy enough that I'm Vice President but forget about me ever being your successor."

"Well, just keep your options open, Morrígan."

The driver signaled they were approaching her rented compound. They moved quickly inside the mansion, and this essential day was now in the history books.

Chapter Four

"I*'m the first leader to stand at the future Center of American Government, the main speaker's podium in the American Village Conference Center,"* Wallyce thought. She suddenly felt insignificant, as if she were a bit actor in a vast production. This was not the role she imagined for herself. The Conference Center was the largest platform in the country—somewhere between cavernous and ridiculous. It was created to host over seventy-five thousand participants, some in person and some in hologram.

Many had tried to create venues of similar proportions—churches and indoor sporting stadiums. Still, none succeeded, and eventually, they were either repurposed or destroyed. Wallyce played this one nicely. She hired some of the best architectural minds, added a few top business psychologists, then assigned her best technologists to understand why others had failed. Finally, she figured out how to make them succeed. It was easy to see what caused the failures. First, the psychologists determined that colossal venues were too impersonal. Next, the architects grappled with the need to design a forum that allowed people nearly fifty yards apart to converse as if they were next to each other. Finally, the technologists took those problems and turned them inside out. The solution was a laser-driven holographic projection system. It enabled projection from outside the arena to any spot inside. The result was a giant arena that often felt like a home conversation pit. It was a masterstroke.

"Goh lights up a half step." As the lights came alive, Wallyce could see the layout of the Center. The place was decked out to remind everyone that this was a United States Government installation for today. Flags and buntings were placed strategically around the entire stadium. Groups would be seated around risers with podiums that would elevate a speaker on demand. Emblems and state seals were in place over specific risers that identified the section as Senate, House of Representatives, various States, local governments, and more. Over the central riser was the Great Seal of the President of the United States, slightly larger than any others.

Things would change in the dim light as a riser became active and the riser's residents spoke. The emblem would be softly lit so all could see who the speaker was.

Everything was sparkling clean. The air was filled with the smell of newness, new seats, new paint, new flooring, and the mere idea of the place celebrated that newness.

The wizards of Barca Corp took care of every detail. Gone was the constant roar of commercial jets flying overhead on their way into San Francisco Airport. Barca had secured a protected airway over the newly designated Western White House. Details were in place to satisfy the ecologists. Barca City was a conservation model, with solar, wind, and water forces all harnessed to reverse the damage centuries of pollution and carbon-based energy had wrought. Who could have imagined a floating city of such proportions that was nearly self-sustaining?

"Goh, lower lights and have Vice President Morrígan come to meet me on the Central Riser."

"Is now soon enough?" Morrígan chirped. "I was watching from over there for the last ten minutes. Impressive lighting."

"Morrígan, I'm so nervous. We need to have all systems tested in the next half hour. Wouldn't it be horrible for things to fail during such a critical gathering?"

"Like what? Which systems are you most concerned about?" Morrígan paused, then let her sister off the hook. "I had them all tested this morning before breakfast. All risers work on whisper command, and activation of a riser performs as designed. Try one."

Wallyce allowed a smile to show as she commanded, "Activate Test Riser Four." That was the command to activate all systems of a particular riser with seats filled with robots. On her order, the riser lifted above the floor just high enough that those in the Center's reach could see the participants on the riser. The lights increased in intensity as they rose, and the system announced who was taking the floor. "Please give your attention to Test Riser Group 4."

Once the riser reached the needed elevation, a dome slowly descended, imperceptible, but Wallyce knew it was there. Within seconds, the dome took on an eerie glow, and the participant robots on the riser seemed to grow in size, almost by magic. Visual magnification systems were placed at predetermined intervals throughout the Center. They added size and detail to the images of people speaking. To those on distant risers, the speaker appeared to be full-size. This was the secret ingredient to making this colossal venue work where others had failed. Add the most perfect sound replication system in the world, and you have created something that people would come to see, no matter what the event was. Of course, the dome over the Presidential Riser magnified ever so slightly more than any other.

"Morrígan, I'm so impressed. What about the participants who aren't here in person. Will there be a similar experience with the holographs?"

"Even better. The system is designed to enhance the holographic image when it comes in from wherever. It'll be difficult to distinguish between in-person and remote participants. They're in their own environment, but the signal we enhance will be clearer and better than anything they have ever seen virtually. We'll dazzle them, for sure. So, are you ready to go with this?"

"I can hardly wait, Morrígan. Let's grab a bite to eat, then get changed."

* * *

This presentation of Barca City's American Village Conference Center would set the tone for how the country, especially the Bay Area, would view the importance of Barca Holdings for the future of America. Wallyce and Morrígan knew how much riding on the successful show was.

The guests began to arrive a half hour before the event was scheduled to start, much later than Wallyce expected them to show up. Morrígan saw trouble right away.

Wally don't get that look. I can see it coming. Just don't get that look."

"Look? What the hell are you talking about?"

"Since we were kids, I could always tell when you were about to lose your stuff. You'd get that look that means you're about to panic. So, what's the trigger?"

"Nothing. I'm not about to panic. You think you know me. Everything's fine. I'm about to go into the biggest dog-and-pony show of my life, facing down some massive power who just might try to run me out of town, and they decide to show up at the last minute? But, no panic, just a little nervous."

Morrígan pretended to be surprised. "Massive power? You mean ABAG – the Bay Area Government powers?"

"Of course, ABAG," Wallyce said. "Think about what we represent to them. This group held nearly complete control over the Bay Area for over two centuries. Power brokers of the worst kind. The mayors of the largest cities in Northern California have held sway over it all; Bart rapid Transit, Airports, and the growth and near demise of the most significant industry in the world happened under their control. Silicon Valley wouldn't have happened without their approval and guidance, crafting laws and tax structures that favored technological growth. The truth is Barca would never have been as powerful as it is without the support of ABAG."

"Okay, I get that they're important. But you represent the entire country. They only represent the Bay Area. So why are you worried?" Morrígan said. "Why even give them the time of day? They mean little compared to the federal government."

"Dear sister," You are so bright, yet so naïve. Barca City is built on Bay Area reclaimed land. Our very existence here required the approval of the state and the cities and counties of the Bay Area. Now that we're in, I'd sure hate to start a battle that would seek to throw us out. And think about this: We are not on federal lands. Barca City falls under city and county laws ruled by several ABAG members. Those very local politicians see us as a threat to their little empires. We are. So, the last thing we want is a public battle with the political power brokers in Northern California. We must either keep them happy or force them to step aside. To keep them happy, they must believe in how important we are to them. Today's show is the keystone to build that importance."

Morrígan responded with just the right thing to say. "So, it has more to do with the show not coming off as a success, and there's no putting that in a closet. It is what it is; we must be ready to run with it. They're more afraid of you than you should be of them. You hold all the cards."

Wallyce was quiet for a moment. "Yeah, you're right. I'm going to put it back in their laps. I'll start the meeting late, just to put them off guard. They come late, and I start late. Maybe they won't love waiting for me like I hate waiting for them."

"Okay, Wallyce. Your call."

Wallyce nodded to the Secret Service detail to indicate they were ready to enter the holding room and wait for the crowd to be seated. All virtual connections are to be made before the grand entrance.

The Presidential Holding room was more than just a place to wait. The room had been dimmed, with little light except for the bank of monitors on the far wall that could scan every riser section with voice command. Wallyce and Morrígan each sat at one of the control stations and placed their eyes in front of the retina scanner that would give them full access. Wallyce started right in and scanned around the Center.

"Senate Section," she commanded. The screen in front of her went momentarily blank. Then, before she could blink, the image of the U.S. Senate riser appeared, the Seal of the U.S. Senate lit up, and the riser became visible. "Morrígan, where the hell are the senators?"

"Oh, sorry. It was in the check sheets. The Senate doesn't take their seat until everyone else, except you and I are seated. Kind of a sign of respect. But we can see them right now if you wish."

"Yes, please show me."

Morrígan turned to her console and commanded, "Senate Holding room, stealth mode." Her screen quickly opened to the Senate Holding room, where they could see and hear the Senators as they waited to enter.

"Stealth mode? They don't know we're watching? I like that. Let's see who showed up." Her mood turned dark. Only a handful of the fifty Senators were there, and they were from the closest states, Nevada, Utah, Oregon, and Washington. "What is this? Nobody showed?"

"Oh. No, that's because the rest of the Senators will be here virtually," Morrígan assured her. "We can mix in-person and virtual participants in every riser."

Wallyce smiled. "This is the basis for my plan to revolutionize business and government. So watch me shake the roof off this show today."

* * *

This presentation of Barca City's American Village Conference Center would set the tone for how the country, and especially the Bay Area would view the importance of Barca Holdings for the future of America. Both Wallyce and Morrígan knew just how much was riding on the successful show.

The guests began to arrive a half hour before the event was scheduled to start, much later than Wallyce expected them to show up. Morrígan saw trouble right away.

Wally, don't get that look. I can see it coming. Just don't get that look."

"Look? What the hell are you talking about?"

"Since we were kids, I could always tell when you were about to lose your stuff. You'd get that look that means you're about to panic. So, what's the trigger?"

"Nothing. I'm not about to panic. You think you know me. Everything's fine. I'm about to go into the biggest dog-and-pony show of my life, facing down some massive power who just might try to run me out of town, and they decide to show up at the last minute? But, no panic, just a little nervous."

Morrígan pretended to be surprised. "Massive power? You mean ABAG – the Bay Area Government powers?"

"Of course, ABAG," Wallyce said. "Think about what we represent to them. This group held nearly complete control over the Bay Area for more than two centuries. Power brokers of the worst kind. The mayors of the largest cities in Northern California have held sway over it all; Bart rapid Transit, Airports, and the growth and near demise of the most significant industry in the world happened under their control. Silicon Valley wouldn't have happened without their approval and guidance, crafting laws and tax structures that favored technological growth. The truth is

Barca would never have been as powerful as it is without the support of ABAG."

"Okay, I get that they're important. But you represent the entire country. They only represent the Bay Area. So why are you worried?" Morrígan said. "Why even give them the time of day? They mean little compared to the federal government."

"Dear sister," You are so bright, yet so naïve. Barca City is built on Bay Area reclaimed land. Our very existence here required the approval of the state and the cities and counties of the Bay Area. Now that we're in, I'd sure hate to start a battle that would seek to throw us out. And think about this: We are not on federal lands. Barca City falls under city and county laws ruled by several ABAG members. Those very local politicians see us as a threat to their little empires. We are. So, the last thing we want is a public battle with the political power brokers in Northern California. We must either keep them happy or force them to step aside. To keep them happy, they must believe in how important we are to them. Today's show is the keystone to build that importance."

Morrígan responded with just the right thing to say. "So, it has more to do with the show not coming off as a success, and there's no putting that in a closet. It is what it is; we must be ready to run with it. They're more afraid of you than you should be of them. You hold all the cards."

Wallyce was quiet for a moment. "Yeah, you're right. I'm going to put it back in their laps. I'll start the meeting late, just to put them off guard. They come late, and I start late. Maybe they won't love waiting for me just like I hate waiting for them."

"Okay, Wallyce. Your call."

Wallyce nodded to the Secret Service detail to indicate they were ready to go inside, into the holding room where they would wait for the crowd to be seated. All virtual connections are to be made before the grand entrance.

The Presidential Holding room was more than just a place to wait. The room had been dimmed, with little light except for the bank of monitors on the far wall that could scan every riser section with voice command. Wallyce and Morrígan each took a seat at one of the control stations and placed their eyes in front of the retina scanner that would give them full access. Wallyce started right in and scanned around the Center.

"Senate Section," she commanded. The screen in front of her went momentarily blank. Then, before she could blink, the image of the U.S. Senate riser appeared, the Seal of the U.S. Senate lit up, and the riser became visible. "Morrígan, where the hell are the senators?"

"Oh, sorry. It was in the check sheets. The Senate doesn't take their seat until everyone else, except you and I are seated. Kind of a sign of respect. But we can see them right now if you wish."

"Yes, please show me."

Morrígan turned to her console and commanded, "Senate Holding room, stealth mode." Her screen quickly opened to the Senate Holding room, where they could see and hear the Senators as they waited to enter.

"Stealth mode? They don't know we're watching? I like that. Let's see who showed up." Her mood turned dark. Only a handful of the fifty Senators were there, and they were from the closest states, Nevada, Utah, Oregon, and Washington. "What is this? Nobody showed?"

"Oh. No, that's because the rest of the Senators will be

here virtually," Morrígan assured her. "We can mix in-person and virtual participants in every riser."

Wallyce smiled. "This is the basis for my plan to revolutionize business and government. So watch me shake the roof off this show today."

Chapter Five

Goh's active light beamed from the central screen, indicating he had a message.

Wallyce responded. "Yes, Goh. What is it?"

"Madam President and Madam Vice President, the in-person attendees are in place, and the core-intelligence system indicates that all virtual attendees are now connected. Shall I present the Senate?"

Wallyce gripped Morrígan by the arm. "Yes, however, I wish you to slow the process. In fact, introduce every Senator, one at a time, and take your time. They deserve the acknowledgment." She winked at Morrígan. It felt schoolgirl-like, but she wanted to make her point.

"Yes, Madam President. I will return to begin your introduction after completing the Senate's introduction." His active light faded off. Wallyce turned to the Secret Service team. "We'll enter the Center five minutes after the Senate has been formally seated."

"Yes, Ma'am."

They could only take about ten minutes of Goh's droning introductions before they were bored.

Morrígan took the initiative. "Have they had enough?"

"Yes. I think we can cut to the chase," Wallyce agreed. "Go ahead, signal Goh to speed things up."

Goh shifted gears on the spot and had the introductions over in less than two minutes. Morrígan signaled the Secret Service to be ready to go. The team took their positions. The red "ready" light went on over the viewing screens, and they could hear Goh make the introductions, one at a time, as protocol dictated.

"Honored guests and participants in the first annual Barca City State of the Union, please join me in welcoming the Vice President of the United States, Morrígan Meath Tilton."

Morrígan entered the Center from the main access ramp. Lights bathed her in a soft green glow. The applause was loud enough to drown out the corny trumpeting heralds. Without further fanfare, she stepped up to the Presidential riser and turned to wave to the crowds. Her riser pad was lifted a foot above the riser platform, a signal that she was slightly more critical than the general participant, but only slightly. She was slowly rotated so she could wave to all in attendance, then the riser pad lowered her to the riser platform. In an apparent show of respect, she turned to face the entrance ramp and bowed slightly in that direction. This was Goh's cue.

"And now, honored guests, please stand to greet the President of the United States, Wallyce Elliott Tilton."

A light show began with spots beaming around the Center for a few moments, finally settling on the entrance to the ramp, where Wallyce appeared as if by some technological trick of magic. Applause shook people close to the speakers. Whether genuine applause or system-generated sound, it was terrific. President Wallyce Tilton walked toward the Presidential riser, smiling all the way. "Hail to the Chief" played in the background to thunderous applause, with Wallyce stopping to shake hands with a few preselected participants along the way. When she reached the riser, she stepped onto the marked platform that lifted her up to the riser and above, ten feet above, the riser platform. She reached out her hand to lightly grip the safety rail in front of her as a clear crystalline dome descended over her. A soft blue light haloed her image on the faceted dome in several sizes and angles, then projected via laser to hologram repeaters throughout the venue. The repeaters magnified her image as needed. The effect was that every person in every seat might be convinced she was standing right in front of them, only a few feet away. The result was better than hoped. A sudden gasp rose from the Center as participants struggled to understand what had happened.

Wallyce smiled and nodded in a greeting as if to each person there. Then, she motioned to them to take their seats. It took some coaxing, but the assembly quieted down enough for her to begin her speech.

"My friends, I am excited to have you here for the unveiling of Barca City. You will see firsthand our plan for the future of technology as we bridge the gap between business and technology today and for generations to come. Everything changes from this point forward." The crowd went silent. Wallyce paused long enough for the statement to sink in.

"First, let me acknowledge some of our distinguished guests." Lights outlined the Senate riser on cue. "I believe we've already introduced the Senate of the United States." The member, Senators became visible. "Senator Argen, I believe there's an item on your table for Senator Reynolds. I selected it myself just minutes before I entered the arena. Would you mind giving it to her?"

Bill Argen knew what to do. They reviewed this a few times this morning.

"Yes, Madam President, happily." He reached for the large red envelope and held it up for all to see. Argen wrote in black marker on the strip of tape and inserted his personal comm unit into the envelope. He pushed the envelope toward Reynolds but moved too fast and too far. The envelope seemed to pass right through the Senator's midsection. Instead of injury, it caused her to smile widely. Argen withdrew the envelope. Maura waved her hands toward the crowd, saying, "As you see, I am not there in person. So, I will not be able to receive the important envelope from Senator Argen. Too bad, though, as it might contain vital information of a classified nature, and he might not want anyone else to see it."

"Perhaps there is a way, Senator," President Tilton said. She nodded toward Senator Argen. Bill Argen turned toward the table that held what looked like some form of old-style printer and placed the envelope into a feeder slot. The device dragged the envelope into itself, then out the other side. Then, next to Senator Reynolds, lights shone on what seemed to be a 3D printer as it quickly produced a red envelope identical to the one Argen fed into the machine.

President Wallyce Tilton asked Argen to empty his envelope. He opened it and showed the item on which Argen had handwritten a message. Wallyce then asked him to open it and show the envelope's contents to the assembly.

Argen made a show of opening the envelope and sliding out the comm. On the tape, in large print, was a message that read, "Who Needs Magic?"

President Tilton turned to Senator Reynolds. "Maura?" Senator Reynolds held up the envelope that had just been printed. She withdrew an exact duplicate of the comm. It was identical to the one Argen held in his hands. "Now, please show us what is on the tape." The assembly gasped as each piece bore the handwritten message, "Who Needs Magic?" A closer look showed that the handwriting and position on the original were identical to the message on the copy.

President Tilton continued. "We can recreate anything within reason. But, of course, cost plays a role. Using this technology to recreate items you could pick up and carry will be easy. Still, it's impossible to recreate a military vehicle, for example. The audience laughed.

"Think of the impact. Virtual collaboration, confidential document sharing, and any new invention can be passed to team members for their review and input without requiring them to travel and without the risk of hackers. We are demonstrating for you today the beginning of worldwide collaboration. The combination of transporter re-creation and holographic participation changes everything. Just one tiny example, the ability to send replacement parts to the field of battle, and updated technologies directly to the soldiers in the field, can save lives and ensure victory. In business, we can update physical products just like logical ones. We can perform hardware updates just as we perform software updates. And we are just getting started. Barca City will be the birthplace of the new world."

Wallyce basked in the ovation.

Wallyce continued. "As you know, the companies of Barca Holding are invested in technology and innovation. One of these innovations, the Video Enhancement Dome, VED, enables you to see me up close, even though I am sometimes more than fifty yards away. Another, Holographic Image Transport, or HIT, makes it possible to participate in meetings with people who can remain in place without traveling. This is far more efficient than the incredible loss of time and focus due to excessive travel requirements. More on this later. Each of these is important, but the shining light of all this technology is this place we are introducing today, Barca City. Please turn your attention to our Vice President, Morrígan Tilton."

Wallyce's platform dimmed as she was lowered to the riser level before taking her seat. Morrígan's platform began to rise as her dome descended, and new holographic images appeared throughout the Center. They projected images of the now nearly complete Barca City. Next to each hologram was the projected image of Morrígan. It seemed she was floating above Barca City and could move from one section to the next. She was an electronic tour guide.

"Welcome, my friends, to the American Village Conference Center, the core of Barca City and the world's most advanced meeting place. Here, we hope to present the future of business and government. You've already witnessed the incredible Video Enhancement Dome and the equally unique Holographic Image Transport Systems. You could hardly help but be excited by them. They are impressive but only a small part of the advanced technologies that make a place like Barca City possible." On the mention of Barca City, the entire hologram of the city came alive. It began to turn slowly in different directions so all attendees could see each of the villages that make up this the largest connected city in America.

Vice President Morrígan Tilton continued. First, I would like to express our thanks and gratitude for the vital support we have been given by all levels of government. In particular, thank you for granting Barca Holding the right to use the South Bay waterway and shorelines to make this miracle happen under the Navigable Servitude rights within the Constitution's Commerce Clause. Although many opposed this agreement, a true spirit of cooperation and search for this area's best and highest use won. As a result, work began a few years ago to create the City of the Future that we are proud to call Barca City." The image of the façade of Barca City glowed and was met by energetic applause.

Section-by-section, she paused to identify and say a bit about each before moving on to the next. For example, from the impressive Main Façade, she moved on to the government section labeled American Village, to a series of floating villages used for Research and Development, Manufacturing, Worker Recreation, a Medical Village, and one labeled Redirection Village.

The most impressive was the Main Façade, so many stories high, covered in a new form of windows that could change in terms of tint, reflectivity, color, and privacy. It was a technological work of art.

"Barca City has been designed to function as self-supporting. Note the far-left end of the cityscape. You can make out the beginnings of Barca City Air Village—soon to be a complete international-capable airport. Air Village will be able to provide all incoming and outgoing flights to and from anywhere in the world, intended for Barca business and U.S. Government purposes. However, for now, Military flights will be limited to nearby air bases. When we are up and running, we expect a significant reduction in business and government use of the three Bay Area airports; San Jose, Oakland, and San Francisco. If and when that happens, we will petition for segmented use of parts of these airports to be open to minor military uses, but that's a discussion for the future."

A low rumble of dissatisfaction came from several sections of the Center. But, of course, Morrígan knew to expect this, so she gave no response.

"The right side of the cityscape will house Barca City Port, an ocean-capable functioning port that will serve our shipping needs. It's already under design. This port facility will provide services for our raw materials, incoming parts, and finished products out of California. I'll admit to additional minor usage for government purposes but only for special needs on an as-required basis. In all, we expect our port facility will impact commercial ports, such as Oakland, very little, if at all.

"It's important to add we have created a dozen smaller, yet no less capable, Barca Corporation/Cities in strategic locations throughout the country. This will form our corporate network and function as satellite government centers."

"In the next few weeks, I plan to host several Barca City tours for many of you. These open information lines between Barca, Local, State, and Federal Governments." She smiled and nodded to the crowd. "Thank you for your kind attention." Morrígan's riser lowered.

Before she reached the platform level, lighted placards over several platforms lit up, indicating requests to speak. The system honored ABAG, The Association of Bay Area Governments, in random order. Wallyce tapped a button on her console and was bathed by a blue spotlight. She saw her sound system was on.

"Although we will have time during the invited tours for in-depth discussions, I'll open the floor to ABAG for three minutes." Then, she waited for the ABAG riser to elevate high enough to see Rachel Perriman, Mayor of San Francisco and current Chair of the Association.

"Mayor Perriman, you have the floor."

"Thank you, Madam President." She looked around at the canyon-like America Village Center.

"Pretty impressive," she began. "Here we are, learning about your plans to change the Bay Area and the rest of the world with your miraculous discoveries, yet you resort to cheap magic tricks to influence us. You would amaze us into just handing over to your private enterprises the largest waterway deals the country has ever allowed. Still, you then just blurt out through your Vice President-Sister that you will be making a move on our airports." She remained silent, just letting the mood in the Center grow tense.

"It's not going to happen, Madam President. The cities represented by my associates here built those airports—maintain those waterways that you seem to lay claim to. "

Morrígan slapped her hand down on her console controller. As hers was a master controller, she was able to override any other controller in the Center, except, of course, President Tilton's. She stood up even before her spotlight completed lighting her.

"Mayor Perriman, this is neither the time nor the place for political discussions. But I'm sure I speak for the President when I say we would be happy to meet one-on-one with you to highlight your concerns. So, please have your staff contact us to schedule it. We will be available as soon as tomorrow afternoon. And thank you for your genuine concern." She tapped another switch, and Mayor Perriman's riser lowered, her spotlight dimmed, and her sound was set to receive-only.

Rachel Perriman knew right away what had happened. With an angry look, she turned to her assistant and ordered her to set the meeting for the next possible date. Now that she had opened the discussion, nothing would keep her from taking it to the conclusion. Damned if I'm going to let this happen without a fight, she thought.

Vice President Morrígan called for any further open discussion with a stipulation. "Please make sure that your questions and concerns are of interest to most of the guests here today. If you have any specific concerns, please feel free to message me. I will answer you or schedule a meeting for the more complex questions." There were several complimentary comments, a few general questions about how Barca City will blend into the surrounding culture, and one from the Senate Minority Leader, Rahm Sizemore.

"Madam President, you said you'll relocate your Administration to Northern California and use the White House as if it were a temporary stopover in our nation's capital. Don't you think this demands more than an executive decision? Shouldn't Congress be able to weigh in on such an important topic?"

President Tilton took the floor.

"Thanks for the question, Minority Leader Sizemore. Rather than hold everyone up, I will state that this is not open for negotiation. Why should it be? President Kennedy had Martha's Vineyard, Johnson and Bush had ranches in Texas, and more recently, President Emmanuel had his banana farm in Hawaii. Were they any less effective for their travels? And please consider it costs a fortune and adds risk every time a President travels any distance from home base, in this case, Washington D.C.

"The world has changed, Mr. Speaker, and we must change with it. A list of changes we've seen over the past century would make you dizzy to read it. Here are just a few: We have evolved to take great advantage of technology, so much so that we have begun to turn the tide on global warming. Video-based meetings have eliminated the need to travel locally for most employees today. Not fifty years ago, we still sat, vehicles running and spewing poison into the air. At the same time, we waited through traffic to move enough that we could make it to work. Then, at the end of every workday, we'd climb into our exhaust-spewing boxes to drive back home; network-based connections and video meetings have reduced the amount of carbon dioxide we produce by a significant amount. Now, and here I'll brag a bit, such powerful tools as the Barca Holographic Network has begun to make virtual meetings so sophisticated that in-person conferences are fast becoming a thing of the past. Air travel, highway commutes, and even high-speed Maglev systems are becoming outdated. Why in the world would we want to return to our old ways? And there are many more examples, too numerous to mention here. I'll be more than happy to meet with you all to discuss this at length. The Vice President will set it up, but the decision has been made. And now," she turned to the cameras, "We will adjourn to the various tours and meetings you have for the rest of the day. Thank you all for coming. We look forward to the future, our future, with you."

Chapter Six

President Tilton enjoyed a task that always brought her warm feelings—reviewing her business success reports. As she was reading the latest sales charts from Barca, Inc., Wallyce's eyes were drawn to the bottom of the screen, where a message trailer was becoming visible. "Vice President Morrígan Tilton wishes to speak."

"Open line. Hi Morrígan, are you calling to let me know we are meeting in five with the mayors from ABAG?"

"Yep."

"All set, just wrapping up my financial review. I'll meet you in the hall outside the conference room in five minutes."

"Okay. See you."

"Close the line." Wallyce gave Goh instructions on what to do with the financial files, then ordered her office to be closed until she returned. Not that anyone could or would try to enter in any event. She headed down the hall to her private conference room.

Already in place, mayors from five of the largest Bay Area cities were reviewing their position on the Barca City question. San Francisco Mayor Rachel Perriman had asked for consensus.

"So, are we agreed? There are no other issues?" Heads nodded. Mayor Perriman made a note on her personal device just before the door opened. Agent Nguyen announced the President and Vice President. Wallyce and Morrígan stepped around him.

"Good day to you all," President Tilton smiled and bowed to them, the traditional greeting. They all bowed in return. "Please, everyone, please, be seated. No formalities. We're here to work. As she took her seat, she nodded to Morrígan and waited.

Morrígan took the lead. "It's no secret, Mayor Perriman, but to set the discussion on track, would you do us a favor and state the focus of this meeting?"

"I'll be happy to, Madam Vice President. Perriman folded her hands on the table before her, a sign she was prepared to take a hard-line stand. "Over the past several months, we've learned that you intend to house all of your employees within Barca City and not allow them to live outside and commute to work. We see this as being against the free enterprise system our country is so invested in. If the workers were housed in the same location as their jobs, there would be little reason to visit our cities. Of course. They might want to visit us for events, sporting or otherwise. Still, I'm speaking of the everyday economy that drives all businesses, small and large, restaurants, clothing shops, medical practitioners, and all forms of entertainment. These things depend on the middle class, the people who build your products, clean your facilities and perform thousands of tasks inside Barca City. If these people are removed from the Bay Area economy, it'll have a detrimental effect on the area."

"Anything more?" Wallyce was direct and to the point.

Ron Andrus, Mayor of Oakland, answered. "Yes. It's flat-out wrong. You're trying to isolate Barcan workers from the rest of society like they're some different class of people. They're people who live in our towns and cities. Imagine that hundreds of thousands of people who live and enjoy the rest of the Bay Area will just up and move into Barca. The hit to our economies is real. It's huge, and it just isn't right."

"Millions," was Wallyce's response.

Mayor Shonna Rimes from San Jose slammed her hand down on the table. "Millions what?"

President Tilton sensed it was time to take the direct route. "Millions of people will work and live in Barca City. Not hundreds of thousands. Eventually, all employees from all Barcan subsidiaries will live and work in Barca City and similar corporate cities across the country. Barca City will grow as needed to accommodate them." She paused as a realization crossed her mind. "Do you believe you have any sway over where and how I will locate my employees?"

Morrígan interjected, "I hope we can bring the tone down here so we can try to reach some understanding."

Rimes stood her ground. "Don't you see, we represent the collective government of the entire San Francisco Bay Area? You don't want to try to steamroll over us. It won't work, Madam. Just who do you think you're dealing with?" The question was directed at President Tilton, who fired right back.

"I'm dealing with a handful of small-time politicians who can be voted into oblivion by signing a large donation check. I hope we can agree, as Morrígan has indicated, but I'll not have the swat team from ABAG try to back me into a corner. Go back to your constituents and think about the reality I've placed before you today. Then, when you're ready to talk, let Vice President Morrígan know."

President Tilton stood up. She'd seen something on her watch that demanded attention. "Now I have to leave. Thank you for your time."

The doors opened on cue, and the Secret Service team signaled that the guests should accompany them to the exit.

"Morrígan, we need to talk. Follow me to my office." They left without further formalities. The ABAG group had no choice but to go with the Secret Service escort.

Once inside the sprawling Presidential Suite, Wallyce didn't waste any time. "Goh, secure the room. Play the advisory from CDC." She looked at Morrígan with a frightened look on her face.

Dr. Emmanuel Walters came to life in hologram form in the viewing area of the room. "Madam President, please forgive the urgent nature of this message, but it is that important. A pause was built into the transmission to allow any who shouldn't hear this classified message to be escorted out. There were none.

"Continue the message, Goh."

Walters resumed. "We're concerned about a possible epidemic we've been tracking. Our data shows that this outbreak has turned aggressive and has the potential to become a pandemic. The positivity rates in several countries are near 12% of those tested—unprecedented. And so far, we hear about death rates well above 25% with no effective vaccine on the horizon. We have no way at hand to fight this thing if it spreads. In clear terms, Madams, we look at what could grow to epic proportions. We will inform you at every step, but we wanted to let you know what we're facing. That is all for now. Of course, I'll be available to take your calls on demand. Dr. Walters, out." The hologram went dark.

"Morrígan, I heard some scary things. Pandemic? No vaccine? This makes the whining from ABAG screechers seem like so much background noise.

Chapter Seven

"Close Environmental Viewer." President Tilton leaned back in her seat and closed her eyes. She needed to adjust them to the brighter lights of the office. Wallyce enjoyed the softer views from the computer-generated scenes that turned her office viewing wall into whatever environment desired. She sat in a lush garden of cultivated plants and rare and beautiful birds this time. An occasional animal skitted by, and a sky filled with puffy, soft bright clouds kept her guessing what they might be. This was what she needed to attain any form of meditative state. Today, she needed to relax.

She opened her eyes, but not enough. The bright lights made her want to close them again. But, instead, sheer will allowed her to force them to stay open, knowing they would soon become accustomed to the harshness of the office.

"Main screen up." On command, the surface of her desk opened to let a widescreen monitor rise from under it. "She tapped her fingernails on the desk. Finally, the screen came to life, and a voice announced, "Dr. Sebastian calling. Do you wish to accept?"

"Yes. Open the call." She sat taller in her seat, hands folded on the desk, as the image of her old friend and therapist, Dr. Sebastian, filled the screen.

"Hello again, Wally. So good to see you."

"Hi, Sebastian. I can't tell you how good it is to see you."

"I can guess. I see the news, and I hear the scuttlebutt on the streets. Local politics trying to undercut national is never a pretty sight. Top that off, the news everywhere talks about a fast-growing threat from some virus. I can imagine the pressures you are under. So, what's the best and worst news you can tell me?"

Wallyce hated those two questions. But, ever since she could remember, he always asked. So she assumed it was his way of framing her focus to see what to start with.

"There is no best. It's all bad today." She hoped he wouldn't press any further.

"Okay. Let's start with the bad news."

"I'll give you a short-list. One, the Senate is trying to block me at every turn. According to my allies, how much time and energy I spend on Barca and Barca City is a big deal. They seem to think I'm unable to multitask. Two, a group of mayors in ABAG wants to prevent me from making Barca City a closed environment, allowing workers to live outside the city and commute. Not gonna happen. Three, you hit the nail on the head with the virus. My insiders tell me it's worse than anything we've ever experienced. The positivity rates alone are off the charts. There seems to be no known way to stop this plague yet, meaning mortality may be headed to 100 percent. If so, then if you get a positive test, you have a death sentence. Holy shit, Sebastian! What can I do about what the world just handed me?"

"Well, as you know, the best way to control a global virus. would be to close the country. Shut down all travel. Lock everything down. But that's supreme overkill and not called for yet. Your best course would be to watch it, learn all you can about the risks and avoidance factors, then act on them if you are forced to. About the ABAG mayors, why are you even concerned? They have no power over the Federal Government. Your friend, Governor Brookfield, could apply enough pressure to keep them busy, looking away, so you can do what you need to. Then, there's the Senate. You've done your homework. Your advisers are assured you can take action to operate from here in the Bay Area. So, again, what are you worried about? They aren't about to rewrite the Constitution. You already knew all this, so what did you want to hear from me?"

"I'm not sure, Sebastian. You know me, how I operate. I just needed some comfort, and you were the one I picked.

"Not much has changed in that regard, right?" Dr. Sebastian softened his tone. "On the bright side, there's no one I'd rather see in charge when we need decisiveness and a quick mind. You got this job for a reason—you're the best one to lead us out of the quagmire. So, let's figure it out, one step at a time."

"Thanks, Sebastian. I needed that support. Okay, I need to gather a team of superheroes. Let's talk through the people I think would be best, and you can keep me focused. Now, the best team I could think of a few months ago to help me lead the country is already in place—my Cabinet. They top my list of team players."

"Bravo, Wallyce."

"Next, as much as I complain about her, Morrígan can out-think any ten people. Then, I'll call in Senator Argen and then Governor Brookfield. Last, or maybe last, depending on results, I'll call in the CDC."

Sebastian smiled. "Good start. What about the other issues, ABAG, and the Senate?"

"Well, I suspect the Senate is preoccupied with the virus. When I gather their help, the issue of where I operate the government will be put on the back shelf. The ABAG is little more than background noise compared to the plague. So, they can sit in their stew for a while."

"And that," Dr. Sebastian replied, "is the Wallyce Tilton I know. Looks like you're on the right track. Anything else?"

"Not that I can think of. Thanks for always being there for me, Sebastian."

"It's my honor. Bye for now."

"Goodbye, friend." The screen lowered.

"Goh, call a session of the Cabinet for one hour from now. I need information on the virus and their input on a plan moving forward."

"I've sent the schedule to all members. Should I include the Vice President?"

"Yes, I need her there. And now, please connect me to Governor Brookfield."

Goh alerted her that Brookfield was standing by.

"Main screen up. Open connection to Governor Brookfield." As the screen rose, she saw he was already on the viewer, ready to talk. "Hello, Jake. Thanks for taking my meeting on short notice."

"You call, I answer, Madam President. What can I do for you?"

"What do you hear about the virus spread across the channels?

"Nothing encouraging. All I hear is pretty grim. I was just informed that healthcare in many major cities east of the Mississippi is already at full capacity. The reports are that this round of virus is the deadliest we have ever seen."

"Yeah. I hear upwards of 25% death rates. Does your info bear that out?"

"Yes, Madam. I'm afraid so. Some locations are worse off than others, but a 25% ratio is supported. To make matters even grimmer, the infection-to-test rates are skyrocketing. I'm scrambling for all the scientific help I can gather. We need to be ready, and right now might even be too late."

"Governor, do you have any preliminary plans? What are your counselors telling you?"

There was a long pause while Governor Brookfield measured his words. Of course, this would be difficult to say to the President of the United States.

"Madam President, it all comes down to how much we believe the threat is real and how devastating we believe the results might be. In general terms, our team leans toward total shutdown."

"Put some detail behind that, Jake. The definition of a shutdown could be very different from one person to another. What is the plan at this point?"

"We are weighing the possibility of closing all borders into the state and all transportation access—busses, planes, cars, travel by water, etc. Your people will be kept abreast of the plan as we develop it further. This would help us to reduce the flow of people into the state, not stop it. And the virus is probably already here. More extreme measures might be needed, and the sooner, the better. Next, there would be a complete shutdown of gatherings and businesses. All businesses would be required to transact "at the curb." In other words, nobody would be able to even enter a restaurant, office building, store, church. . . Everything would be closed down for the foreseeable future. That's the sum of our plan for now. Not very elegant. We have a lot more work to do."

Wallyce wasted no time on formalities. "Thanks. Jake. I knew I could count on you to be honest with me. Sounds like we need to work head-to-head on this right away. You up for it?"

"I'm on your team. We can win this time."

"Okay, Governor. Look for my messages in the next few days. We need to stay connected. Contact me without fail with any news or concerns. I'm out for now." She tapped the switch on her console, and the screen went black and dropped out of sight.

"Goh, get the Joint Chiefs and the brass at the Pentagon. Schedule a formal meeting for tomorrow at 7:00 am our time. I will take all meetings from inside Barca for the time being."

"Yes, Madam."

Chapter Eight

Wallyce wanted to be sure everything was perfect for her dinner/meeting with Governor Jake Brookfield. So she had her personal assistant make the arrangements for an elegant dinner for two in the private dining room at the Presidential Mansion in Hillsborough. No detail was overlooked. There was a tuxedo-wearing staff, a string quartet filling the background with angelic music, and a menu that would be fit for royalty. . . right up to and including the entre. First, Wallyce did some information gathering. She learned Brookfield's favorite food was pizza from a shop on 57th Street in Manhattan—a passion developed when he served as the Attorney General for New York State. "It's fun to have connections," she thought. She had the staff arrange the ingredients and written instructions for preparation to be shipped via a super-fast Air Force jet on a return run to Northern California. Her chef was standing by, ready to assemble and deliver New York pizza to the Bay Area. Brookfield would not soon forget this meeting, and not for the food.

"Jake, thank you for taking time out of your week to meet with me on the issues we discussed. This plague has us all worried, and I want to be sure you and I form an alliance to defeat this thing or at least keep it from ravaging California. As President, I owe it to the people of this country to develop a plan to contain and eradicate the plague. You and I need to become a fighting force against this killer, and I thought it would be a good way to start if we had a nice quiet dinner to get to know each other."

"Madam. . ."

"Please, let's drop the formalities. Call me Wallyce."

"Very well, Wallyce," Brookfield said.

"Okay then, Jake. Why don't we head to dinner? I'm looking forward to your reaction to what I have planned."

Jake was intrigued. "Well, I'm sure I'll be blown away by the dinner if this beautiful dining room is any indication," he said. They had entered a space with a table large enough to accommodate two dozen guests. The walls were a backdrop for many works of art, several Brookfield wouldn't be surprised to have seen in museums. The furnishings were Louis XIV, with gilded soft velvet fabric and beautifully carved wood. At the far end of the table, two seats were set aside for the President and the Governor. The place settings bore the Presidential Seal, and the glassware was of fine crystal. Jake felt out of place.

"I'm, uh, impressed. And I'm also out of my league. Wallyce, I'm a hot dog and burger kind of guy. But this is way too much for me. You shouldn't have gone to such extremes."

"Okay, Jake. I get it. And I'll ask you to hold off on what you think until after dinner." A crooked little smile crossed her face, and Brookfield saw her as a regular person for the first time.

Hell, she's even cute, he thought to himself. "Okay, Wallyce. I promise not to jump to conclusions." He moved to pull her chair back for her but saw one of the white-gloved tuxedoed staff was already there. They sat and watched as the Sommelier poured a first taste for President Tilton. On her nod of approval, she poured a glass for each of them, then placed the wine into a silver cooler on the side table.

Several courses were served in order, and the elegance seemed to continue enough that Jake was beginning to think everything would stay above comfort for him. He felt awkward as the chef brought out the main course. Brookfield laughed out loud when he recognized the cardboard pizza box from his favorite pizzeria in New York.

"Wallyce, I love the thought of pizza, and I'm so impressed you put it in a box from Manny's in New York to serve it in. Now I get it. I'll never second-guess you again."

"Oh, but you just did." Wallyce smiled and nodded to the chef, who opened the box to present what looked like an authentic Manny's pizza. He placed a slice on Jake's plate and stepped back, signaling Brookfield to taste the pizza.

"Well, it looks like Manny's. So I think I'll eat it like Manny's. With that, he grabbed the slice in one hand, folded the two corners, and took a hearty bite. His eyes opened wide. "What the hell? This is Manny's. But how. . .?"

Wallyce winked to the chef, turned to Jake, and gave him a sly smile. "That's my secret. It's as real as we could get without flying Manny here himself to make it. Enjoy it, Jake. It's meant to kick off what I hope will be a long and meaningful working relationship. We're important to each other. California will benefit from moving my administration here, and I've already benefitted from the support of my home state. It can get better from here." She offered her glass, and they toasted each other, and Governor and President sealed their unspoken agreement.

Ice broken; the balance of the evening was spent with the two of them getting to know each other on a more personal level. Soon enough, the talk moved to what she needed in return from California. Wallyce was eager to be sure Governor Brookfield was committed to her personal objectives. For Wallyce, her list was simple: absolute control over her business and governmental domains, a mutual commitment to work as a team to blockade the epidemic, and finally, a promise that the state government would support her more vigorous, centralized style of leadership that would make the United States' new form of government the envy of the modern world. Simple needs, yes, but Wallyce made certain Jake knew there was no room to negotiate. She required a total agreement from him.

For Brookfield, the focus was tighter. He was setting up a close relationship with the single largest taxpayer in the State of California—by far. Whatever he needed to do to make sure this was an agreement that would benefit California in every way, he was ready to do whatever it could take.

"Jake, I'd like to revisit our brief chat about the plague. For starters, let's try to define the undefinable. The enemy is hitting hard in the east and will soon head our way."

"Okay. I'm with you."

"First," Wallyce said, "just the name 'plague' is enough to throw the country into a panic, but I'm okay with that, up to a point. If the populace had a real sense of how dangerous this is, they would give us free rein to do what is needed to save lives. This current epidemic may not be a plague, but it might be a viral infection we can fight. We can't even pinpoint what it is yet, much less know how to deal with it. The numbers are off the charts regarding infection and death, and the scientists are stumped. This scares the hell out of me."

Jake leaned in. "You're not alone. A deadly infection with high transmission and fatalities isn't like past infections. And, as you point out, the scientists don't even know what we're dealing with yet. "

Wallyce took a sip of port. "Worse, I have the Congress hovering overhead looking for answers. I also have a desperate pack of Association of Bay Area Government screechers. They seem hell-bent on saving their cities and counties at the cost of progress and many lives. Jake, I sure hope I can trust you to cover my back. What we're trying to do here is monumental. We must save our country from devastation, streamline corporate and governmental management, and solve the climate mess. Imagine the positive effect we are creating will have on the climate."

"You can count on me for whatever you need and California to pave the way for you to build the infrastructure you dream of," Jake said. "And, we can provide the resources and legislation needed to get there without resistance from anyone, even the ABAG bunch. Wallyce, I've followed your journey for a few years. I know what you accomplished in terms of business success and technological advances. It's been nothing short of miraculous. What you've done and are trying to do is visionary—the stuff of legends. And now, getting to know you has been an unexpected pleasure. You had me at the pizza." Jake held his hand out. Wallyce reached out and put her own in his as if to shake them. But they didn't. Some connection was being made that they both became aware of. They stood for a time, holding hands and looking into each other's eyes. Just a momentary spark, but enough to get their mutual attention. Then, as if she just became aware, Wallyce pulled back a bit, looked down, and turned away to take a sip from her port.

Too soon, she thought. "Well, Governor Brookfield, I've enjoyed getting to know you on a more personal level. It'll help us as we work for our mutual goals." Then, sensing she sounded far too formal, she adjusted the tone. "Jake, I'm looking forward to working together. An ally like you will make these next few months seem less daunting. Let's have our staff set up a regular contact schedule so we're sure to keep the momentum going."

"Yes, good idea, Wallyce." Looking at his wrist comm, he noticed the time. "I am sorry to say I must be heading out. I have meetings in Sacramento in the morning, so I must return. Wallyce, I am so glad we had this chance. Together, we'll build a great team. He nodded to the Secret Service, "If they notify my driver, I must be going. Thanks again, Wallyce. Good night."

They shook hands. "Goodnight, Jake. I look forward to the next time."

Jake Brookfield headed toward the rear exit. Secret Service gave an informal bow along the way. His driver was ready, holding the door to his car open. They soon rolled out and down the long driveway.

Wallyce thought for a while. Something didn't sit well with her. "Build a team together? I'm gonna need to set tight protocol with this one."

Chapter Nine

Morrígan was committed to her work. This was always a sticking point with her father, General Elliott Tilton. She remembered one of his lectures to her.

"A leader does just that—leads. You set up the mission, establish the objectives, assign the team, then monitor and adjust. Those who cross over into what is called 'hands-on' by getting in and doing the jobs you've assigned to others because they aren't getting it done have removed themselves from the leadership role. If the team can't or won't do the job, replace them quickly with someone most suited to get it done. That is required of a leader."

"But, General," Morrígan would argue, "in this case, I believe I am the most suited to do the task. I can't find anyone who can do it as well as I can."

"Then you are not a leader. You're a worker. No shame in that, but you shouldn't try to be both. Leaders lead. Workers do what is assigned. You need to choose which one you will be."

It was always the same with them. Still, Morrígan knew General Tilton adored her, his second daughter. Since the day her birth parents were taken by a truck driver running far behind schedule, she knew The General was committed to her. He did all he could to allow her to become "her best self," as if that could erase her devastating loss. She knew he loved her as his own.

Morrígan also knew Wallyce, unlike her, was a born leader. So, this morning, she handed Morrígan a Barca Logic-Assisted Intelligent Device (BLAID®), already running. The small screen listed the files and a note with instructions for specific tasks she wanted Morrígan to complete.

"This is going to be massive, Morrígan. It's about the plague epidemic hitting the country's eastern half. I need you to get up to speed. Learn everything there is to know, then come to me with a plan for going forward without becoming victims of the potential devastation. I'm gathering a team of experts and leaders who will get into whatever action plan you, and I devise. I've already coordinated with Governor Jake Brookfield, who will take the lead statewide. You need to do the same with Argen and Congress so we can anticipate any roadblocks they come up with. Morrígan, this is pretty scary. From all I hear, this plague, or virus, whatever it is, is hitting with the speed of a lightning bolt and the devastation of a nuclear attack. We need to be ready. Get back to me tomorrow morning, say 7:30 AM. And get hold of me right away if there is anything I need to know about. I'm giving you total control here. Make it happen."

"Okay, boss." Morrígan liked to take the edge off situations by occasionally slipping into a familiar tone.

"Let me know if any of these contacts give you trouble. I'll be available later today." Wallyce turned and walked out before Morrígan had a chance to reply. Left with just herself and the BLAID®, she decided it was a good time to start.

"BLAID® 591717, you will respond to me and recognize my voice alone. I will address you as "Lucid." It was her code name for all of her personal technology devices. Now, show me the first action assignment you have for me."

"Yes. The first action calls for you to contact Dr. Walters at CDC. Your objective is to learn all that's meaningful about the disease infecting many people. Would you like me to connect to Dr. Walters?"

"Wait for further orders. I'll let you know. Lucid, show the action list, then hold." She scanned the list. Some names caught her eye:

- Dr. Walters, CDC – What do we know about the disease? How bad is it? How can it change? Can this become a pandemic?
- Senate Leader Argen – Current status in WDC area, current reactions in Senate/House
- Secretary Fogel (DOD) – If needed, what is the process for the Declaration of Martial Law? Morrígan stopped cold on this one. Why is she even thinking of this at such an early stage? She continued.
- General McCann (Joint Chiefs) – What is the process for population control in the event of Martial Law?
- Rachel Perriman (SF Mayor) - How prepared are you in the event of an extreme State of Emergency?

Morrígan was worried. All current info says a new virus

or plague is coming around the country in some European pockets. That's all we know so far. So why does Wallyce think about Martial Law and the extreme State of Emergency? Does she know something I don't? Did Governor Brookfield tell her something? I'd better get going on this list right now. Morrígan made the first call to Dr. Emmanuel Walters, the head of the Center for Disease Control.

The instant he answered, Morrígan knew she wasn't ready for this.

"Hello, Madam Vice President, Dr. Walters here. How can I help you?"

"Hi, Dr. Walters. Please, you know me well enough. It's Morrígan. You might know from your recent call with the President that we're concerned about this sickness we heard about. So, what's the picture for this? Is it anything to worry about?" She knew right away he was ready.

"Morrígan, it's bad. We're seeing some form of hybrid that acts like a virus one minute and like a bacterial infection the next. We've seen these in the past, but this one is different. Somehow, all those infected by the plague have severe autoimmune diseases. In every case so far, this is how it starts. Sometimes the body, hoping to stop the infection in its tracks, triggers certain immune system responses to thwart it. Sometimes, the infection is unknown and powerful, so the system sends out various immune defenses, almost like dumping everything it can against the viral invaders. In rare cases, and certainly, in the case of this syndrome, the amount of these immune defenses is far excessive. That is called a cytokine storm. In fact, the immune system is out of control in this disease. The body, by now, is desperate to kill any intruder and often begins to attack even good tissue. The results are devastating. Among them is the massive shutdown of most of the body's organs, resulting in death. Cases of this Cyto-47 have all ended in death within a few days. The signs indicate overactive immune systems. That points toward a simultaneous viral/bacterial infection."

"What does that even mean, Dr. Walters?

"It means that until we can develop a vaccine or even a cure, there is no stopping the deaths once the infection hits.?"

What he said, or how he said it, felt unreal to Morrígan. She thought momentarily that the microscopic world was plotting to wrestle power from humans and rule the world from inside a Petrie dish. She fought the idea and refocused on the problem at hand in the real world.

"Unfortunately, I'm starting to understand. How about a plan? Is there any procedure in place to go about defeating this mess? Any timeline?"

"We don't even know what it is yet. We think it's a dual infection, but of what? Don't expect a quick-fix solution until we know what we are dealing with. This isn't looking like anything short-term. I might suggest you and the President put together a strategy team. It should be all science and no politics. We might not have much time with this disease."

"This disease . . . don't you have a name for it?

"The formal name at this point is Severe Cytokine Storm – 47. now referred to by its public name of Cyto-47, for lack of a more appropriate term until we can identify the source viral agent.

* * *

Senate Leader Bill Argen wrestled with a dilemma. President Tilton, through her Vice President, wanted some insight into Congress's status regarding the quickly spreading disease. "The truth is," he thought, "it's like everyone in Washington is passing the buck to everyone else. Congress is at a standstill about this plague, and rightly so. What the hell can a bunch of politicians do about something so complicated even the best scientists in the world have no idea what they are dealing with. So, Congress is passing the buck to medical science and playing a waiting game. So, what to tell the President?" He knew that if you tell the truth, you risk panic. But if you withhold the facts, you risk losing favor with the President (that favor he needed to keep his seat for another six-year term). Wallyce Tilton was that popular. But, on the other hand, he knew he'd lose reelection if she backed someone else.

"Good to hear from you, Madam Vice President," he lied. "What can I do for you?"

"Hello, Leader Argen. I'm afraid this is going to be a somewhat abrupt call. I hope to learn all I can about the Severe Cytokine Storm plague, or what they call Cyto-47. I have a rather shallow understanding, in scientific terms, of what we're facing. What I need from you is a 'street-level' point of view. What are the social and political angles on this? Are people in a panic? Are they ambivalent? Is it even on anyone's radar?"

Argen could tell she was struggling. Even with all her education, he supposed Morrígan had little practice dealing in politics. Her questions were vague—' social and political angles,' indeed.

"Madam Vice President, please forgive me if I'm too bold, but I think I know what you need to know. This Cyto-47 is hitting hard out here, and all of Washington is calling it, is a political football. One side blames the other for something neither side could have had a hand in. Plagues, so to speak, just happen. The public isn't the least bit alarmed. The general sentiment is that this is just another scam foisted on them by the government to get them to do what they want. Politicians are concerned, but politicians don't often consider science the cause. It's far too profitable to blame the opposition for hurricanes, pandemics, droughts, and floods. The legislature gets the pleasure of pointing the political finger. But it lands on you and the President to find a solution. And you need to know this will be something that the opposition will ultimately blame on your administration. Maybe not for causing it, but certainly for not fixing it. Did that answer some of your unasked questions?" He guessed correctly. The proof was in the next move the Vice President made.

"Senator, I need to get back to you after I gather more information from others. Would it be okay if I call you tomorrow?".

"Of course. I'm on your team." She guessed correctly. He needed to see she wasn't one to shoot from the hip just to appear like a strong decision-maker. That was enough for Argen. He would work for her.

"Until tomorrow, Leader Argen." Morrígan ended the call.

Chapter Ten

Wallyce usually met with Dr. Sebastian right after a light lunch when she was still somewhat relaxed, and her thoughts were precise. However, this early morning conference made her feel out of sync. She also felt a shift in Sebastian's demeanor. Does he know something I can't see?

"Sebastian, have I missed something? You seem a bit distant this morning, more professional and not so much Dr. Sebastian I know."

He paused momentarily, then in a somber tone, said, "Madam President, I see a dangerous situation growing. First, you've stirred a hornet's nest in Washington by announcing the move of your administration to here, in Barca City. There are plenty of pissed-off Senators getting ready to strike out politically. Second, you've lit a fire under the Association of Bay Area Governments by calling its senior mayors small-time politicians. Not on the list of How to Win Friends and Influence People. You may have been correct, but perhaps it would have been better left unsaid.

Finally, a deadly plague is headed our way, and not even the brightest scientists know what it is, much less what to do about it. It's a perfect storm for you, Wally, so I may be on edge in that light. I'm wondering why you aren't."

"Maybe I'm skilled at holding back my emotions, Sebastian. You've known me long enough to guess I have a layer of fear that never rises to the light of day. If my father taught me anything, it's to always keep people guessing. Never give them a way to control you through your thoughts and fears. Even you've counseled me many times that mystery is a powerful negotiating tool." She paused to let Sebastian mull that over. Then, when she was sure he wouldn't try again to test her resolve, she opened up to him.

"I understand you only want to help me be aware of a dangerous situation, and I appreciate that. In this case, you can rest assured that I see the risks and rewards. Think of this. When everything works well, and everyone feels secure, there's almost no desire for radical change. Some might use the old cliché – 'If it works, don't try to fix it.' Things are getting pretty dicey in the country. People will be looking for some leadership out of the quagmire, and I can provide that. Am I on edge? No. I'm confident that this perfect storm, as you call it, is my best opportunity to streamline government to everyone's advantage.

"You know me. And you can see through my armor. Yes, I'm a little concerned. This will be a difficult time for the world, and I sometimes feel it's too much, even for me. That's where you step in. I need you to keep my emotions in check—hold me to the path. When I get shaky, bolster me. When I get overconfident, temper me. Most important, don't let me get weak. I need your support. Got it?"

"Of course. But you already knew that. I'm always your

biggest supporter. And, of course, my participation is your decision. I've nothing to say either way."

"Okay, then. Until our next session." She hit the switch to close the connection and lower the screen.

"Goh, please send in the Vice President."

"Yes, Madam President."

The center doorway to Wallyce's office opened as if it simply dissolved. No sound or movement. This was new technology from the architectural minds at Barca. Made of refractive light, electrical impulses, and sound-blocking lasers, the door wasn't solid. However, it functioned as if it were.

Morrígan appeared in the opening where the door once stood.

She marveled at the doorway as she stepped through the opening.

"Good morning, Wallyce. You're up early."

"You're my second meeting of the morning. You know I like to start early. Have a seat."

Morrígan chose to sit at the window end of the conference table, next to the expansive view of San Francisco Bay. Wallyce touched the control board to change the view to an office setting.

"We need to concentrate on the business and not be distracted by the view. Agree?"

Morrígan nodded and looked down at her BLAID®, ready to report her findings.

Wallyce was never one to wait for needed information. "Okay, start talking. I'll let you know if I have any questions."

"Okay," Morrígan said. "First, I should point out that everyone you assigned seemed surprised by the line of questioning. One even asked if you were trying to set up the need for a declaration. I let everyone know that you were just hoping to be fully prepared for any possibility of a full-blown pandemic. So, that said, first was Dr. Walters at CDC. He was clear on what we were dealing with. Most likely, it's a combination of a deadly virus and a bacterial infection simultaneously. Walters says this sets off alarms in the immune system and causes the body to attack itself. Any healthy organ can be attacked as if the organ were a virus or a bacterial invader. This leads to a quick death in most cases. I can give you more detail if needed."

"Not yet. Stay with the overview, and I'll ask questions when we finish."

"Fine. Next, Bill Argen was about as pointed and open as I had seen him. He called the Cyto-47 a political football. He's pretty sure the opposition will try to use it against us. Maybe even try to blame us when it gets worse, and he's confident it'll get worse.

"Secretary Fogel at the Department of Defense was next on the list. He's a team player, but he said he can't help us with any hope of planning for a declaration of Martial Law. He said this is one of the most undefined areas of federal law. Some interpretations confine Martial Law to areas of State Legislature powers. He said it has never been specifically ascribed to the Presidency. The Supreme Court hasn't ruled on where the power to declare Martial Law lies. The Constitution doesn't support Martial Law, in which the government enables the military to place control of the States under the command of the President. So, given that he's hesitant to even be open to discussing Martial Law, we might need to dig deeper. I didn't think you'd be satisfied with his non-answer, so I did some fact-finding. In brief, you could declare Martial Law—no law supports it, but no law prevents it. It could be subject to federal court review, but if we are in the middle of a full-on pandemic, that might not be anything anyone would want to do."

Wallyce knew there was more information Morrígan wasn't telling her, probably for the sake of time. "Is there anything else I need to know on this for now?"

"Only that the right to declare Martial Law is something the Governor of any state can do within the bounds of that state. Anything else will be in my report." She paused, then said, "Wally, why do you need to think about Martial Law?"

"I'm not thinking about it. I just like to have all the options on the table." Wallyce wanted to fast forward. "Okay. Who's next?"

"General McCann, Chairman of the Joint Chiefs. Again, pretty vague. Fighting an attack from within would have to be different than fighting an attack from the outside. In case of some outside military attack or even rapid growth of Cyto-47, we'd need total control over the population to protect all. In the revolution scenario, we need to determine the good guys and the enemy. Then we control them according to their category."

"What a stiff," Wallyce said. "It leaves me to wonder if McCann would be on our side or against us if we had to take control. Now, what about Perriman in San Francisco. What do you think about her emergency plans?"

"Little to none. The Mayor is all fluff and has no substance. We can pass her right by if needed."

Wallyce was troubled by this answer. "All fluff, no substance, and has an army of friends to protect her. But don't count her out. She could turn the people against us in a heartbeat. So be careful with that one.

"Now," Wallyce was to the point. "Which of these asked if I was trying to set it up for Martial Law?"

"Mayor Perriman."

"As I suspected. I'll deal with Perriman directly. Thanks for the report. I'll get back to you if I have any questions." The door appeared to open again, and Morrígan understood it was time to leave.

Chapter Eleven

On the way out of her home, Morrígan stopped to look in the mirror, hoping she would like what she saw. She looked good, and it comforted her. She was excited about Daylight Project but was over the moon about the chance to see one person in particular. Her thoughts focused on seeing her long-time dear friend, Aaron Rollins, venture capitalist and the original funding source of the Daylight Project. They were very close when she was lucky enough to be in the Bay Area while Aaron was there. She was sure they would have been lovers but for the massive pressures of their businesses. Morrígan could hardly think of anything else all afternoon. It was over a year since she last saw him. She wouldn't let the evening end without telling him how she felt. No matter how formal this evening would be, she would find a way to break free and spend some time alone with Aaron.

As her caravan approached the event, Morrígan felt a rush of excitement. She could see the intersection of Funston Avenue and Presidio Boulevard glowing with flashing lights atop the dozen police, military, and Secret Service vehicles as she turned onto Funston Avenue. The entourage made their way up Funston, turned onto Presidio, stopping in front of the headquarters of Daylight Project. Daylight was the fund she created to pay for higher education for kids from low-income environments. She was there this evening to support the organization on its tenth anniversary. They had so far funded college for more than one hundred thousand students. In addition, tonight marked the formal installation of new members to the Board of Directors.

It was one of those rare San Francisco evenings—there wasn't even a puff of fog. Instead, a mild sea breeze lifted the smells of the ocean up from where the crossroads of bay and ocean formed the Golden Gate. The moon joined the festivities, providing a bright early sky as hundreds of gulls danced their magic. The show delighted the folks assembled on the wrap-around porch of the modernized 19th Century Union Army Officers' quarters.

On rare occasions, the Secret Service might skip the safer rear entrance and pull up in front of the building. Morrígan gave strict instructions that she wanted this to be a press opportunity, so the front door was selected. She wasn't disappointed when she saw more than two dozen cameras and reporters standing by across the street.

Almost before the vehicle stopped rolling, a Secret Service officer moved in, grabbed the handle, and waited for a go-ahead signal before opening the door. She reached in with her other hand and offered it to Morrígan, who stepped from the vehicle. Morrigan walked directly up the sidewalk, her escorts on either side. The closer she got to the building, the more she could see faces and some of the people she had known through the past ten years. She didn't see one in particular but passed it off as trying to find one face in a crowd. Well, maybe he's inside.

Smiles and applause started before she stepped onto the porch and continued as she moved through the small crowd. Then, she entered the parlor, smiling and greeting familiar faces as her escort opened the path. And, in a blink, he was there, smiling and reaching for her hand, looking better than she remembered. The night just got better than I hoped for, she thought.

"Hello, Madam Vice President," he said. "It's a pleasure to see you again."

"Aaron, it's been too long. So good to see you too. There's so much catching up to do. I hope you'll stay around after the event so we can spend some time together." Her smile was sincere, and she hoped he was too. She also hoped it masked her giggly school-girl feeling when she saw him.

"Of course, I'll stay. Your security would have to tear me away." Aaron smiled at the Secret Service escort.

"Welcome, Madam Vice President." Morrígan turned around to see Rachel Perriman holding out her hand in greeting. "We are so happy you could be here for this." Having The San Francisco Mayor open ceremonial events in and around the Presidio was tradition.

"Mayor Perriman. So good to see you," Morrígan replied, shaking her hand. "I wouldn't miss this for the world." She turned back to see that Aaron had moved to another part of the room.

The Mayor said, "Sorry your sister couldn't make it."

"My sister? Oh, you mean President Tilton. I'll be sure to tell her you asked about her." The cynicism was apparent, but Perriman let it slide. She knows this is not the time for a political battle, Morrígan thought. This is my world, filled with my people. She's a barely-welcome guest speaker. There will come a time, but this is not it. Morrígan turned away from her and continued greeting people, friends, one and all.

"May I get you something, Madam? A drink, some hors d'oeuvre?" Morrígan turned to face a young lady, just old enough to serve alcohol. She wore a name tag identifying her as a Stanford University graduate student named Manda Watson.

"Thank you, Manda. White wine would be perfect." The girl nodded and turned to leave. "Wait a minute, Manda. I know you, don't I"

"Yes, Madam. I was among the General Tilton Leadership Award winners five years ago."

"Yes. I remember. Stanford, right? And please call me Morrígan."

"Oh, I could never do that," the girl blushed. "You're the Vice President."

Well, then, just call me Vice President if you wish. It's just that Madam is so formal, and you and I are old friends," Morrígan smiled and winked. "It's good to see you, Manda."

"It's good to see you too, Vice President." Manda smiled back, then went off to get the wine. Morrígan worked the room like an expert, greeting everyone, those she knew and the few who were new to Daylight Project. She was genuinely happy to see each one and made sure they knew it. Morrígan was skilled at making people feel good about knowing her. She would mention their kids' names, the member's businesses, or something special about the last time they were together. It was an effective tool, and she used it well. And when Manda brought her the wine, she put her arm around the young woman's shoulder. She told the group, "This is my friend Manda Watson, one of the General Tilton Award winners from a few years back. Even though she likely has a ton of work as a Stanford Grad student, she's volunteering here tonight. Thanks for being you, Manda. We're proud to know you."

Manda was caught slightly off guard, but she loved the recognition. "Thank you, Vice President. You can count on me any time."

The room lights flashed once, and Mayor Perriman stepped onto the small platform meant to serve as a stage for the night. She paused for the chatter to subside.

"Dear friends, thank you for allowing me to open the evening's program. We are here tonight on behalf of The Daylight Project. As you all know, tonight marks the tenth anniversary of the Daylight Project's first awards ceremony. It's to honor the recipients, the Board of Directors, and Benefactors who make this possible." She referred to the notes she had been given. "The Daylight Project has provided funds for college educations for thousands of deserving youth and offers counseling and support for those who have completed their education and are ready to start their careers. And, as is tradition, the Project will present one of its students with an honorarium tonight. This award signifies recognition for outstanding achievement, the General Tilton Leadership Award. And now, let me introduce the Chairman of the Board for Daylight Project, The Vice President of the United States, Morrígan Meath Tilton.

On cue, the crowd parted to make a path for Morrígan to reach the podium. It was interesting. She thought that she imagined the room's mood changing to a formal, somber one on mentioning her title. People stood more erect and clapped less enthusiastically as if it were expected and not out of genuine feeling. But, looking directly at some of the faces, she realized the mood swing was a figment of her own insecurity. These people were her friends and associates. They cared about her. One quick look over her friends' genuine smiles and happy faces erased the insecurity from her thoughts.

"Friends, I am so lucky to do this every year, spend some time with all of you, and then announce the General Tilton Award winner for the year. But, as lucky as I am, I also feel the loss of being able to work day in and day out on the Project.

"I've been proud to be a part of the project for many years. I know how hard you all work, and I'm proud of you and what you do. I've watched for so long the young people who receive your support. They mirror your hard work and commitment, and their results have been astounding; doctors, research fellowships, and corporate leaders. A few have started their own groups designed to help others who are less fortunate but no less deserving. You exemplify leadership to them every day.

And now, as you know, we had the impossible task of selecting this year's recipient of the General Tilton Award for Leadership. Of course, picking one out of the many you work with daily is difficult. I don't envy you that. But, on the other hand, I take pride in the fact that every one of the young people we work with year after year is an example of hope for our future. They bring daylight to an often-dark world.

"The time has come to announce the General Elliott Tilton Award recipient for this year." The award goes to a promising young woman who founded and brought her organization of committed volunteers and donors called Fast

Forward to life. They acquire and refurbish older, abandoned buildings in San Francisco and Oakland. These buildings are repurposed as apartment villages to house people recently left homeless. This project has become a start-to-finish solution in which the homeless are taken in and enrolled in a self-sufficient community. Fast Forward is a shining example of how to repurpose buildings, provide homes, feed and clothe people, and build a self-sustaining community caring for people like themselves. This group has become quite a success, and the founder has been awarded the Pulitzer for her work. Friends, I present our Tilton Leader and my friend, Soba Parkasian."

A screen behind Morrígan came to life, showing the presentation team standing with a young woman at her home as she has just been told of the award.

"Hi, Soba," Morrígan shouted over the applause. "We are all so proud to be associated with you. Congratulations. We'll see you on our worldwide broadcast tomorrow night, but we'd love to hear a few words about how you're feeling right now."

"Oh, thank you so much," The young lady beamed. "This means more to me than you can know. The Daylight Project has changed my life, and we can change others' lives through your support. You all should be getting this award. I'm only doing what you have made possible. Thank you, from the bottom of my heart, thank you." Tears welled in her eyes as she waved to the camera. As the applause continued, the screen faded, and Morrígan returned to the group.

"Many of you know, Soba and I share childhood trauma. After a kidnapper stole her from her parents, Soba spent much of her youth as an abused child. In her early teens, she managed to escape, living on the streets, afraid to go to the police for help, as the kidnapper convinced her they would only lock her up for life. Soba was left homeless and without a family. She wandered the streets, asking at every opportunity if there was any work, so she could earn enough to buy food. One day, she happened to walk into our offices in the mission district. One of our volunteers saw a fire in her eyes and sat the girl down for lunch, where she was able to learn the girl's story. That, as they say, was that. Soba became one of us on the spot, and you have all seen the results of her determination; Fast Forward. And the best news, Soba's parents happened to see her story on the news in a promotional ad for Daylight Project. They knew right away that this was their daughter. And now, Soba and her parents are being reunited.

Because of who she is—her core spirit—Soba turned difficulty into opportunity. Her commitment and her genius are inspirational. So please give her another hand and donate to her project, Fast Forward Fund.

"And now, I need to make a couple of announcements. First, as you can imagine, since my campaign for Vice President, I find my time is no longer my own to schedule. I'm committed to working on behalf of the country. I must tell you that this commitment leaves no room for other endeavors, including the Board of Directors of the Daylight Project. Therefore, I must now turn the leadership role over to someone who will hold the organization as dear as I have these many years. I am excited to have found the one person I feel will protect and promote the Project above all else. I present to you our dear friend, Aaron Rollins.

* * *

Aaron stepped onto the platform, reached for Morrígan's hand, and shook it. He stepped to the podium. "First, I'd like to congratulate Morrígan on her election to the Vice Presidency. This proves the American Voters actually are smart." He paused for the laughter. "Next, I wish to accept this honor and thank the Board for their confidence. I'll add that I'm confident that I wasn't chosen for this position just because I run a business that raises and invests millions of dollars every month." He looked at Morrígan and chuckled as he nodded his head, the nod slowly changing into a head shake. The group laughed, getting the joke right away. He looked down at his notes, then back at Morrígan. In all honesty, I accepted this role for several reasons, not the least of which is my total devotion to the one who made this organization possible in the first place. If not for Morrígan Tilton, there would be no Daylight Project. You wouldn't be here ready to work your butts off to help the next generation of miracles happen. I wouldn't be standing at this podium accepting a job that will inevitably be the most difficult one in my life, yet the most rewarding. The plain truth is, I would do anything Morrígan Tilton asked me to do. And I am asking the same of you as we begin another year of opportunities and challenges. And so, I wish to announce that my company, Nor Bay Ventures, pledges ten percent of our profits for the next six months to provide a fast start to success for this year." The applause was as generous as his gift.

"Now, what do you say we move into the dining room for dinner?"

Aaron sat next to Morrígan during the meal. The seating chart served him well. He hoped to use the dinner as a means of reconnection—an opportunity to somehow rekindle the closeness they were beginning to feel the last time they were together.

Aaron thought he had never met a more fascinating woman in his life. "Morrígan, it's so good to spend time with you again. Seeing you this evening has made the last year worth the wait." He wondered if he was too forward, based on the look of surprise on her face. Did I move too fast?

"Aaron, I was just thinking the same. I've often thought of you over the year since we spent the weekend in Carmel. Other than your business, which I see all over the news, how are you?"

"Well, besides business, as you say, there's not much to discuss. I'm more boring than ever," Aaron half-joked. "I've spent a great deal of time and money building a support team I can trust to handle things as I would, allowing me the luxury of taking some brief escape time. But, unfortunately, about all I've been able to use the time for is the occasional wilderness week."

"I recall you told me about them. If I remember, you go as deep into the forest as possible, and there you stay, living off the land for a whole week. Right?

"Pretty much. My last trip was two weeks long. My favorite escape is in the redwood forests up the coast. I won't bore you with the details, just to say I can find near-total peace up there. No one else there, no questions, no pressures, no critical decisions. More than anything, I've found out who I am. Imagine you're given a week to spend alone, no unnatural sounds, no voices with their incessant questions that mean everything to them but very little to you. Sure, you're stuck thinking about your normal pressures, work, and the like for a few days. But, after about three days alone, the subconscious begins to look for the familiar—that which it knows, people and social trappings. Then, absent the presence of others, without thinking about it, you begin to look inside yourself, the only human within social distance. And you start to ask questions."

"Like what questions?"

"Well, like mundane crap you think you're supposed to ask yourself. Questions like do you like the person you've become? Are you happy with your business? Do you ever think you'll find someone to share your life with? Soon, you're aware that those questions are just scratching the surface, superficial. It's not long before you dive right in and hit some nerves with things like Who are you, really, who? What would that word be if you had to describe yourself in one word? Finally, I asked myself the difficult question that I've never been willing to ask, much less answer, even less do something about it. Now, I must determine if I'm willing to act on the answer." He paused. "I can see I've confused you. It's hard to describe without giving all the details."

"So? Is this something you would share?

"Not sure. If I shared the answer, you'd be at the top of the list of those I might share it with. I will, however, tell you the question that now haunts me. I asked myself if you knew that you had a very brief time left here on Earth; if you knew you would die on a certain date, what is the one thing that devastates you to know you could never do or be because time has run out?"

Morrígan sat quietly for a time. A tear trickled silently down her cheek. "Thank you," she whispered. "It must have taken so much trust to tell me that." She was moved by the question, remembering her parents and wishing she could spend more life with them.

"It takes more trust to tell you that the answer to the

question surprised me. And I can't stop thinking about it. It's unlike anything else in my life. I've been unable to resolve the answer in my mind, much less in my heart. It's life-changing. I hope you'll let me share it if and when it's right to do so. But that's for another time."

They sat silently, looking at each other for a long time. By then, the demeanor of the crowd had shifted. "Looks like the party's over," Aaron said.

Guests lined up to pay their respects before leaving. Morrígan was surprised by Aaron's following comment. "I'd like to see you again. The sooner, the better."

"Well, how about tomorrow?" she said. There's a tour of Barca City I'm scheduled to lead, and I'd love to show you around."

"I'll clear my schedule. What time should I show up?"

"I'll send a car for you at 11. It'll make it easier. That way, you don't have to pass through security. Where should they meet you?"

"My office will be fine." He leaned in to kiss her cheek. Morrígan turned quickly and kissed his lips.

She smiled. "See you tomorrow." With that, she was escorted out to the waiting transport.

Chapter Twelve

Morrígan had much to do to contact all team members. She had to enroll them in the new Pandemic Control Team, open an initial introductory session, establish a contact meeting schedule, then close the session. When that was all set, she would be ready to greet Aaron and the diplomats to start the tour of Barca City. She opened the list on her BLAID® and selected the Contact Group function. The system activated the communications screen above her desk, which showed in large fonts Establishing Group Meeting.

She could feel the pulse throbbing in her neck, indicating she was under too much pressure. It wasn't just because she had so much to do before the tour. The look she saw on her sister's face shook her. She knew Wallyce like she knew herself, and she could tell that Wallyce Tilton, the President of the United States, was frightened.

The Communication Screen changed as the notification chimed, Group Established. Morrígan clicked the Open tab on her BLAID®, and the group members appeared on her wall screen. She needed a fast connection, so she opted for simple projection.

"Good day, all, and thank you for taking my call. I'll get right to the point. President Tilton has appointed you to The Control Team, a special task force. If you accept this, you must be sworn into a very high level of Top-Secret confidentiality. In other words, you can't discuss or hint at this to anyone, including your family. This must be clear. Please signify your intent to comply under oath." One by one, the words Oath Affirmed appeared under each person's image onscreen.

"Thank you. The purpose of this group is to determine the exact risk we face with the Cyto-47 plague. Do we stand any chance, or is this enemy impossible to defeat? Over the past thousand years, we've witnessed many epidemics, pandemics, and viral attacks. We now believe we should be able to develop some form of vaccine, medical treatment, or genetic manipulation to defeat such an attack. However, some tell us that this time is different. Cyto-47 is the exception, the one we have always suspected would be among us at some time—the one we may not be able to defeat. We expect you to give us your initial findings later today.

It's now 10:00 am, West Coast. You should expect to meet with us online at 5:00 pm Pacific Time today. However, we may have other reasons to contact you beforehand, so be prepared. Thank you again for your service. Until later." She closed the meeting and lowered her screen.

Morrígan spoke to her comm, "Call Aaron." Her BLAID® flashed silently.

"Hi, Morrígan. I was just thinking of you."

"Good morning, Aaron. How's your day going?"

"Great, and soon it'll be better," he said. How about yours?"

"Like running away from snarling dogs uphill on ice, but otherwise terrific. I could use an army of assistants to manage so many things. In fact, I will probably bring on a new virtual AI assistant this week to focus on the critical issues a bit closer. Let's talk when you get here."

"Oh, good. I was worried you were calling to cancel the tour.

I'm really looking forward to it. Does it still look like the car will get here around 11:00?"

"Well, we operate on a tight schedule," she laughed. "I'll bet it arrives exactly one minute before 11:00. They'll drop you at the Executive Entrance in the tunnel, and you'll be escorted into Stanford Hall. I'll be there waiting, along with a handful of diplomats. Not to worry, though. You and I will leave them in that hall. They'll follow us electronically—holographically, to be clear. We're pretty careful with visitors from outside the country. Diplomats and Embassies have a continuous flow of couriers and dignitaries, so we restrict their movement inside the City."

"The plague?"

Well, partly. It's never too early to take strict precautions if we've learned anything from past pandemics. This one is super-deadly. It could be hundreds of thousands, maybe even millions of deaths. We can discuss that later, but you'll likely be scanned at the entrance. Is that going to be a problem?"

"Probably not. Depends on the definition of a scan." His little joke fell flat.

"One of our companies has developed a special scanning system that can detect certain viral and some bacterial anomalies. It's non-contact, and there is no risk to your health. Assuming you're virus-free, no alarms will flash, and you can just walk in. If I hadn't mentioned it, you'd never have known. But, I'd feel creepy about not telling you like I was somehow tricking you, and I couldn't do that."

Aaron chuckled. "Okay, as long as you put it that way, I'll let you scan me. But you'll have to sign a Non-disclosure agreement about anything your scanner learns about my tattoos."

"You? Tattoos?" I'm so surprised. I didn't see you as the type."

He started to laugh. "I Gotcha. I don't have any tattoos. I'm just playing with you. But, hey, time's flying and I have things to do before I leave here. See you soon."

"Yep. See you soon," Morrígan said. "And for the record, I'm really looking forward to this. Bye for now." A smile stayed on her face. What a great feeling, she thought after she disconnected. The world's in crisis, and I'm partly responsible for building a plan to minimize the horror we're facing. I'm about as happy as I can ever remember being. Look out, Mr. Aaron Rollins. You're becoming very important to me.

She had a quick snack before meeting the visitors at Stanford Hall. "Goh, please bring a small order of crab sushi to my office as soon as possible. And add an iced tea fixed my way." Morrígan rarely used the AI assistant for trivial things like snacks, but she was in a hurry.

"The order is in, Madam."

"On second thought, double the order and add a tuna roll. Mr. Rollins may not have time to eat before he arrives."

"Yes, Madam."

Morrígan wanted to learn as much as she could about the

Cyto-47 plague in the little time she had before the tour. "BLAID®, scan all available reports dealing with the Cyto-47 worldwide. Order by date, most recent first, then by subtopic equal to positivity rates, and then by mortality percentages." The screen flashed three times quickly, then a new custom app displayed. The heading read, "Vice Presidential Briefing on Plague Status," and several columns of thumbnails were too small to read the text, although the headlines were readable. She clicked through a few more interesting titles. Still, their headlines were much more informative than the actual text of the reports and articles. Then, one caught her eye. The title read 'Pandemic: What the Government Isn't Telling You?' published by the leading anti-government rag, Never Again Publications. Morrígan knew right away that a quick scan wouldn't be enough to get the critical points of this story. She also knew that Never Again was adept at turning the truth in their desired direction. They often broke factual reports the traditional media hesitated to bring to the press. Sometimes, it seems, the reality is just too frightening to look at. Morrígan guessed that some of the horror stories already a part of this infection were frightening. The sushi arrived, and the server set it up on the side table.

"That's okay," Morrígan said. "We can handle that. You can go now." Without looking up from her reading, she could sense that the server was still there.

"Can I help you?"

The young lady looked up. There were tears in her eyes. Morrígan approached her, put a hand on her shoulder, and asked, "What's wrong? Don't cry. Let me help." The girl broke down sobbing. Morrígan could feel the girl's entire body wracked with sobs. She hugged her, hoping the girl would be able to gather herself. After a minute, the sobs slowed to gentle crying. Morrígan held her off enough to look in her eyes.

"I'm sorry, Ma'am. I just found out my Mom has some kind of sickness, something they are getting back east where she lives, and they say some people are dying from it." Her sobs threatened to return.

"Did they tell you what the name of the sickness is?"

"I don't know. . . some kind of plague, something. I was too scared to hear it all." Then, the girl must have realized she had lost it in front of the Vice President. "I'm sorry, Ma'am." Her look betrayed her embarrassment, and she left before Morrígan could stop her.

Morrígan was too shaken by the girl's bad news to continue reading. She couldn't help but think that according to what she had just heard, this young girl might receive worse news soon. For Morrígan, the Plague became more real. This girl will soon lose her mother, and there is no way to stop it. Morrígan vowed to do everything she could to fight this monster, Cyto-47.

The wall screen beeped once. Aaron's face filled the screen, and the announcement came that he had arrived in the tunnel.

"Please bring him to my office right away." She looked at her BLAID® and saw they still had time to eat before meeting the diplomats. Less than two minutes later, the door opened, and Aaron stood there. Morrígan walked over to greet him. A respectful handshake and kiss on the cheek in greeting were designed to be the formal greeting any passersby would expect. Morrígan wasn't in the mood for any office rumors to start. As soon as he was entirely inside, she hugged him and gave him a more affectionate kiss, which he was only too happy to return. They stood there, looking into each other's eyes. When she began to feel uncomfortable, Morrígan broke it off, turning to the food. "I recall you enjoyed crab sushi, and I took a guess on the tuna roll. "

"You didn't have to feed me. I feel like a kid at the amusement park, and I can't wait to see this magnificent Barca City inside."

"I'm happy to hear that. But I need to eat a bit. I won't have any time later. Please join me."

"Well. Since you put it so nicely, I may have to try some of this sushi. It looks great." They ate the food, drank the iced tea, and stared into each other's eyes the entire time. Morrígan chuckled when Aaron accidentally put a roll with a large glob of wasabi into his mouth. Then made a feeble attempt to pretend he meant to do it. When the tears rolled down his face, and he quickly drank half of his iced tea in one draft, it was too much, and she laughed out loud.

"I'm so sorry, Aaron." She fought the laugh enough to get the words out. He tried to speak, but the words came out scratchy and muffled.

Morrígan went into action. Goh, a cold glass of milk, quickly." It arrived as if by magic, and she said, "Drink the milk slowly, letting it cool the burn. He was soon able to speak.

"How did you know to do that? Milk and wasabi?"

"My Dad once did the same for me. You never forget it happens to you. Are you okay?"

"He touched his throat, coughed softly as a test, then nodded. 'Yeah, I think I'm going to make it. Judging by your laugh, I must have been quite the picture of cool."

"Well, you had this look that was just too much. Sorry for laughing, but I have to admit, it was pretty funny. I thought your eyes were gonna pop right out of your head." She chuckled again. This time he joined her. They had some fun with the thought of his eyes popping right out. Morrígan knew they were acting like a couple of school kids, but maybe, she thought, it's just what we need now.

"So, what's on the agenda? He asked."

Her BLAID® showed seven minutes until the guests were due to arrive.

"Well, we'll meet up with the tour group, a few diplomats downstairs in Stanford Hall. I'll spend a few minutes explaining their experience, then their food will be served. In the center of the tables is a presentation platform for holographic display. I'll introduce you as the newly appointed head of the Daylight Project. They don't need to know more about your business or anything else. Then you and I will tour the facilities, and a crew will film the tour, projecting it all holographically to them as they enjoy their lunches."

"Well, I hope they aren't having sushi," he giggled." They stepped into the transport lift system, and Morrígan gave the voice command, "Stanford Hall at Presentation Access Doors." The transport traveled westward 100 feet, then glided downward for more than 30 floors. Finally, it transitioned southward fifteen feet toward the requested stop. The transitions were seamless and nearly imperceptible. Aaron told Morrígan he was surprised he barely felt anything when they shifted to straight descent. The entire trip took less than half a minute. Gliding softly to a stop, the doors opened without a sound, and the access doors to the Hall opened, ready for their access.

Entering the room, Morrígan noticed everyone wearing a clear full-face covering, including the ever-present Secret Service agents. She could also hear the low steady hum of the air filtration system as it exchanged the air in the room at high volume. She thought to herself, looks like Wallyce enacted Phase II Medical Precaution in the last half hour. She stepped to the podium and found a box of face covers. She handed one to Aaron and put one on herself.

"Aaron, there's a seat next to the podium." As he took his seat, she stepped to the platform. The instant she approached the podium, the lights focused on her and bathed her in a soft glow. The sound system targeted her, and sound levels were established and verified. She was good to go.

"Hello to all of our visiting dignitaries. I am Morrígan Tilton. We're excited to introduce you to the future of corporate living, our new state-of-the-art Barca City. I hope you'll see unexpected things here. Some of our new technologies certainly are that. But, some technologies are in testing, many in design, and a few are confidential and proprietary. Those are things we can't show you today. You will see some things that surprise you, and you may ask questions as we go along. We will answer some of these questions, and some will not. We hope you understand. For your comfort, you won't need to leave your tables to take this tour. In fact, your lunch will be served as we speak.

"As you have probably heard, Barca is a leading provider of holographic technologies. My friend and associate, Mr. Aaron Rollins, and I will tour Barca City in person. Our hologram images will come to life right here, in the middle of your table grouping." As she said, a fully functioning medical facility grew from the floor in enough detail. It was a hologram of the Barca City Medical Center. "Here is our Med Center. If I were there, I might walk into the waiting room like this . . ." The image zoomed in to show the actual waiting room, with people seated and walking about. "As you see, we can drill down to full-sized holograms. Aaron and I will be in the rooms as we tour them, and I'll explain where we are at any time. At the end of the tour, I will rejoin you. So, unless there are any questions now, Let's get started.

* * *

The room lights dimmed as a holographic model of the entire Barca City Bio-environment was constructed in the middle of the room. Some areas, as they were shown, were labeled in general terms, such as Medical Centers or Manufacturing. Others were not.

"I encourage you to pay attention to details as we progress through the City. Every building operates separately within Barca City, except most are physically connected within the Main City building. You can see this master structure from Observation Park, accessible from the San Mateo Bridge, about mid-bridge. Spanning two-thirds of the distance from the western San Mateo shoreline to the Eastern Hayward Hills shoreline, and reaching the center portion to more than 40 stories, is the main structure of the City. You are seated in Stanford Hall in honor of Stanford University, my and the President's alma mater. We are loyal to the place that gave us the education President Tilton has relied on to create the great Barca Corporation.

"With all of our buildings and businesses directly connected here, we needed to develop the world's first multi-directional/ multi-speed Inside transport system. This replaces traditional stairs, elevators, and many hallways. To understand the value of this system, consider this. If you wanted to leave Stanford Hall, on the first floor of Barca, and walk to our Training and classrooms, located on the 20th floor of the Southeast corner of the City, it would take the better part of an hour. We have a solution called Mag-Glide Transport, or MGT. Borrowing from the old Maglev designs of the last century, MGT operates on a cushion-of-air principle afforded by magnetic-levitation systems. The magnets are programmed to move the transport capsule in nearly any direction, quickly, silently, and without a feeling of speed. For example, when Mr. Rollins and I left my office and came here, our trip was the following: We entered the transport capsule. I told the system where we wished to go and which specific access point we wanted. We traveled westward 100 feet, then descended for more than 30 floors. Then once we arrived at the first floor, the MGT quickly transitioned and took us southward fifteen feet, where it stopped and opened the doors." Turning to Aaron, she asked, "Aaron, what did that trip, which took a matter of seconds, feel like to you. Did you feel the speed? What did the 30-floor drop feel like, and what surprises you the most about it?"

Aaron stood and faced the guests. "Honestly, I had no idea we left the 30th floor and are now at ground level. And as far as the speed and directional changes, I can hardly believe it. I'm amazed." His reaction was better than any technical description. The guests were whispering among themselves about this game-changing technology.

"And now," Morrígan said, "Please follow us through the magic of Barcan Technology as we take a tour of Barca City. You will see, hear, smell, and experience several of our facilities. Of course, there will be many leading-edge products in use that you won't understand how we do what we do. In fact, you might have an interest in using some of these new technologies in your own countries. Feel free to ask questions as we go along.

* * *

While digging into the chilled crab salad in front of them, the guests got to know each other. Of course, it helped that they were forewarned, and most didn't eat earlier before arriving. The Barca kitchens had earned quite a reputation as top-grade, and the crab didn't disappoint. Served on a crystal plate, the salad was chilled to perfection. It was clear that the Tilton Administration knew how to entertain.

After only a brief pause, the south wall of Stanford Hall came to life. A vibrant logo announced that the viewers could join the tour of Barca City as it took place, figuratively speaking, on the low platform area between their tables. A voice announced, "Please continue to enjoy your lunch as it is served. You are seated far enough apart, and your scans show you are each free of any infection, so you may remove your face covers to eat.

"As you can see, the space reserved for the holographic tour experience is relatively small. Therefore, it doesn't allow a life-sized representation of the places visited. Instead, a more detailed version of the toured places will be displayed in 3-D video format on this larger screen.

The screen faded to black as the area between tables began to glow. A deep, almost imperceptible hum began. The room lighting softened, just dark enough to create a feeling of mystery, adding to the curiosity about what would happen. The guests looked at each other. Someone whispered, "Okay, this is special." Others smiled and nodded in agreement.

"By now, you're probably enjoying the crab salad and wondering what's next on tour." Their eyes were drawn to the hologram platform, where a smaller version of Morrígan rose slowly up from the floor, revolving. She smiled at each guest as she turned to face them. "I can tell you, the food will be great, but you'll have to force yourselves to remember to eat, as the tour will challenge your thinking. We are now across from Stanford Hall, at the American Village Conference Center and Arena entrance. This is the world's largest, most sophisticated, fully indoor arena today, capable of hosting more than One Hundred Thousand people at a time. Let's take a look."

Above Morrígan's head, the image of the Conference Center and Arena took holographic form. She described the significant design nuances of the Center, such as the unique sound system. Soon, a tiny image of Aaron Rollins began to take shape on the opposite end of the arena seating, in one of the riser platforms.

"As you can see, Aaron is about as far away from me as normal vision can tolerate. Imagine trying to carry on a deep discussion with such a distant person. At the same time, the Conference Center is filled with, oh, let's say, fifty thousand people. You might think the discussion would be impossible." She turned toward the direction of Aaron and whispered loudly, "What do you think, Mr. Rollins?" She flipped a switch on the controller in her hand. Suddenly, Aaron appeared to be standing right in front of her. The guests, as a group, let out an audible gasp.

"What you see is a brand new, revolutionary technology from Barca, best described as repeating image transport. First, Aaron's image from where he is standing is slightly enlarged, then passed to another repeating station, where it is again enlarged, and so on. Next, it's transferred to a life-sized hologram in true-life detail closer to me. From where I stand, I can tell he seems to be standing right next to me. Finally, his sound is projected into my ear by a similar technology to the hearing aids from past centuries. I hear him clearly if he whispers, but no one else does unless he allows it. This Is just one of the hundreds of innovative breakthroughs we have applied to our home, Barca City. Some are in beta mode, and others are available on the world marketplace.

"Similar new technologies you might enjoy include the ability to host meetings here that are a hybrid combination of in-person participants and those here in hologram only. I would not exaggerate to tell you that you might have difficulty deciding which are here and which are holograms. To underscore her claim, she added, Ladies and Gentlemen, allow me to introduce The President of the United States, Wallyce Tilton." In a heartbeat, President Tilton appeared standing on the other side of Morrígan. "Now, I challenge you. Which of us is actually standing here, and which is a hologram?" she waited. When no answer came, she continued, "It's a trick question. In truth, as you know, we are all holograms standing before you in miniature form. Now, look at the projection wall and try to discern the difference. They all were there, on the wall, but slowly, Aaron and Wallyce faded to black. Soon, Morrígan also disappeared. Then, her holographic image grew in both size and quality on the platform between tables until she seemed to stand there.

"I am now a life-sized hologram standing with you. Could you tell unless I told you? This is the most advanced image system, Holographic Image Transport, or HIT. We are revolutionizing how people and companies will meet soon. Think of the positive impact of significant reductions in business and government travel. Imagine the time now wasted getting from one point to another just to have a face-to-face meeting being reduced or eliminated. Certain levels of employees will be able to spend all their work time actually productive and with no more travel downtime. Now, imagine the benefit to those who seek a better world, free from the fear of global warming and the need to burn fuels.

"Now, she added, "Let's meet up in the Manufacturing Operations community." She and Aaron left the view of the active hologram of the Arena. Once they were no longer in sight or sound range, she spoke to Aaron.

"Follow me. I know a shortcut." She was only half joking. Although the Manufacturing and Operations sector was straight down the hall and on the ground follow level, Morrígan had learned that the movement of materials and products had not yet been fine-tuned. There were often traffic jams in the main corridor. It was faster and safer to go up one level, then cross to the east before returning to the main level at the entrance to the Manufacturing building. It took them out of the planned tour and the vision of the Secret Service detail for a minute. She scanned her eye into the route sensor, then gave their destination as ManOps. When the door closed with a slight whooshing sound, Morrígan put her arms around Aaron's neck. They kissed, a kiss of new lovers trying to find their connection. At the same time, they were transported up one level, across the mile distance past Accounting, Past Design and Testing, finally down one level, stopping at the main entrance to the sprawling Manufacturing and Operations Center for all of Barca City. They parted just a moment before the door opened in front of a team of workers probably heading out to the Break Center. Although sure they weren't seen,

Morrígan felt herself blush like a schoolgirl on her first date. She looked over to Aaron and was surprised to see him standing at the entrance, seeming dumbfounded. They were stopped in their tracks by a small Secret Service detail who separated them and asked Morrígan to identify the man she was with. She gave his name and the reason for his visit, and they allowed them to pass. But they stayed behind them a bit closer in case she violated her security again. They had their mission, and they were committed to it.

"Morrígan, I had no idea. I didn't expect anything like this." He was staring into the Center, where visitors were greeted by the image of a woman in what might be a Barca Security uniform. Behind her, groups of robots hustled back and forth, carrying packages and pulling carts laden with more boxes. Some robots were trimmed in official-looking designs, wearing badges and weapons, and set up to look like police officers. Past the non-human crowds were several of what could best be called tunnels. In fact, they were more like roadways, two lanes wide and fifteen feet high. "Morrígan, where do they go?" Aaron asked.

"Funny you should ask. We're headed there now. So rather than tell you, let's just go. But first, the tour." She turned so the central part of the entrance was directly behind her, clicked on her BLAID®, and waited a few seconds. Then she spoke to the visitors.

"Welcome back. I hope you're enjoying the meal. If there's anything else you need, simply ask. Behind me is the main entrance to Barca's Manufacturing and Operations. We manufacture many leading-edge products, including our revolutionary communications, holographic environments, and transport systems. Much of this is assembled robotically, right here behind me. We'll take a brief tour through the center, mostly from the vantage point of the interior roadways you can see just over my shoulder. Shall we go?" An electric transport vehicle rode up and stopped for Morrígan and Aaron to climb aboard. There was no human driver; it was just a cart with seats. Morrígan and Aaron took the seats in the front while a second cart carried the Secret Service detail. Once they were seated, a chime sounded, and a message on the dashboard told them to raise their arms to their chest level. As they did, padded seats and shoulder belts snaked around them and snapped into place.

"Convenient and clever," Aaron said. You've finally solved the question of personal choice. Choose not to comply; the belts will wrap around your arms like a straitjacket."

"Shhh," Morrígan whispered. "We're on tour, right?" She winked, and Aaron nodded that he understood. And the tour proceeded.

Chapter Thirteen

The cart signaled it was about to proceed by sounding low-beep noises. Turning in place often surprised the passengers, who might have assumed the cart rolled on traditional wheels. It didn't. Instead, these transport carts floated on a cushion of air. Riding only an inch off the surface, they could add pressure to ride even higher if there was an obstacle in their path. The ride was like a small boat on a still lake—smooth, quiet, and very comfortable. It could also be surprisingly fast.

As they approached the center corridor, the tunnel walls began to glow softly and then ripple like small, soft waves bathed in a glow reminiscent of the ocean. They offered a comfortable, almost hypnotic rhythm.

"What you see here with the movement and light patterns is pretty and functional." Morrígan spoke to the Hologram laser cameras slightly in front of her and attached to the tunnel's roof. "The glowing lights result from our system-wide UVC sanitation effort. The Ultraviolet-C light, supported by our solar power generation and refined to a level strong enough to kill viruses and bacteria yet soft enough, so there is no damage to our eyes, comes from the wall itself. The movement prevents dust and pollution from sticking to the wall. Air-screen jets at the top of each tunnel wall move the debris downward, where powerful vacuums draw it out of the building all day long. The result is a cleaner environment for man and machine inside Barca City. Plus, as you can see, it makes for a beautiful display. Now, we'll move ahead to see the BLAID® production." A light flashed on the dashboard, indicating a question from the visitors. Morrígan tapped the light, and a voice message played.

"Please, what is the blade you speak of?"

Morrígan gave a voice command to her own BLAID® device. "Transport hologram of BLAID® device to Stanford Hall Display wall." A chime indicated it had been done.

"You may have seen me use my own BLAID® today. One of its functions is to monitor our progress, analyze our next moves and needs, then send the results to the holographic display in front of you. At the same time, BLAID® is managing my schedules and sending out all communications per my pre-set list of contacts. In addition, it continuously evaluates my success rate for my efforts, giving me an on-demand display that pretty much tells me how I'm doing. Based on the statistics, BLAID® will eventually advise me of my possible success rates, allowing me to make the best decisions based on my past successes. How's that for a pocket device?" She knew the answer. "Now, let's turn up the speed. We have another mile and a half before we reach the BLAID® Manufacturing Sector."

On her command, a warning sounded, telling all to sit back and hold onto the arm rails. Within fifteen seconds, the alarm stopped, and the cart began to gain speed, slow at first, then ramping up to what might be called too fast if on an outside highway. But, here in Barca, all traffic movement is tightly controlled, and the chance of collision is nil. But the speed was scary. Morrígan glanced at Aaron and noticed the knuckles on his hands were white. He was death-gripping the rails.

"You okay, Aaron?"

"Oh, yeah, I love it. His wide eyes belied his claim. He was more than a little nervous.

For those seeing this via HIT display from Stanford Hall, the camera view shifted to emphasize the feeling Morrígan and Aaron must have felt from the front seats. They watched the speed ramp up. The effect was so real several of them let out a moan as they grabbed their seats in involuntary reaction. Thirty seconds later, they felt the reversers engage to slow the speed. The reversers had to perform the same action as reversing the engines on an airplane as it landed—even more so since there were no wheels with brakes to finish the job.

Morrígan stood to face the cameras to her right as their seat harnesses retracted. "As you now see, behind me, we appear to have stopped too soon, as we're up against the same wall we saw before we took this ride. No expected doorway in sight." The wall was as blank as it had been the entire trip. "Looks here can be deceiving." She raised her BLAID® device toward the wall, and the device chirped rhythmically. The wall disappeared, and they found they were staring inside BLAID® Village. In this secure environment, all Barca Logic-Assisted Intelligent Devices were built, customized to their new owners, then tested against the owner's history files.

"We're very proud and protective of our BLAID® technology. As you see, the entire operation is performed robotically. To your left is the assembly operation. There, assembly and final testing are performed. There's no human intervention in this process. Next, they move on to the BarcaGenius stations, where the new owner's history, intelligence, personality traits, genetics, and habits are loaded. Then they are tested against our known data for that owner. Since these devices serve as an extension of their owner, we infuse as much of that owner's personality into the device itself as possible."

Three similar questions rang out on the dashboard. In effect, they all wanted to know how that could be possible.

"First," Morrígan explained, "with the permission of the BLAID® buyer, we gather all known history of the person we are making this device for. We search medical, government, educational, religious, military, and the details of any police records. This gives us a basis. Next, we interview the person at length, then, if needed, we interview their friends and family. Finally, they are given a battery of personality tests. All of this is fed into the Intelligence Engine of the BLAID®. Of course, Barca controls the world's largest social media database, the benefit of owning nearly all of the network sources and their associated data. That is what enables us to make each device close to the intelligence and personality of the user. Naturally, long-term use will add an even tighter personality factor. As I said, we're both proud and protective of this technology. I've told you what I can tell you, so please, no questions."

Morrígan focused on Employee Community Housing, Education, Medical, and Research and Development. She concluded with a return to Stanford Hall. Finally, she bid them a good day, and they were escorted out of the City. Aaron was glad she saved some time for him at the end.

"Morrígan, I'm blown away. I could never begin to imagine anything like Barca City. There's so much I'm trying to wrap my thoughts around. I may have some questions for you over time, but right now, I have one thought that keeps tapping me on the shoulder. It seems to me that the Employee Community section is massive—larger than I would have imagined. That indicates an expectation of a great deal of growth. Then, too, many services and even housing are set aside for these employees. Does that mean you expect them to all live and work here inside Barca City?"

"Great question. I'm not surprised you'd get it. I'll answer you directly, but I'll tell you we're trying to keep this closeted in the public eye for now. Yes, we expect at some point to have all employees live in, work in, and enjoy Barca City. Details to follow," she smiled. "I am surprised you haven't asked about the separation of Corporation and State. In other words, where does Barca end and America begin? This issue is more complicated. We expect the government will become more and more distributed. We hope to reduce our habit of gathering everyone into face-to-face meeting rooms, with associated scheduling nightmares and expensive travel budgets. We believe it'll become a thing of the past. We're convinced that Barcan technologies, such as HIT, and all you saw in the American Village Conference Center will make this possible. The ability to speak to someone in a different location, as if they are right next to you, changes everything. And that's what we're all about."

"What was your goal in presenting the company to these diplomats?"

"Well, it's complicated. On a governmental level, offering other first-line countries a peek under the wrappers is always a good idea. It lets them know we're pretty much on the leading edge. On a business level, these countries are potential customers, suppliers, and possible partners in the big picture. You were surprised and excited at what we saw today, and so were they. It's a win-win all the way." She looked at the BLAID® screen for a time check. "Wow, it's getting late."

Aaron looked at his phone. "Wow, how did it get to be 3:00 already? I need to think about heading out. I have a list of things I must handle before the day ends."

"I have to prepare for a meeting this afternoon," Morrígan added. So, you and I may have to fight for some alone time." She smiled, hoping he understood her direct approach.

"Well," Aaron replied, "I might have an idea. Every year I spend a couple weeks in the redwood forests, just me and nature. No technology, no access. Would you consider going with me next trip? I have a feeling you could use the break."

This caught Morrígan off guard. She had to think this through before answering. "Of course, I'd love nothing more than a couple of weeks alone with you and pure nature. But then I'd have to imagine what that would be like. So. It would be just you, me, and six Secret Service agents.

And, as far as no technology, I can imagine the friendly chat between President Wallyce and Vice President Morrígan."

"Well, when you put it in those terms," he said, "I can't find anything to argue with. Secret Service always watching, an obligation to your oath of office, and who's to even say that you might even want some time alone with me anyway?" A wry smile showed, if only for a second or two.

Morrígan took the challenge. She turned toward the agents on duty, gave a quick nod, and they turned away momentarily. Morrígan took that moment to its full advantage. She reached over to Aaron, wrapped her hand around his neck, pulled him toward her, and kissed him, a long, meaningful kiss. He was right there with her, careful to be sure she knew how he felt.

"That should answer your question clearly," she said. She smiled, kissed him again, and they held each other long enough that the lead agent became concerned. With a soft, throaty cough, the agent said, "We need to turn around again, Madam Vice President." And they did just that. Morrígan and Aaron didn't hear him, or they ignored his caution.

Morrígan was amused at seeing Aaron act like this was his first date. "Morrígan, I feel like a clumsy kid. After all, what's the protocol to let the United States Vice President know how you feel about her? Not that I'm impressed by titles, but you sure have a whole set of rules and restrictions. I don't want to mess it up."

"Then don't tell the Vice President–tell the woman. Say it to me. There doesn't need to be any protocol between you and me. So, say it to me. I'll make sure the V.P. gets the message." She smiled.

As if ordered to do so, the Secret Service team turned away once more.

"Morrígan, I can't get you out of my thoughts. But the truth is, I haven't thought of anyone else since the first time we met, and I've been waiting this past year for the time to pass so I would see you again. Now that it's on the table, I must be sure you know how I feel." She raised her hand as if to stop him from saying the inevitable.

"I'm in love with you, Aaron. Always have been, since we became close working on Daylight Project." She paused, waiting for him to absorb what she was telling him. "Oh, sorry." She winked. "I interrupted you. You were saying . . .?"

"All this time, all the worry that you'd reject me or not take me seriously. And," Aaron said, "we've managed to wipe away all the "awkward lover" anxiety and replaced it with a new reality—trying to build a relationship under a microscope. At the same time, the whole world watches your every move."

Morrígan saw that he was sincere, and he was concerned. But she also knew the pressure they would have to deal with as they learned to separate personal needs from the responsibilities of her office.

"Aaron, we can work this out. Others have done it. Some even expect Wallyce to allow someone into her life one of these days. But, I promise you, we will have plenty of time and opportunity to share alone time. Isn't that right, Agent Farley?"

Caught off guard, the Secret Service lead agent waited before answering them. "Yes, Ma'am. We have a protocol for the separation of personal and official time. We won't be intrusive, and you can interact freely without fear that we will be listening. Our concern begins outside your personal circle and extends to any possible threat to your safety. So, to simplify, we don't listen to you. We don't watch you except to evaluate your surroundings. And, an added benefit might be that we provide even more privacy than most others enjoy in their lives."

"Thanks for the explanation, Agent Farley," Morrígan added.

Now, the pressure of time was getting stronger. "Aaron, we must cut this short to get back to work. But I promise that this is the beginning. And I meant what I said. I love you."

Aaron held her close and looked deep into her eyes. It was as if his emotions were ready to overflow. "And I love you, Morrígan. Now, you need to tell me how I can focus on my work."

"I was thinking the same. Luck has it. I'll be with Wally, and she has a way of commanding focus from everyone. Otherwise, I'd be lost." She sensed that she had to make the next move. "Goh, please have the car ready for Mr. Rollins."

"Orders have been sent, Madam."

"Agent Farley, can you send an agent to accompany Mr. Rollins to the car?"

"Yes, Madam." He tapped the agent next to him, nodded, and the agent moved to ready the doorway.

"So, Aaron Rollins," she said. "We'll talk tomorrow."

There was another quick hug and kiss, and Aaron was soon gone. Morrígan didn't allow herself the luxury of quiet reflection. She turned and headed to the Executive Offices.

Chapter Fourteen

Wallyce Tilton checked the time before heading from her Barca business office to the Western Oval Office. She gave it that name in deference to the White House in Washington D.C., the traditional Home of the Executive Branch. It was a sign, but the truth was that Wallyce had no plans to ever use the White House as her base of Administration. But, she recognized that Washington prefers to move slowly, at a measured pace.

She entered the Oval Office and began to list orders for Goh to complete, even though he had already finished each task well ahead of schedule. "Goh, please prepare the room for myself and the Vice President, open the Holographic Platform, and establish connections with the following participants: Dr. Walters, Leader Argen, General McCann, Mayor Rachel Perriman, and Governor Brookfield. Have the connections established, but leave them in Hold State until I've had a chance to give last-minute instructions to the Vice President. Then, I'll signal you when to take them off hold."

"Yes, Madam, all is completed as directed. I await your further instructions."

The entrance security system announced the arrival of Morrígan and her contingent of Secret Service agents. "Madam, the Vice President, and her Security have arrived."

"Let them enter."

Morrígan and two Secret Service walked in through the central doorway. "She must have left her other agents in the foyer," Wallyce thought.

"Hi, Morrígan. Thanks for being here a bit early. I'd like to cover a few things with you before the others connect and the system begins recording the meeting. Goh, please order coffee for Morrígan and me?" she looked to Morrígan for agreement.

"Nothing, thanks. I'll just have water."

In a moment, the service doorway opened, and a staff server brought in a complete setup of coffees.

"Just put that on the table, thanks. We can take it from there."

"Yes, Madam," the server placed the setup down and left the room.

Wally, typically a high-energy person, seemed pensive. There was no smile as she signaled Morrígan to sit on one of the two sofas.

"Morrígan, this is going to be hard to say, but I must tell you that the news is frightening." She didn't pause. The news from the CDC is much worse than expected." Now, she paused to give Morrígan time to prepare for what would come next. "Two sources have told me that the death toll from Cyto-47 is already at more than one hundred thousand people in the United States alone. There's an average mortality rate of 75 percent. That means for every four identified cases, three have already died. Inside discussions tell me that the balance of those infected are not expected to survive for more than a couple of days. These numbers are vague, at best. The deaths can be from any organ failure or from sepsis. We have instituted a national mask mandate, as we always do, but this takes time to enforce and to see positive results. Dr. Walters insists there's no simple way to diagnose this plague, much less a way to cure or even prevent it. He even hints that masks are useless in this case. The bottom line is, we have to act immediately and decisively if we hope to come through this with any humans still alive."

"Yeah, that is scary, but Walters is an alarmist. You said so yourself."

"Morrígan, Argen has reported thirty-five Representatives and eight Senators have been diagnosed. Does that sound like an alarmist? Okay. Let me cut to the chase. I've ordered our operating companies in-country to call all employees into our Barcan facilities and place the facilities on lockdown for now. They have the choice of bringing in their immediate family members. All food and supplies are to be provided. We'll ship food and supplies to them weekly from our internal storage. All buildings are filtered by BioChem filters already, and we have sanitation stations with UV sanitation at every entry and many stations placed throughout the buildings.

"Anyone who refuses to lockdown will be fired and not allowed to re-enter our buildings. Our site-wide medical staff will have authority over our security staff regarding entry and exit authority. There will be no access to our facilities from the outside. Any contact will be online, holographic if available, and face-com usage only. Does this make sense to you?"

"Are you asking if I agree? No. I disagree. You're setting the stage for a massive panic. Okay, I agree with protecting the employees and the facilities. But, still, to lock everything down, that's a bit over the top, don't you think?"

"No, I don't think it's over the top, and I've already decided. This is such a deadly plague. If you wait, you die. My people are not going to die. I need your full support on this one."

"Regarding Barca Corporation and the employees and management, yes, full support. You're in charge. What about the government?"

"Let me hold off on answering that. I'm not sure yet. I have some ideas about the government but I need to see what we deal with. Let's talk again after the meeting, Okay? And, by the way, what we just talked about is strictly confidential, just between you, me, and my adviser. And I mean that in the real sense, He's been right so far, and I've never been up against an enemy that frightens me, much less one that could kill millions of people in a month. I want you to know I've been in close contact with Dr. Sebastian, and I trust him as much as I trust you, maybe even more. No offense."

"None taken. So, Dr. Sebastian sounds like a good one. Maybe I need a counselor too. Can I talk to this Dr. Sebastian or his cohorts? I'd prefer one skilled with affairs of the heart." She winked and giggled.

"Nope. Afraid Dr. Sebastian is my personal therapist. I'll leave it at that. He has no associates to refer you to. Sorry. Now, you need to let me in on this affair of the heart. It's so not like you. Who is he, or is it she?"

"Nope, right back at you. I'll be happy to tell you when the time is right, but now we have a country full of people to save."

Wallyce made a mental note to have the Secret Service look into this potential lover. But, her instinct told her you can't be too careful in these situations. Everyone must be checked closely when there's the possibility of power over the Vice President.

"Okay. Let's start the meeting, and let me take the lead. Keep a careful eye on that Perriman. I don't trust her, and I'd like your opinion."

Morrígan knew her sister well enough to know the hidden meaning of her comment. Wallyce wanted her to find a reason to go after Perriman in front of the others. She might have tried to get some detail from Wallyce about what she should look for, but the Holograms were beginning to take form, and she thought it best to wait until after the meeting. So, for now, she'd just note any strange behavior, probing questions, or comments that seemed too aggressive. She sat at the table, activated her BLAID®, and closed her eyes momentarily. This never failed to catch everyone's attention.

"Good evening, everyone," Wallyce began. "Thank each of you for your willingness to take on this challenge. I'll open by asking if there are any questions or misgivings. Please use the "raised hand" icon to let us know you wish to speak." Before she was even finished, Mayor Perriman's hand was raised. "Ms. Mayor, we'll start with you. Questions? Thoughts?"

"Thank you, President Tilton. Yes, I have a question, and the answer may trigger some thoughts. My first question revolves around the scope of this group. I note there are local and federal government representatives, including military leaders. I ask if you intend to establish global control over all of our efforts to fight off this plague. Do you intend to assert federal authority over state and local domains without the benefit of any laws supporting that and without any emergency being declared?"

Well, Wallyce thought. There it is. We didn't have to wait long for that. "Mayor, I will answer the obvious and implied questions just under the surface. Do I intend to assert power over the various governmental authorities without getting Congressional support for such a move? More to the point, you ask if I intend to take global control over any effort to fight Cyto-47. I'll be direct. I will take control if it's needed to fight our common enemy. Now, the unasked question of how far I am willing to take this. If needed, I will seek Congressional support beyond the powers already available through the Constitution. Just as each of you is responsible for protecting and defending the people within your domain, I have that responsibility for all people of the United States. Some might even say I have a similar obligation to protect the world's people by working directly with various governments. I have sworn to protect and defend the Constitution against any threats, foreign or domestic. I promise you that I see Cyto-47 as a threat, possibly the most dangerous enemy we have ever encountered. Of course, I'll do whatever it takes to protect and defend the country. Have I answered your questions?"

Mayor Perriman sat shaken. She didn't expect President Tilton to be so open about her intentions. She thought she might try to soften things by pretending that this task force was merely a means to evaluate the dangers. She thought Wallyce would dance around her real intentions. Her instinct told her that she was being set up to be the scapegoat if one were needed. She knew this could be a dangerous position, so she tried to move the attention off herself and onto the plague. "Madam President, I am clear that yours is an awesome responsibility. I give you my total commitment to support your efforts to eradicate this plague. We know there has never been a worse threat, and we understand the need to dedicate all of our resources in a combined effort to fight this evil."

"And that is just what you will do. Is that clear?

"Why, yes, President Tilton. I'm with you all the way."

Morrígan saw the danger signs. This woman is a considerable threat. We need to move her away from any mission-critical work—maybe assign her busy work to keep her occupied while the rest of us do what's required. But we can't remove her from the group unless she releases control over the city and county resources of San Francisco. Maybe then. . . "Mayor Perriman," Morrígan interrupted. "I'll be happy to be your focal point with the task force. Maybe you and I can talk after this meeting to discuss it."

"Yes, Madam Vice President."

Wallyce looked across the platform to see if anyone else had raised a hand. None had. "Now, I'll ask several of you for your input. You've been briefed on the level of confidentiality for this session and the specific information areas you will be directly responsible for. I'll begin with a general update from Dr. Walters of the CDC. Doctor, what are the major details we need to know?"

Walters was more than ready. He had already updated the President on all the information he knew. Hence, she could prompt him to feed information as she called.

"Yes, Madam President. I have the latest information here. I can give you an overview first, then add detail, or I can just dive into the heart of the matter? Which would you prefer?"

"Overview, then we can ask questions as needed."

"Yes, Madam. First, a dose of reality. We're only a few days into recognizing this as a true pandemic. Most people haven't even heard of Cyto-47. Yet, we have over a hundred thousand dead out of an identified one hundred thirty-five thousand cases. As we identify them, many victims are dead or quickly dying. And seventy-five percent of all cases, thus far, have become terminal. We expect more of these identified cases to end in the patient's death. For all we know, we might be looking at a plague that has a 100% fatality rate. If you become infected, you will die. We haven't yet determined the cause or isolated the agent—the infection that dooms the patient. As we already know, Cyto-47 triggers a storm of the autoimmune variety that causes the body to attack itself, ultimately destroying otherwise healthy organs and causing death. Unfortunately, many healthy organs have been destroyed when the plague is diagnosed. Death is imminent.

"Now, the worst news. Based on infection rates, we will likely lose five million of our citizens every month until we can find a way to stop this evil threat." He stopped, looked down briefly, then lifted his face to the cameras. "I'll tell you we're losing medical staff at alarming rates. We've also lost several Senators and Representatives. One of our parochial schools in Washington, D.C., has closed due to a near-total infection of all staff and students. This happened in two days. I add this last bit to help you understand that we may face an unbeatable enemy. I am sorry to have to make this report. He paused to be sure his words had the right impact. Seeing the looks on all the faces, he was certain they'd been fully impacted. Thank you, Madam President. I'm finished for now."

Wallyce thanked him and called on the next speaker, Senator Argen, Senate Majority Leader. "Senator Argen, as I listened to the Doctor's dire warning, I was stunned to hear of several Senate and Representatives deaths. The most recent information I had prior was the note of thirty-five Representatives and eight Senators infected. Can you add to this detail?"

She had difficulty hearing his answer, as it was almost a whisper. "Yes, I have to report that fifty-two Representatives have been hospitalized since yesterday. We have lost the eight Senators. No reports yet of additional infections."

As he spoke, Morrígan received a notification on her BLAID® that she felt needed to be shared. "Excuse me, President. I've just been informed that the thirty-five infected House Members succumbed. The remaining seventeen are in guarded health in ICU."

"Thank you for the update, Vice President, and from you, Leader Argen. We'll hear from Governor Brookfield. Governor, how tightly can you lock down California, and how long would it take?"

Rachel Perriman interrupted. "President Tilton, isn't that far too early? You're asking about completely shutting down the most important State in the country on the off chance we will be infected by this unknown disease? What about containing it in the East? What about coming up with a vaccine or a treatment? If you try to shut down California, you'll be lighting a fire that could destroy everything. If you think you've seen violent protests in your time, I am willing to bet you could be igniting a statewide revolt to make these protests look tame."

"Is that a threat, Rachel? Are you drawing a line here?"

Perriman was confused by the direct attack from the

President. Her heart rate climbed as her anxiety jumped to a new high. No, Madam, I can't support such a knee-jerk reaction without looking for better plans. I'd like to hear from our Governor on this. Jake, what do you think. Shut down without looking at the options?"

Governor Brookfield looked to President Tilton in case she wanted to speak. But, instead, she put her comm on the table, folded her hands, and leaned back. He knew she wanted him to answer Perriman.

"President Tilton, I will speak directly, if I may. I listened closely to Dr. Walters and Senator Argen. I heard enough to convince me we were attacked by the most dangerous enemy people have ever faced. Five million deaths in a single month are what I heard from the CDC. No known cure or even treatment exists. Congress has been attacked, and we've already lost too many members, with more deaths likely. We can't say if the plague is headed our way soon. Still, all it takes is one passenger landing in the Bay Area on a crowded plane to infect the entire State. We've seen, in past pandemics, that hesitancy has dire consequences. Waiting to act is not an option. I fully support your strategy. Do I think closing the state down will be an effective strategy in the long run? It's going to be similar to finding and stopping a roof leak. Water travels by gravity and seeks the path of least resistance. This plague may do the same. So, lockdown is a temporary strategy, at best. But it must be done sooner than later. I intend to institute lockdown statewide immediately."

Dr. Walters jumped in, ignoring protocol. "To hesitate even a week could be the worst thing we could do, but what levels of lockdown do you propose?"

The Governor resumed, "The state of California will

close its borders. No flights in, except through the military airports, and only on the approval of myself and the State Assembly. Freeway access, a difficult target, will be closed to all except to bring in food and critical medical supplies. All ports will be closed to both shipping traffic and private boats. We'll call up the California National Guard to enforce these restrictions. The Coast Guard will be needed for port restrictions, and all State police will be activated to enforce the roadway restrictions. I'll need help from the Air Force to open access to the State government to give us limited military airport access. This is my initial volley, and I plan to refine it if things worsen. I'll temporarily put these rules in place until we can determine what works and what doesn't. We'll modify as we're able to gauge our success or failures against Cyto-47." He paused. Looking at the President. Then, he addressed her. "Does this general plan meet with your approval, President Tilton?"

"Yes, at least for the next few weeks. As you indicated, this is a temporary strategy. Now, I'd like to go to another level with you. Since we must protect this country and our citizens, we may be called on to make tough decisions. One of those times could be when we know that the only way to save lives is a full lockdown—the country's total lockdown. We'll do what is necessary to save the country. But, if this sparks any blockade by people who feel we have taken on too much authority, we'll do what must be done. I assure you that my Administration will be prepared to declare Martial Law and activate it under the Insurrection Act. I've sworn to uphold and defend the Constitution against all enemies. For the record, I see this plague as an enemy. And I will give you this to think about. I would also vigorously defend against any of our own who might try to prevent us from defeating the Cyto-47. This is not yet a stated plan, just something to get you all thinking clearly. I'll adjourn for now. You'll be informed of our next meeting in advance. As we adjourn, I'd like General McCann, the Joint Chiefs of Staff Chairman, Vice President Morrígan, Governor Brookfield, and Senator Argen to remain. All others are now free to disconnect."

Mayor Perriman raised her hand. "May I stay to speak with you for a few moments?"

"No. I'll speak with you soon,"

"Goh, please verify all of the connections, except for those I wish to remain, have been disconnected,"

Goh closed Perriman's connection.

"Verified, Madam. Also, per your earlier instructions, all other sound and video signals have been blocked. Therefore, the room is in isolation."

"Thank you, Goh, she said, catching the absurdity in thanking a non-human intelligence. It was now time to speak with candor to the remaining core team.

"Undoubtedly, each of you is well aware of the terrifying danger coming our way. One of the obstacles we need to overcome is public apathy. We know how many have died thus far. Sadly, most people wouldn't believe the numbers if we showed them names and pictures of the dead. This is the deadliest invader the world has ever seen. So, here's my first reaction. Given the kill rate of this monster, we'd be foolish to ignore the danger. Cyto-47 must be stopped quickly, or we face the possible end of humanity. Remember, Dr. Walters mentioned a possible 100 percent mortality rate. The prediction of five million deaths in a month will only accelerate. And we must protect the people from themselves and their deadly skepticism.

"I've shared with the Vice President that I am locking

down all Barca Enterprise facilities here in the U. S. effective immediately. All employees can bring their family members inside following a brief quarantine. Once inside, they will remain inside. There will be no revolving door. You're in to stay. Leave, and you're out for good. I'm issuing similar orders to the Administration's staff and their families. All other governmental personnel under my control will be asked to join us. Of course, many will not be able to, given the nature of their responsibilities. I ask that those required to be out and at risk, you institute an immediate requirement of Bio/Chem protective gear for all under you. All military have been issued CBRN equipment, and I would like to see orders to use them asap. General McCann, is that possible?"

The General sat back in his chair, his hand cupping his chin, eyes closed for a long time. Then, as if he had an epiphany, he said, "We can do it, but it would create a panic situation. Seeing troops walking around in full CBRN gear can frighten the average civilian. So, instead, I propose, for now, a slightly less frightening solution. We can order all to wear masks and gloves at all times, with basic hazmat suits. We can leave the full hooded and tanked suits for later if needed. So, to be clear, our people will be outside wearing what might look like scuba wetsuits. We can get the best protection with full face masks, the new chin-to-top clear-view masks. These have a filtration system that rests under the shirt, so no one will see them. And, since everyone will be required to wear masks, they won't be much more frightening than what people are accustomed to seeing. Also, I would want our people to wear gloves and boot wraps. Keep the outside air from infiltrating the clothing. We can monitor this closely, and if it isn't working, we can require full

CBRN, chemical, biological, radiological, or nuclear protective gear."

"Thanks, General, but I'm not sure Bio/Chem will do the job. I'll get back to you." Wallyce said. She turned to Governor Brookfield. "Jake, as Governor, you have the best legal shot at calling up Martial Law if needed. Do you have the stomach for it?" It was a point-blank shot designed to test his commitment.

"If it's determined to be a situation of deadly violence or insurrection, hell, yes. I'd implement Martial Law for the state of California in a second. But that's only one state. What about the country?"

"Leave that to me, Governor. I'm prepared. Now, back to you, General. If we have to declare Martial Law, are you prepared to put boots on the streets all over the United States, even if they'll be fighting our citizens?"

"Madam President, I have sworn the same oath as you. This is not in any way vague. All enemies include our own citizens who are deemed to be in the act of or plotting to overthrow the duly elected government of this country. Anyone engaged in any form of insurrection is considered to be an enemy. It's reasonable to consider those who have decided to remain unprotected outside and at risk of infection a deadly risk to our government, our people, and more. Therefore, they can be considered insurrectionists. I hope to be clear. I will not hesitate to support the Insurrection Act in such cases."

Yes, General. You've stated your position clearly, and I appreciate it. But, Senator Argen, I asked you to stay behind because I need to better understand what happens when a Senator or Representative dies. How are they replaced, and how long does it take?"

"Well, it depends on the State. Most have the Governor appoint a replacement. Several require a special election, but even they allow the. Governor to appoint a temporary replacement if needed. The process can happen overnight. Now, suppose both the Senator and the Governor die or become incapacitated. In that case, the states each have a method to immediately transfer power to the second-in-command—either a Lieutenant Governor or Vice Governor —some such title.

"But in the House of Representatives, the Constitution requires replacements be by special elections. The answer to your question of how long it takes? It depends on how far we are out of the next scheduled election. Worst case, more than a hundred days."

Wallyce was stunned. She hadn't seen any need to research the topic before tonight. Still, this could be a massive pothole in whatever path she takes in the event of Martial Law. But, if Congress were somehow disabled, it might also be good for her. Need to wait and see, she thought.

"So, I understand that we need to be ready immediately for any number of contingencies. And we need to lock down both Houses of Congress right away. Senator, am I reading this correctly?"

"I will put this to my advisers tonight to test the theory that you can even require anything from Congress unless we are under full Martial Law conditions. Even then, it's pretty dicey, but It would appear you're right. I'll keep you updated in any case."

"That will be all, then, folks. I'd like to keep this under Top Secret

for now, and I'll have Goh schedule daily briefings for

now. Does anyone have any questions before we wrap up for the night?" No hands raised. "Then, thank you all, and good night. Goh, disconnect the meeting."

She looked at Morrígan and frowned. "Breakfast, 6:00 AM, my office. We have much to talk about. I need to discuss our friend, the Mayor of San Francisco. See you then." She closed her own BLAID® while Morrígan packed up and left.

Chapter Fifteen

Her personal residence in the Corporate village of Barca City was far beyond anything Morrígan had ever dreamed. Standing at the Northwest-facing windows, the old remains of Alcatraz Island floated on the bay's surface in the distance. Barca's designers thought ahead and built an on-demand magnification system into the glass, so she could see the island as if it was right below her. The sunset off to the left cast a surreal glow that helped the waves that lapped at the base of Alcatraz and seemed to lift and drop the island rhythmically in a "Dance of Alcatraz." Her logical mind told her that the island was stationary and it was the bay waters that rose and fell with the tides, but the little girl in her knew otherwise. It was magic, plain and simple.

"Madam, your guest has arrived," came the announcement over the Res-comm system. "Shall I send him in?" Agent Corey Gaiters, a Secret Service agent, waited for instructions. She wanted to make him wait a few minutes just to test his reaction, but she was so excited to see Aaron she almost shouted. "Yes, Corey, please show him in. I'm in the formal room. Thanks."

Aaron's smile was so worth the wait. She had a hard time concentrating on the job most of the day, knowing she would finally be able to have some alone time with him. Morrígan planned to move their relationship forward as much as possible, given the horror she felt was about to become a reality in the Bay Area. She reminded herself so much of what she learned about the scary plague currently spinning out of control all over the east coast was highly classified. She couldn't even tell Aaron about it.

On the other hand, she was super resourceful, and if she was determined to give Aaron a heads-up, that's what she'd do. Now, about that alone time. After giving Aaron a welcome hug and kiss, she turned her attention to Agent Gaiters.

"Corey, we'll be heading over for our dinner service, and please set the room at max security." Max security was code for total privacy, even privacy from the prying eyes of the Secret Service. Why not? The entire apartment was secure and under their constant watch. No one comes in or out without their approval. Even Vice Presidents had at least a right to that, and she was determined to take advantage of their time.

"Yes, Madam." The agent left them.

"Aaron, I've looked forward to this all day. It's been a crazy day, but now you're here, and the crazy just faded away." She hugged him as if to pass her feelings over to him. So many emotions rushed through her, and she was unprepared for the shock that hit the moment their lips touched.

"Static," he mumbled.

"What? Static?" she blurted out.

"Yeah, static electricity. Like what you drag your feet and touch a doorknob, and you get that tiny shock."

Her smile turned to a giggle, then a full, hearty laugh. "You're gonna think I'm a novice at this, and maybe so, but I thought it was a genuine spark between us. Like we have so many feelings for each other, it caused a spark. I'm such a twit."

"No, not a twit, he answered. I felt that too. It was something like this." The kiss he started this time was magical. She felt the connection, heart-to-heart, a profound expression of love. Dinner would have to wait.

Morrígan turned toward her bedroom. "Wait until you see this view, she teased, pulling Aaron toward the hallway. He didn't hesitate.

"It's a stunning view," he commented. But he never looked toward the bay. Instead, his eyes never left Morrígan. Without another word, she softly pulled him to the bed.

Afterward, it left them feeling there had never been a closeness like this for either of them, and there would never be another. They sat for a long time, taking in the expanse of the Bay view. Seeing so much of the Bay Area from such a high vantage point was special. Still, it was only a backdrop to the moment when Aaron and Morrígan shared their love for each other as only brand-new lovers can.

* * *

"Aaron, do you want any wine with dinner? We're having something special. It's my favorite delicacy from California's finest producers. Dare to guess?"

"I'd rather skip the food and return to where we left off fifteen minutes ago." He was more than a little serious.

"Don't tempt me," she replied. "We do have to eat, though. So, come on. Guess."

"Okay. Stop me if I get warm. How about Dungeness Crab?" No reaction. "Then maybe lamb chops? No? Then I think I know. Some of the best Chinese specialties are from San Francisco. Right? No? Warm?"

"Not even lukewarm," she answered.

"Okay. I give. What type of wine goes with what the staff has prepared?"

"I usually like a nice cold beer with a lime wedge. We have my favorite," Morrígan said. "Burritos de Camaron."

"Shrimp Burritos. I love them too. So, two beers and burritos. Sounds like the perfect meal for a night like this."

They were both hungry, but neither did more than pick at the food. Morrígan kept going over everything in her mind —mostly their new relationship. Still, her thoughts were haunted by Wally's plans to fight the plague. What could happen to any of them if this plan went horribly wrong? She wavered between her need for confidentiality and her desire to give Aaron at least some warning about the mess brewing in the East. But, of course, this was probably a matter of national security, which Maybe he already knew about Cyto-47.

"Aaron, what have you heard about some sickness or flu taking hold in the world? "She knew she was on the edge of violating confidentiality, but. . .

He stiffened, and she regretted asking.

"Do you mean Cyto-47? Yeah, I heard some background noise, but not enough to get excited about. Why"

"So, what do you hear? What do people think about it?"

"Not much at all. I hear the typical blown-out-of-proportion rumors. People just like to have controversy to pass around. They say it kills everyone, and it's traveling at light speed. I hear it can kill hundreds of thousands each month and that we should expect it to hit the Bay Area sometime soon. Just the usual cocktail chatter. So, Morrígan, what do you hear?"

"Well, I can only talk in general terms about it. Some things are confidential, and some aren't. So, I'll tell you what I can. This Cyto -47 is a bad one, much worse than any we've seen in our lifetime. Think of it as fast and deadly. That's it in general terms. Now take your imagination on a trip. Imagine the worst plague you've ever learned about in history. That might seem like a common cold in comparison."

"What the hell? Are you serious?" Aaron's fork dropped t the floor, and his eyes opened wide.

"So, I got your attention. Good. Now, listen. What would you say if, at some point, I asked you to move inside Barca City for an extended stay? Don't ask why. Just answer."

"Now I'm worried. Morrígan, I'd do anything you asked without question, but that's a pretty big ask. I have a business to conduct, so I need to be available, but this sounds like it might have to take a back seat. Are you trying to tell me this is apocalyptic?

"No. Well, in a way, yes. Maybe that's part of what I'm saying. I hope to alert you to the possibilities that might come our way soon. If scientific predictions are close to correct, these events could change our lives, at least for a while. I'm not saying they will happen, just that there is a possibility, and I don't want you to be off guard if and when they do. Damn it. I wish I didn't have to be so cryptic. There are things I need to tell you." She stopped suddenly, sat upright, looked him in the eyes, and moved so that her lips were brushing his ear. She whispered softly, hoping to not be heard by whatever listening devices her sister must have placed all over the room.

"Aaron, listen to everything I say, and don't ask any questions. This is going to be pretty risky for me."

"Then, why take a chance?"

"Because I love you. I need to tell you so we can have some kind of plan for when things go wrong. Okay?" He held her hands and looked into her eyes. She knew he was ready. She moved back to whispering in his ear. "Aaron, Cyto-47 is a monster. It has the highest infection rate; some have speculated the death rate might be close to 100 percent. It is killing so fast in other parts of the country. We're looking at some extreme methods to minimize the devastation it might cause here in California, including a total lockdown of the entire state. If that doesn't work, we might have to consider imposing martial law to enforce strict isolation and containment. I'm guessing that could even include some form of internment, like during the World Wars. More on that later. For now, I need to know what we might need to set up for ourselves. What if there's a lockdown? How could we be together? Would you be willing to come into Barca under lockdown?"

"Hey, whoa. Are we getting ahead of ourselves? This plague hasn't even hit the California population yet."

"Aaron, Wallyce is finalizing a plan to lock the state down. That plan should be in place in days, and the speed this plague travels indicates a week might even be too late. Ahead of ourselves? No. We might be behind the curve. At least. I need access to your private comm—the one you think no one knows about. I'll give you mine. I want to be able to contact you in a heartbeat, anytime. As it sounds, we may have one chance and very little time to get together in case of isolation."

"Morrígan, are you sure you want to do this?"

"Aaron, all that I just told you gives me no way to back down. I've already committed to you that can't be undone." She was arguing with herself, testing her commitment to Aaron and her ethics. "I may have violated national security by mentioning Wallyce's plan for Statewide lockdown. Aaron, I'm the Vice President, and I'm disclosing some sensitive information to you that could cause a massive panic if it got out. Suppose I was willing to do my job, according to Wallyce. In that case, I'd be up to my elbows helping the President just let the majority die, believing she can save a tiny portion of mankind. I don't happen to see it that way. I see her as a madwoman amid a plot to become the Queen of the World. However small the final population is. I can't have any part in that. Aaron. She's decided to sacrifice most of our people just to save the few who will do her bidding? And there is no way I can be a part of that.

"I might be able to defend myself since there hasn't been an emergency declared yet, but for certain, I'd be impeached and possibly removed from office. At worst, I could be charged with serious security violations and then prosecuted as a criminal." I know she would fire me if it were in her power. She'd have to impeach me, but there's no time for that. To get me out of the way, and I'm confident she will do that at some point, I would have to quit, or she would have to bring in an assassin to kill me. I'm convinced she will do that if it's her only option."

Aaron stood silently, eyes wide, hands clenched, visibly shocked by what she had told him.

Her argument ended, and her commitment was solid; she looked at him directly, then spoke. "You ask if I'm sure? I've never been surer. Would I take these chances if I weren't ready to take this all the way? It's you and me, Aaron. You're the one. And, yes, I'm sure."

"Then, I'm with you all the way, he said. I won't let anything come between us. Do you remember when I told you the one question I ask myself that keeps me focused on what's important? What is the one thing that devastates you to know you could never do or be because time has run out? I promised to tell you what the answer is. It's all about you, Morrígan. It would devastate me knowing I couldn't be with you for the rest of my life. If I could never live that dream, it would make everything else meaningless." Time stopped for that moment. Each of them sat silently, Aaron because he finally crossed the line and told her, and Morrígan because she just saw her dream come to life when she least expected it. After a pause, Aaron broke the spell.

"I'm in love with you. If you feel the same, we need to leave here as soon as possible, or we might not have any future. Here's my private access comm. Link it to yours, and send me a message about how we can communicate in private as soon as possible. But, Morrígan?" he hesitated. "you know you're the one for me, too, don't you? I'm with you no matter what. So maybe we can get beyond the new boyfriend jitters," he laughed. "From now on, I promise we'll never keep secrets between us, and all that we share is sacred."

She was sure the smile would never leave her face. "So, it's to be an Oath Between Conspiring Lovers, right? Absolutely. I pledge to you." The smile faded a bit as she remembered what they were facing. "Now, we need to start coming up with a fallback plan in case things get as bad as we think they're going to, and Wallyce takes the next step in fighting this plague. We'll have to go into a sustained lockdown, probably here in Barca City."

"Or, maybe there are other ways to be safe together."

Morrígan wasn't prepared for that. "You mean outside Barca? But everything we know says Cyto-47 might soon be worldwide, and only completely sealed environments will be the least safe."

Aaron looked around the room, wondering how many ways Wallyce and her non-human, Goh, might be watching and listening to everything they say. He decided to be cautious. "Of course, I agree. But we aren't locked down yet, and the order could come when we're somewhere outside the City. Just makes good sense to be ready for any eventuality, is all I'm saying."

Morrígan caught on. Yeah, you're right. By the way, let me link our comms now. She quickly tapped her fingers over Aaron's screen and then returned it to him without closing the app.

Aaron understood the strange look in her eyes meant he needed to look at the screen. He glanced while saying, "It seems you made the connection. Thanks." The screen held a simple message. "Wait until we're not here in Barca so we can talk." He smiled at her and the comm, put it in his pocket then followed her to the bedroom.

Chapter Sixteen

Wallyce spent the final five minutes of her meditation thinking about the upcoming meeting. She knew her plan would be controversial and must move the group's mindset in the right direction. This was a one-shot attempt to get all to agree. Failing that, she'd have to resort to more forceful tactics.

The program would start, as usual, with an outline/status from Dr. Walters. Wallyce set him up to hit the team hard with the bad news. There'd be no doubt they were in grave danger from the Plague.

Next, California Governor Jake Brookfield would detail the plan for the complete lockdown of California. This was certain to trigger waves of protest from some of the group, especially the ABAG members. In fact, Wallyce counted on it, starting with Rachel Perriman. This would allow Wallyce to take a hard line, letting everyone know she wasn't about to compromise. There would be no negotiation. At this point, the stage would be set, and Wallyce would be commanding.

Wallyce opened her eyes to the bright light, breaking the

spell of meditation. "Goh, please bring my salad and beverage to my residence, and have my formal meeting uniform laid out. I'll meet my pandemic team in thirty minutes, so this needs to be done quickly." She reminded herself to work on breaking the habit of using please and thank you when speaking to her electronic Assistant.

"Yes, Madam. The orders have been sent, and all should be in place by the time you arrive in residence."

Wallyce fought the urge to thank Goh. Instead, she headed to the private transport, where her Secret Service agent awaited her arrival. Together, they rode up to the Presidential Penthouse.

* * *

To Aaron, the shower was a gift. The right temperature and pressure reminded him of standing under a warm waterfall. He almost didn't want it to end. He was also impressed that Morrígan had his clothes cleaned and pressed while they slept, if one could call what they did sleeping. By his analysis, they took a few naps between several incredible lovemaking sessions. He also didn't want that to end so soon.

"Morrígan, why not join me in this shower. I promise to be a good boy."

"Darling, that sounds like a good idea." She knew she had to get up and move soon or risk being late for the meeting. "A great idea as long as you'd be okay with Wallyce popping up on every screen in the residence shouting about how I had better get my butt down to the meeting in five seconds. Oh, and when she's in that mode, she never asks permission to open video lines—just pops right up no matter what I'm doing."

"Yeah. I get the point. I'll be out in a couple minutes. Can we get a cup of coffee brought up?"

"Breakfast should be here any time. Just a quick scone and some coffee. Is that okay?"

He surprised her by stepping from the closet room, already dry and half-dressed. "I hope that was quick enough." As he spoke, the door chimed, and Morrígan called for the server to enter. Aaron laughed when he saw the food laid out on the cart. There were a half dozen scones, assorted bagels, cheeses and jams, and a large bowl of berries.

"I see you're in the habit of understatement. So, this is a quick scone and some coffee?"

"Well, they do like to give me choices. So I'll probably nibble on a few of these and gulp down the coffee. The meeting starts in a half hour."

"So, I need to see what the next two days offer regarding us being together. After that, I'm headed for my wilderness trip for two weeks. Does the Vice President get to take a vacation? Maybe you can join me."

There's not much I'd enjoy more. Sorry, but I'm booked solid for the next three days. We're in the middle of pandemic planning, and every second counts when you're trying to save the world. She winked at him, but the thought of Cyto-47 sent chills down her spine. "Aaron, I would feel much better if you passed up the trip for this year. You don't know how deadly this plague is; things can change instantly. Our state could be fully immersed in it by this time tomorrow. That's how fast it can happen."

"Then I'd be in a safer place than you. I'd be so far from other people that the plague monster would never find me. Come with me."

"I can't. Let's keep in close contact."

The only way I could is if we were on a sat-comm line, which I could set up. Unfortunately, there's no regular comm out where I go. It's like being on Earth before humans. That's the goal for my trip—two weeks away from people and all their crap. No comm, no noise, no crime, no pressure. Nothing but me and mother nature. I'd go nuts if I didn't take this trip every so often."

"Then we won't even talk for the next two weeks? How sad."

"Oh, we'll talk. Heart to heart, we'll talk. And you'll hear me, and I'll hear you. You'll see. It'll be magical. Then at the end of two weeks, I'll come home, and we can meet up in the Presidio and tell each other how much we love each other. In fact, I'll call you when I'm on my way and back in comm coverage. But, if you need to contact me for any reason, use the comm. If you're in trouble, I'd much rather take a break from my Zen pursuit. I will say it's gonna be impossible to clear my mind and become one with nature when my mind is so fixed on you."

"And it's also sad that we must break this off right now. I'm almost late." She nearly jumped into his arms, gave him a loving goodbye kiss, then turned to the screen. "Goh, please bring Mr. Rollin's car to the executive ramp. Thanks. Now, Mr. Aaron Rollins, I really have to go. I'm gonna miss the hell out of you." They kissed goodbye, and she left for the transport ahead of him. He waited for the next carrier to give her some alone time before her meeting.

* * *

Wallyce gave instructions. "Goh, classify the upcoming meeting as Confidential and Top Secret. Ask Secret Service

Agent Nguyen to meet me here in five minutes. When the meeting closes, create access for the record only to me, the Vice President, and General McCann. And remember to alert me when anyone requests access to the files."

"Yes, Madam. It will be as you have ordered."

Wallyce moved to the Executive Conference Suite and began to note the name of each participant on the individual seating screens to establish the strategic positions she had in mind. Vice President Morrígan would be at the opposite end of the table from her so they could watch for any member-to-member personal looks and eye-rolling. She wasn't going to miss a thing. Dr. Walters and General McCann would be at her end of the table, while Mayor Perriman and Governor Brookfield would be at Morrígan's end. Senator Argen will sit at the middle of the table, and the seat opposite Argen will remain available for hologram participants.

"Yes, Madam. You asked for me to meet you here."

"Hi, Agent Nguyen. Thanks for being on time." Wallyce greeted the senior agent at the back of the conference table. "We're about to begin a Top-Secret meeting here, and I want to let you know some of my concerns about the people who will participate. First, I would like to focus on Rachel Perriman, S.F. Mayor. She's proven to be a provocateur at these gatherings, and I don't trust her to participate without causing a stir. Frankly, she scares me. If things turn ugly and we can't stay on track, I may ask her to leave. But, if she refuses, I would like your team to handle it quickly and with as little struggle as possible. Am I being clear?"

"Yes, Madam. Perfectly clear. Any others?"

"No. The rest will be either remote participants or no threat to our purposes. Thank you, Nguyen."

Yes, Madam."

Agent Nguyen walked out and took his station just outside the door.

"Madam President," Goh said, "you have guests in the outer chamber. Should I bring them in?"

"Not just yet, Goh. Who are they?"

The simulated human voice responded from the desktop speaker. "All indicated local participants are here, and the remote participants are available for connection."

"Go ahead and signal the Vice President to enter, and let the others know we'll open the room for them in a few minutes.?

"Yes, Madam."

Morrígan entered immediately, and they spent a few minutes reviewing last-minute details. Then, satisfied they were ready, Wallyce ordered Goh to bring in the local participants and connect the remote ones. The room was ready within three minutes, and she opened the meeting.

The locals, those who would be there in person in addition to the President and Vice President, were Governor Jake Brookfield and Mayor Rachel Perriman. They took their seats as the room lighting dimmed to allow for a brighter hologram for those participating remotely. They were Dr. Walters, Senate Majority Leader Argen, and Chairman General McCann. The available projector/seat was for others as needed. She wasted no time.

"Let me set the ground rules. So, we can avoid falling off track, I will call on individuals, in turn, who will present their portion of the information we've gathered. Some may update us on their progress, and others may pose scenarios and propose solutions. Any questions or disagreements will be reserved until I open the floor for them. Now, we'll begin, as usual, with Dr. Walters and the latest data from CDC." Goh understood the cue and connected the communication link to the hologram that was Dr. Walters.

"Am I connected?" Goh responded that he was. "Thank you, and good day to you all. Madam President, I wish the news from CDC was better. Still, reality forces me to tell you that things are desperate on the east coast and quickly ramping up everywhere else. I've uploaded a detailed report to you and the Vice President, which you can review at your discretion. In a nutshell, we have lost nearly five million citizens from all sectors. The good news is that we hear of possible scientific breakthroughs almost daily. The bad news is none of them have panned out so far. But we will continue to race against time to defeat this monster. I want to caution you to approach the rumors of miracle cures and medical breakthroughs with skepticism. Only believe it if you hear it from me. I can't stress this enough. We have no known cure or breakthrough coming down the road, and things are as bleak as possible. The citizens haven't yet gotten the message, as shown by the small percentage who bother to wear hazmat gear we are starting to provide in certain high-infection areas.

"There's a solid movement to discredit everything we tell them about Cyto-47. Many now protest our steps toward isolation and stay-at-home mandates. We have some large protests taking place, followed by reports of the deaths of many of these protestors. But the masses hear about them yet don't believe them. They think it's a plot against their freedom and rights.

"On the plan to save lives, we have a hundred labs working night and day to develop a vaccine and a cure for those infected. This will increase. I'm still hopeful. But I offer that hope with a dose of reality. We're running out of time. It's that simple."

"Thank you, Dr. Walters," Wallyce struggled to hide the terror that invaded her thoughts as Dr. Walters spoke. "Next, Let's hear from Governor Brookfield. Jake, what's the status of our efforts here in California?"

"Thank you, President Tilton. As of this morning, we've made progress in sealing off all access to the state. All main freeways and many local inroads have been closed—some by police checkpoint barricades and some by placing physical barriers across the roadway. All airports, except U.S. Military bases, have been on limited initial lockdown since yesterday, noon. The limits are in place to allow certain required shipments into the state only when they have been passed through our authorization checklist processes to ensure they have been cleared by the government and only after we pass the shipments through strict disinfection and three-day isolation. Airport police and County sheriff forces have been stationed on all roadways leading in and out of the airports. No one is getting in or out through the airports. Similar measures have been taken at railroad terminals and all ports, large and small. On the downside, I have to say, we pulled too many agents from border patrol and left the southern border vulnerable. Near as we can tell, a couple thousand border jumpers made it in and have disappeared into the barrios and homeless camps in and around San Diego. We launched a strong roundup effort and have grabbed over twice that many illegals, probably including the jumpers. So far, no reports of sickness from the area. We might be lucky. The border is now secured by armed-drone activation."

"Jake," Wallyce said, "on the one hand, it sounds like

you've done a fine job securing the state in a hurry. On the other, this border problem is a huge failure. If just one infected illegal gets in, the state is at risk. We have to be perfect. From what we heard in Dr. Walters's report, being pretty good will kill us all. Double up, triple if you have to, but get those holes plugged today." She smiled a bit, letting Jake know she was still on his side, but her words left no wiggle room. He had to do better.

She put her Blaid® down, put both hands on the table, and leaned forward. "This applies to every one of us. We're in a deadly battle here. News from the rest of the country is that things can turn toward hell in a blink. Less than perfect will not be tolerated. Are we clear?" Each of them, in turn, told her they understood. Wallyce was only a second or two from a panic attack and insisted that each team member saw Cyto-47 as seriously as she did.

Wallyce's thoughts drifted back to her nightmares in which she couldn't keep any American people alive. In a flash, Cyto-47 rolled over the country, leaving nothing but death and silence. The plague was a demon in her dream, changing shape and size so often and quickly that she couldn't keep up. At every turn, a new monster rose up to devour the people, all people. But, as it passed, there was an eerie silence, as all machines, broadcasts, engines, and wheels rolling down roads stopped in silence. Other sounds of animals barking, whinnying, howling, and growling died with the animals who made them.

Sounds were a product of life. When life ended, sounds ended, except the sounds of nature. But even natural sounds need a living being to hear them. Lightning was becoming silent, and the staccato rain on a roof was unheard of in some places. Wallyce's dream was most frightening. She believed in dead silence. She thought it was the most frightened she had ever been until she heard the sound of death itself. The voice of Cyto-47 called to her in her dream.

"WALLYCE." It screamed into her soul in a voice that held the sounds of every former living being. "You can never defeat me. I will drown you in the ocean of the dying. They will become a sea of decay, ever-growing, faster and bigger, until the crushing waves pull you in and drag you to the bottom. You will fight, screaming in unending fear, until even you are one of the dead, putrid corpses who have fallen to the plague. COME TO ME, WALLYCE."

Her lungs failed her, and her throat closed in fear. Unable to breathe, a horrible scream burst from her throat, pushing all of the air out until, at last, a desperate gush of air refilled her lungs. She heard the unearthly scream as it woke her. She realized she had defeated death—this time. She also understood it would revisit her mind often, haunting her sleep until she either surrendered or defeated the monster. She also knew she would never give in to it. She would beat it, no matter what that meant, what she needed to do, or who she needed to overcome.

The sudden revisit to the nightmare lasted only a second, but it shook her soul. The others noticed as the deadly panic flashed across her face as the too-real memory jolted her back to the meeting. Glancing at the faces, she felt they knew Cyto-47 was destructive but not as horrific as she knew it was. She had to make them feel the fear and understand the critical importance of their mission. This fear caused her to be point-blank-focused in her dealings with Mayor Rachel Perriman.

Still shaken but trying to regain composure, Wallyce looked to the head of the Association of Bay Area Governments. "Mayor, please give us the report from ABAG. What's the current status?"

Mayor Rachel Perriman grabbed her comm device so fast that she nearly dropped it onto her coffee cup. Her face reddened, and she looked down at the table, moving her cup far enough that she might not complete the show of nerves by actually spilling it in her haste.

"Yes, Madam President," Mayor Perriman spoke. "The Association of Bay Area Governments held an emergency meeting to inform all members of your status and concerns about Cyto-47. I presented your plan as it stood two days ago. There were many questions, and several of our members did not agree with your assessment. In a nutshell, most of the mayors of Northern California aren't ready to accept the situation as you've described it. There's a general feeling that the federal government is blowing things out of proportion.

"As you know, we've been down this road many times. A threat suddenly appears, there seems to be no hope of defeating the threat, and the Federal System comes to the rescue, bending, breaking, and voiding the rules along the way. A result we've seen too often is a power play by the Feds. We in local government have been forced to fight long and hard for our constituents against the never-ending stream of federal oversight. Unfortunately, this is a repeating cycle we're no longer willing to accept without deep negotiations.

"I am certain Governor Brookfield will agree. States and Municipal rights must no longer be weakened and removed due to some game of political fear-mongering."

"So, mayor, what are you proposing?" Wallyce was controlled, emotionless.

"Madam President, we hope you will agree to meet with

us on Monday. We have prepared a tentative agenda that will meet your approval. I will transfer it to you if you accept the file." She held her comm in one hand, the finger on her other hand ready to click the "send" button.

Wallyce rose to her feet. She looked at each member in turn. Then, she walked to Mayor Perriman and stood directly over her. She responded in a dry, emotionless tone. "No, Rachel. I will not accept the file. You are free to push whatever theory you wish. Still, I am not willing to go down the road of negotiation while our country stands on the edge of extinction. Believe what you will, and I will believe what the evidence supports. Millions have already died from Cyto-47, and hundreds of millions are in immediate danger. However, I will not shirk my responsibilities to the people of the United States just so you and others like you can play your power politics game. Governor Brookfield, please have someone on your team sit with the ABAG group right away to make certain ABAG has all of the same information that we have based our plan on. If they see the facts and still wish to hold onto their conspiracy theory, then replace them immediately on this team. At the very least, Rachel, you do not need to remain in this room today. After you meet with the Governor's team and have the facts, and you can agree that we are headed down the right path, then contact the Vice President. She will possibly put you back on this panel. Otherwise, good day." She turned to Agent Nguyen, gave a single nod, then returned to her seat. Agent Nguyen opened the door to the exit corridor and motioned Mayor Perriman to leave. But Perriman refused

"Madam President, it's clear that you have no idea how our group operates. ABAG represents all of the citizens and businesses in the Bay Area. If we return to them with a report describing what you are trying to do, they will take up arms. So, you might want to rethink your decision."

"Perhaps you are right, Rachel. I have rethought it. I have now decided that you will be replaced. Thank you for your time. Agent Nguyen, please escort Mayor Perriman to the exit and see that she is given transportation back to her office in San Francisco."

When Nguyen reached to take Mayor Perriman's arm, she stood abruptly and began to leave alone. "Wallyce, you'll live to regret this. You have just declared political war on the local and state governments."

Governor Brookfield spoke with force. "No, Perriman. The State of California is in full support of the President's plan. Please don't get in our way. It will be messy if you do." Perriman left.

Wallyce waited long enough for Calm to return. Then she addressed the Senate Leader, Bill Argen. "Senator Argen, please give us an update. What is the level of support we can expect from Congress?"

"Madam President, the better question might be to ask if there is any Congress to work with. Data from my staff indicates both halls of Congress have been devastated. We have lost seventeen Senators and one hundred twelve Representatives to Cyto-47."

"Bill, clarify. What do you mean by lost?"

"Dead, President. These are the numbers of dead Senators and Representatives so far today. This doesn't include others who have reported being sick. If they have the plague, we might look at many more losses in a few days. I project we will be unable to reach any quorum soon, leaving Congress unable to reach any meaningful decisions."

"Dear God, Bill. Are you telling us that the legislative

branch of our government is helpless? There must be some fallback position. What's the process for moving forward?"

"It's not clear, Madam. Some states have a rapid-recovery program in which the Governor can appoint a replacement in the event of death. Others require their state legislature to act, assuming they haven't lost too many members, which makes them similarly locked out. Finally, several of the states require a special election. In short, it's a mess that I have my staff working around the clock to try to unravel."

"Dr. Walters. Do you have any idea of the safe incubation timeframe for this plague? In other words, how many days would someone need to be in complete isolation before we can say they are not infected?"

The CDC head looked at his notes. "A guess would be three days. A safe bet would be one week. So, if there are no symptoms within a week, we call them safe to be with others."

"And, Dr., is there any procedure we can define that would reasonably sanitize a closed indoor area?"

"We have seen good results with super-strong air evacuation and filtration combined with the typical alcohol and betadine wash. It must be 100% coverage in a tightly secured room thrice daily. All isolants, the people being isolated, must be in biological suits at all times—from when they enter isolation to when they are released out of the chamber."

"Can you make that happen in a place like the Senate chambers and the House of Representatives?"

"Yes," Dr. Walters was quick to answer. "My team has already been designing a plan and checklist for that purpose."

"Senator Argen. . . Make it happen."

"Yes, Madam President."

"Now, I'd like to hear from General McCann. Chairman, your thoughts?"

Jim McCann, Chairman of the Joint Chiefs of Staff and the ranking military member for the country stood at attention. "President Tilton, do I have permission to speak candidly in front of those assembled here?"

Wallyce felt the bile rise in her throat. She knew McCann wouldn't speak so formally unless what he had to say was earth-shaking. "Yes, General. Of course. We need your insight and don't want you to mince words."

Ever the West Point strategist, General McCann walked over to the podium, where a projectable screen waited. He had it set before the meeting in case they wanted reality, not just boot-shining. Then, the General picked up the stylus and began to write on the screen. Everything he wrote was projected on the wall behind where Mayor Perriman had recently vacated.

"You may wonder why I'm handwriting my report for you now. Two reasons: Things have been changing so fast that there's no time to be fancy. There's no record of this, so it can't be hacked. So now, I will speak to you like you've probably never been spoken to in years. I call it plain-speak. No bullshit, just plain-speak.

"Okay, that's outta the way. Here's the deal. Our beloved country is about to be destroyed by the fiercest enemy known to mankind. This Cyto-47 is only a tiny part of it. The real enemy is our incredible ability to bullshit ourselves. Yeah, it's true. We have lost more than 5 million people and are only five yards into this game. We lost them simply because they either didn't know or they didn't believe this was a real thing, this plague.

"Our citizens figure that we are lying to them about this pandemic and trying to scare them into some form of submission, or they just don't understand how deadly this is. It's pretty intense, this denial thing. But what people refuse to believe can't be real, and unreal things can't hurt them. Just like your Daddy coming into your bedroom at night and pretending to look under your bed, then telling you there are no monsters there. But, sometimes, there are monsters there. Daddy just didn't look because he decided they weren't real.

"So, the problem is, once you deny something's existence, accepting it might be real destroys your safety. Where you once were invincible, you are now vulnerable. There are real monsters, but people will never believe in them. This presents a problem for us, who are responsible for saving those people. The problem is, they'll never believe us. So, we can't save them by convincing them to become vulnerable, can we? We can only save them by taking full control and making them do what we need to save them."

Bill Argen interrupted. "What are you saying, General? What do we need to do?"

"Martial Law, Senator," the General said. We have to force them to listen to reality or abandon them. No other way."

Leader Argen jumped to his feet. "All respect, General, but I think there might be some real problems. First, I'm not convinced that would be a lawful thing to do. Nothing in the Constitution gives the President the authority to declare Martial Law. Next, what are the grounds you would use to justify this?"

President Tilton stepped in. "Bill, we've had a team of Constitutional Lawyers study this problem in anticipation of the possible scenario the General is describing. They have advised us that there's enough precedence to support going forward under the Insurrection Act and declare an attempted overthrow if the general population refuses to accept the orders to isolate and lock down once we give them. The basic premise is that they would be committing a deadly assault on the country by willingly spreading Cyto-47, especially after we issue Orders of National Emergency describing the nature of the deadly threat and adding the specification that anyone in violation of the order will be deemed guilty of insurrection. Once that line is crossed, Martial Law becomes the logical next step we will use to protect the United States and her citizens."

Argen was shocked. "Do you really think you can get away with this? Madam President, I'm your biggest fan, and you know I'm committed to you. Absolutely committed. I'll support whichever direction you choose with this, but how can you hope to get away with calling up the National Guard and other military branches and have them become a federalized police force? It's never been done."

General McCann stepped close to Argen—face-to-face. "Who the hell would stop it? You heard today Congress is wasted. People are dying by the millions. President Tilton will do whatever it takes to save as much of our country as possible. So, who the hell is gonna stop her?"

The room went silent.

President Tilton took control. "Everyone, please be seated. It's time for a dose of the truth. Dr. Walters states this monster is rolling across the country, leaving nothing but death and destruction. Senate Leader Argen reports that our Legislature is on the brink of collapse due to deaths in Congress caused by this plague. Five million of our citizens have been killed by Cyto-47, with a promise of many more deaths in a hurry. What would you do if we spoke of an invading army instead of a plague? Or a very effective army of terrorists? Would any of us hesitate to do everything we could to stop this deadly assault on America? No. We would act without hesitation. And that's just what I intend to do. I need each of you to make the same commitment. Can you? Do you?" She looked down the length of the table, her eyes stopping to stare into her sister's eyes. Morrígan, was silent, unshaken. Morrígan, what are you thinking?"

Vice President Morrígan Tilton sat upright in her chair, making a process out of the slow, deliberate way she closed her Blaid® screen, pushed the stylus into its holder, folded her hands on the table, then scanned the room, with a focused look into each person's eyes. Then her attention landed on Wallyce, and she stayed emotionless for a half minute. Finally, as if the room held its collective breath, she sighed. "What am I thinking? Assuming that is a genuine question, I offer my sincere answer."

Wallyce imagined she could actually hear her heart beating in her chest. What's Morrígan's game here, she wondered.

"So that you get what I am about to say, let's assume a major resistance and protests spring up when we try to corral our own people into herds and move them into some place, wherever that could be, and subject them to extreme isolation and lockdown. We can define what we mean by lockdown, for how long, and the procedures for sequestration." She stopped talking, more to collect herself than to decide what to say next. Her face darkened, and her jaw tightened. A hint of sarcasm crept into her voice. "But for now, use your imaginations. Of course, as we've heard, we'll consider any protest and refusal to be an act of terrorism or even an assault on our country. Remember, these are Americans we're talking about. But, now they're terrorists. Got that?" Her speech got louder, more intense. "Good. Now, General McCann activates National Guard forces, maybe even the Marines, and they march into downtown anywhere U.S.A., armed and ready to protect our America. Busses and vans are quickly loaded with these terrorists, also called Americans." By now, she was standing, leaning over the table toward them. Her voice was louder, and her words came faster. "They're driven to the nearest isolation camp, stadium, arena, military base, or just wherever you find a place suitable for housing the millions of our friends and neighbors who we need to protect from themselves." She sat back down, opened her Blaid®, then nearly whispered. "That's what I'm thinking, President Wallyce. I'm too frightened by the reality to accept the fantasy, wherein we tell more than four hundred million people to do what we order them to do, and they actually comply."

Wallyce fixed a smile on her face and waited long enough to sense that the room had recovered to continue the discussion if that's what it would be called. She restarted the meeting. "Thanks for your candor, Morrígan. We've all had similar thoughts, concerns, and fears. I've had a massive guilt trip since we started this process. But I had to bring it back to reality several times. The one looming question, the idea that forces me to keep going down such a horrible path as to isolate and lock down our people, is the question none of us would ever want to answer for ourselves. Being unable to admit we have no choice is as close to defeat as we ever want to get. But, nevertheless, that frightening question looms large—it must be answered. That question is this: What options do we have to save as many of our friends and neighbors, as you pointed out, from dying a terrible and frightening death from Cyto-47? So, as you've been open enough to point out the horror of isolation and lockdown, I'll ask you, Morrígan. What options do you see for us to save any of our people? I'm open to ideas."

"President Tilton, if only I had any ideas. I'm as stumped as you all are. And, I must admit I'm afraid of what I see coming. We are about to lose most of our citizens to an unknown plague. We have no idea where it came from, how it kills us, where to look for a cure. . . we are screwed. And if we're about to be destroyed, America, the leader of the free world, then by default, the rest of the world is in far worse shape. They may already be over the line of no return. Any international reports, Dr.?"

Walters looked to the President for permission to speak. She nodded consent.

"I've held back on the status of the rest-of-world so we could focus on our own situation. Here is what we know: The Third World seems okay so far. Our best guess is that they haven't had much exposure, given the limited amount of travel they do. We expect, however, that this will change dramatically in a hurry. All it takes is a few cases of Cyto-47 for this monster to devour an entire population. We're watching closely, and I'll keep you up to speed. Europe and South America are in worse shape. Case counts are ten times our own. Tens of millions are dead, and more are infected. Australia is in pretty good shape. They caught it early, closed their island to all traffic in or out, isolated anyone sick, and cremated their dead immediately after they passed. Tight control meant better results. The Empire of Korea is closed to the outside world, as they have been since the North Korean Nuclear War. There is no news in or out of China or

Japan, and India cannot keep up. Dead are left in the streets, burned on the beaches, or hastily buried. I expect the entire country to fail to recover, and they may be the first large-scale population to disappear. Are there any questions?"

Governor Brookfield raised his hand. "Dr., where would you rate us at this point, on a scale of Third World on the low side to Australia on the high?"

"I'll give you two ratings. The first is where we are now. We are better off than Europe and South America, but not by much. The second is where we'll be in a month unless we adopt President Tilton's plan. We'll be worse off than Europe is today and headed downward in a hurry. Remember, nothing so far has been able to stop this plague. Our only hope is avoidance. And there is only one way for that to happen; through isolation and lockdown. This program is heartbreaking at best and devastating at worst. But it is a walk in the park compared to what will happen if we fail to control our population immediately."

President Tilton spoke next. "I've ordered O2 Regenerator Systems to be installed at the Capitol Building and the Supreme Court. The buildings are being encapsulated in a super-strong steel/glass enclosure, similar to the one encapsulating the entire Barca City complex. Those who move into the facilities for their safety must remain inside for the run of the plague. However, their immediate family members can live with them, and food supplies will be planted and grown inside a new construction farm next to the Capitol building. These projects have been approved and funded by Congress. They're being built by the firm that produced most of Barca City and our newest remote facilities. Regarding Barca recovery plans, we have ordered all employees and immediate families to move into their local

Barca Corp facilities, which are already sealed environments. Employees will commit to staying inside for at least three full years and must renew as needed if the plague is not under control by then.

"Now comes a decision point. We all agree that the only hope is to isolate and lock down as many Americans as possible. Undoubtedly, this extreme measure will only enable us to save a small percentage of our country. Also, when we issue the order, there will be an immediate and violent backlash. As I see it, the decision is what will we do with those who wish to isolate? I can take a good number into Barca City, but there will be a need to house many more. Ideas?"

General McCann spoke first. "Since the airports will be closed to all traffic, perhaps the empty terminal buildings can be repurposed. Then, too, several airlines have large maintenance facilities at each of the three airports. They might serve as biofarms."

Wallyce agreed. "Excellent ideas, General. That's the kind of thinking we need to engage. Next?"

Dr. Walters raised his hand. "Yes, Dr.?"

"Universities and hospitals. Stanford, Berkeley, UCSF, and all the rest. Perfect facilities for this type of effort."

"Great, Dr., Wallyce smiled. Who's next?"

Morrígan spoke. "As I said, stadiums and arenas. I can see them easily turned into the modern-day version of internment camps. Maybe they can be used more readily for isolation. Isolate those who may have some form of sickness. Hold them until we determine they are free of the Plague, then move them into the longer-term lockdown facilities. That way, you don't need to separate healthy from sick in the lockdown."

Jake Brookfield spoke. "So, as Governor, I'll probably be

the first to act by calling up the national guard so you can federalize them. I'm ready to do that when you give the signal. But, and I ask this in all seriousness, what do we expect will happen when hundreds of thousands of California citizens flat-out refuse to isolate or go into lockdown? Hell, Madam President, there's likely to be a major revolt in our state's northern and southern sectors. What line must be crossed before we send the troops out to forcefully meet the resistance?"

"I don't know, Jake. That question is the hardest one to answer. First, it forces me to consider when to wage war against our citizens. And then, I have to rethink that question many times, at least once for every state. I've been over this in my mind time and time again. The only thing I've come up with is to make these decisions case-by-case. For example, is the protest benign? Are the people marching and waving flags? Then we might be able to pretty much ignore it. It's painful to admit, but they'll probably die out before they're any threat to those in compliance.

"On the other hand, what changes when the crowds turn violent and begin to attack us? They may take up arms and attempt to sabotage our secure isolation lockdown facilities. What if they're an actual threat to the survival of those in full compliance? My current thinking tells me they're to be considered the enemy and should be treated as such. That will be where I ask General McCann to take action to protect the rest of the population. Please, if anyone else has any different ideas, speak now."

"Make your lockdown strong enough that they can't possibly break through the security. Then you don't have to kill anyone." Again, it was Morrígan who dared to speak.

"Or, are you afraid your encapsulated world won't be as strong as it needs to be?"

Wallyce realized her sister had just crossed a line. "Interesting question, Morrígan. Why don't we discuss it over supper after this meeting" She looked around the room. "Does anyone else have anything to add? No? Okay, we'll meet again tomorrow at the same time. From here on, we will be meeting remotely, so be sure to have your comm location/ready so that the system can quickly locate you. That's it for now." Goh disconnected all remotes while the others present, except the President and Vice President, were escorted out.

Wallyce didn't hesitate. She was ready to end this charade between her and her sister. "Morrígan, are you sure you're on my team? It seemed you were fighting me at every step. Your last suggestion was not only unworkable, but it was also clearly antagonistic. I need an answer. Are you with me or against me?"

Morrígan was ready. "Your team? Is that what this is about, Wally? Your side?" She stood up to leave. "Make no mistake. I'm on the side of the people of the United States. I took an oath to protect and defend the Constitution. How does this thing you call your side balance with the right of life, guaranteed by the Constitution? I heard you, and I understood your goal. You're about to take autocratic control of the country–forget why. You're ready to grab it all. The problem is, you can only do this if you're willing to sacrifice those who aren't on your side. Those who aren't willing to follow your plan for isolation and lockdown should be killed? If that's it, then no. I'm not with you. If you're open to my simple suggestion to make the lockdowns secure enough so desperate rebellions don't threaten our very survival, then maybe. Maybe I can be on that side. Your choice, Wally. Or should I say yours and that so-called adviser you depend on, Dr. Sebastian? I have a strong feeling he's behind this."

That was too much for Wallyce. She let her temper come out. Now, she shouted in anger. "What the hell do you know about him? Sebastian's been my close friend and adviser for a very long time. He's helped me become the mega-successful person I am. He's kept me from losing my shit when things came crashing down on me. He was the only one to keep me from jumping off the damn bridge when Dad died, and I had nowhere to turn. Don't you presume you know him and how I make my decisions. This is between you and me. Leave Sebastian out of this."

The mention of Sebastian, not Dr. Sebastian, as she referred to him before, must have jolted Morrígan. "Sebastian? Sebastian, as in that playmate you made up when we were kids? Your imaginary friend who showed up when Dad died? Is that what you're calling, Dr. Sebastian? Wally, tell me I'm wrong. You don't depend on some imaginary friend to tell you how to run a country, do you? Oh my God! No. For a moment, I thought . . ."

"You can shut the fuck up, dear sister. Those I seek for advice and ideas are of no concern to you. Imaginary friend? Sure, believe what you want. I know you better than most, so your imagination does not surprise me. Just some advice for you: better keep this crap to yourself. Others might not be as generous as I am. Tell them what you told me, and you might be poking a bear. And you know what bears do when you poke them? Sure, you do. Now, this leaves me with a different problem. As of this minute, consider yourself on reassignment. We'll handle this without you. And tell your new sweetheart, this Aaron guy, that you can go with him on his two-week jaunt in the forest. I'll tell the others you're on a secret assignment."

"You spied on us? In my own home, you spied on us?"

"Oh, be serious, Morrígan. This is the national security we deal in. You didn't think you wouldn't be under the microscope all day, every day, did you? Here's a news flash. People are dying by the hundreds of thousands every day. You and I are charged with the most important mission ever known to mankind. We have to save the world. How important is your love life compared to the extinction we face if we get this wrong? I'm sorry, but I must use everything in my reach to beat Cyto-47. I mean everything."

"Wally, is that a threat?"

"No. You're my sister, my friend. I would never do anything to hurt you. But I can't let anyone get in the way of people's future. No, not a threat. However, I need to be able to move forward without feeling the need to look over my shoulder to see what the Vice President is doing to undermine the strategy I'm putting in place. I know you believe we can defeat Cyto-47 without sacrificing the hordes of our own people. You were pretty clear about that. But I can't take the chance that you're wrong. People will die; no way to stop that. Some will die because they make an incorrect choice. They'll refuse isolation and lockdown as their best chance for survival. Others will die because they took their refusal too far and chose to attack our isolation facilities and government forces—the very ones we're counting on to save them. Your thought of strengthening the isolation and lockdown facilities falls short. I see something else. I see a war of good versus evil soon. This is Armageddon, dear sister. You had better line up on the right side. Have any thoughts about your future?"

Morrígan noted something in her sister's words that she had never heard before. She heard a note of insanity. Of course, she thought. Anyone who seeks advice on how to run the country from her imaginary friend can't be reasoning. Now she imagines the end of days in Biblical proportions. "Maybe you're right. I need a break. I guess I'm so confused by the speed at which things are happening and the terrible power of Cyto-47. I might take you up on that break. I'll see my schedule, then let you know if I decide to head out for a week or so."

"Good, Morrígan. I'm not gonna lie. It'll be good for both of us. But, whatever you do, coordinate with the Secret Service detail."

"Yep. Will do." Morrígan could hardly wait to get out of there.

Chapter Seventeen

Governor Jake Brookfield straightened his tie, checked his bag to see if he had all he needed for the meeting, then scooted forward in the seat, ready to go. His driver stopped the car in front of the Civic Center in San Francisco, waited for the security team to park behind him, and signal-flash that they were also ready. The driver stepped out of the limo and walked to the right rear door at the curbside. He touched the brim of his cap and nodded to the car behind him. On cue, three security members exited the vehicle and surrounded the Governor as he left his car. As they moved closer to him, Governor Brookfield pulled back, feeling awkward.

"I wonder if I'll ever get used to this routine?" he said to no one. As if in response, the lead security guard spoke.

"President's order, sir. We are to be your protection today."

After six years at the helm of the nation's most prosperous state, Jake Brookfield felt the need for tight security for the first time. General McCann called him last night to alert him that there were credible threats against all of the members of the Plague team, including himself. His warning left no room for discussion. The danger was real and scary. The feelings nearly overcame him as he exited the elevator into the garage. The security team met him when they arrived to escort him.

Today's meeting held another concern for Jake. He was asked to meet with the Association of Bay Area Governments, ABAG, to hear their questions and demands of President Tilton. Jake knew the President would never let ABAG prevent the isolation plan from taking effect. But, he thought, two rock-solid forces, each trying to move the other at all costs, could never produce a good result. No matter, Jake's mission for this morning was two parts: First, he needed to find out if the ABAG group was operating as a team in its opposition, and next, he would make a sincere effort to convince them otherwise. The best outcome would be for ABAG to support isolation and lockdown. Jake knew the probability was slim, but he had to try.

The Governor and his team passed through the security at the entrance to City Hall. Mayor Perriman was there to greet them. "Welcome, Governor," she said, shaking his hand. "I'm looking forward to discussing our individual points of view. I'm even more excited that we may reach an agreement that the President can accept."

Rachel, call me Jake, and let's also cut the pretense from the start. You knew Wallyce Tilton even before she was elected. You've had many business bang-ups with her in the recent past. So, I guess you know what we're up against regarding any agreement. Will she be open to negotiation? My bet is no. She is about as locked in as I've ever seen her."

"Then why the hell did she agree to this meeting?

"My question, exactly. I suspect there are two overriding reasons. First, the President believes holding your enemies closer than your friends is wise. Second, she's interested in understanding how you could be willing to gamble with the future of humanity for any reason. She believes we're on the brink of destruction and isn't willing to take that risk. I'm sure I know why you wanted this get-together, but I'd like to hear it from you."

"And you will, in the meeting. Shall we go in?" Rachael Perriman didn't wait for an answer. Instead, she turned her back on the Governor, went right into the meeting room, and sat at the head of the table. She pointed to a chair at the side of the table, a move that Jake assumed he was to take that seat. Jake saw this as a slapback for the seating she was given in the President's last meeting.

Rachael didn't wait. As the Governor took a seat, she started with her personal agenda. "Governor Brookfield, I'm curious where your allegiance lies. Are you a State of California leader or a Federal Government lackey?"

Well, there it was. Jake expected resistance, but this was well beyond that. No beating around it. Perriman was locked and loaded and ready for a battle.

"That question is more aggressive than I expected, even from you, Mayor. Although it doesn't deserve an answer, I will say this: I'm an American loyal to the United States of America. I serve the people of California as Governor so that I can represent their best interests in all dealings with the federal government. I see no conflict in this and play no favorites in my dealings. The State of California is a member of the United States, and we have sworn to uphold the Constitution of that union. Now, I will ask you a similar question. Would you seek the best interests of the City and

County of San Francisco if those interests would directly conflict with the needs of California, even if those are opposed to the needs of all Americans? Look, Mayor Perriman, we have a situation where the people of America are at great risk of dying in huge, unthinkable numbers. Are you going to sit there and tell me you're sorry about that, but if it means doing all you can to stop this plague will require the City of San Francisco to make some serious trade-offs, you'll refuse?"

"No, governor. You never heard me say anything of the sort. My big concern isn't that San Francisco will have to make tough decisions just like every city and every state will. We're in this together and will win this as a team. I am, however, greatly concerned about who's calling the shots. Are the strategies laid out by President Tilton based on sound logic, or is she shooting from the hip with her sights set on what's best for Barca and Wallyce Tilton?"

"Get to the point, Mayor. What's your biggest concern?"

"Okay. More than the other things that concern me about Wallyce's plan, I'm convinced much of it is centered around what's best for Barca Enterprises and places America second. I'm talking about this plan to lockdown and force those who are willing to work to move into Barca City under a long-term contract, while the others are going to be forced to live in stadiums, places like The Cow Palace, and military lockdown reminiscent of the Japanese Internment Camps of the Second World War. It's so transparent. She's saying, 'Join my team or suffer the consequences.' What about the people who don't support that plan? Will they have a third option, the choice to live freely apart from others until this crap blows over?"

"Mayor, what the hell makes you think it will ever just

blow over? This plague might be here for a long time from all we hear. President Tilton believes in science. Science tells us it may be years before we can safely venture back outside unprotected, if ever. Look, Rachael and the rest of you ABAG leaders, you might think our President has some agenda to profit from misery. It couldn't be farther from the truth. Suppose you know anything about her and Barca. In that case, you know her success is tied to technology, design, creation, integration, and sale of all forms of technology. Let's look at the next five years under her plan. Factories worldwide will close. Think tanks will slow to a trickle, and innovation will suffer. Transportation will grind to a halt. Nobody will commute when everyone is locked safely away from harm. The economy will implode, and no one will suffer more loss than the head of Barca, Wallyce Tilton. Mayor, she stands to lose most of her vast fortune, hoping that she may help save a few million people. And you think she's self-interested?

"There are a few things nobody knows about her. Let me just tell you in confidence what she said last night. She asked me what I thought about her plan. I told her I didn't like any of it, but I couldn't think of another path. She was silent for a long time. Then Wallyce told me that she hated that she would probably be forced to do this lockdown. Still, she said, 'Maybe, when this is over, we can salvage a little of humanity, enough to start over again. Maybe, we can learn from our mistakes and build a better world for all who haven't been born yet.' She cried, Mayor. You see her as some tough-as-nails leader, but I know the Wallyce Tilton that only comes out when the public can't see her. She cares so much for the people; she's willing to risk everything if she can save even a few of us to be able to begin again. So, now.

What's it going to be? Are each of you willing to support her?"

Rachael spoke for the group. "Governor, you've told a heart-wrenching story about a wonderful and passionate leader. Too bad none of us believed it for a second. We'll discuss this today, and if we need more information, we'll contact you. Is there anything else to add?"

This told Governor Brookfield all he needed to know. "Nope. I don't suppose there is. Good day." He and his team left quickly.

The Governor's vehicle was just turning onto the 101 Freeway, headed toward Barca City, when his comm lit up. It was Wallyce.

"Jake, where are you?"

"Just headed south on the freeway. What's up?"

Some bad news, Governor. I received a call two minutes ago. The mayor and two others of the ABAG team started out of the City Center parking garage when an assassin stepped in front of the car and opened fire, killing everyone inside. The killer was run over and died."

Governor Brookfield sat in silence for a few moments. "Holy Shit!" He sat quietly for a few more moments, then, lifting his eyes to meet hers, he said, "I can't say I'm sorry. Perriman was impossible to deal with, and she'd surely have been a huge barricade to your success. But unfortunately, we didn't have time to reach a meaningful conclusion for our meeting. I'm worried now that the opposition will try to use this heinous crime to claim your administration had something to do with it. What's our next step?"

"We can talk when you get here. Meet me in my office." She disconnected. Jake Brookfield instructed his driver to head to the Executive Tunnel into Barca City. The security team was ordered to wait for him in the parking garage and to watch for any signs of danger.

Jake Brookfield was troubled. He remembered that three security guards accompanied him into the building. He wondered why only two were with him when he left. Governor Jake Brookfield gained a new perspective on President Wallyce Tilton. It shook him.

* * *

Morrígan sat looking at her comm for a long time. She knew what she had to do, but it scared the hell out of her. She couldn't support what her sister planned for the lockdown. Too many would die. Others would gather force and rebel against what would be seen as tyranny. Depending on who and how many became rebels, this could easily lead to the Armageddon she feared. Wallyce was insane—that much was certain. But was there really any alternative? Cyto-47 was death itself. So many had died in such a short time that severe and immediate action was needed. Maybe Wallyce was right. Maybe there was no alternative. But, as evil and insane as it was, her plan might just be the only plan that had any chance of saving the future of humanity. Morrígan knew she needed to talk to Aaron right away. He was already going to the deep forest to start his two-week disconnect from the world. She remembered he gave her access to his direct comm line. Hoping he still had it with him, she activated her internal headset, so no one else could hear their private comm discussion, tapped on his picture, and the line came to life.

"Thanks for contacting me," came a recording of Aaron's voice. "Please leave a message." Her heart sank.

"Aaron, it's me, Morrígan. If you get this message, please contact me as soon as possible. It's urgent." She didn't want to panic, but she needed him to know things were worsening. Her use of "urgent" was an attempt to let him know to call as soon as possible. She closed the comm. Now, she thought, I can only wait. She focused on their recent conversations, hoping to remember how much she had told him what she thought Wallyce was planning to do. Did I tell him enough? Will he see the urgency in what I have to say?

She didn't have long to wait. The comm flashed in her hand. Seeing Aaron's face on the screen filled her with both comfort and panic at the same time.

"Hi, Morrígan. Couldn't stand to be without me for even a day, huh?"

"Oh my God, I'm so glad you called back. I feared you'd be in the deep forest and might not get my comm. Hold on a second. I need to wash my hands." She hoped Aaron would get that she needed background noise to muffle her voice as she talked. Then, leaning over the sink, she placed the comm close to her mouth and spoke softly. "I'm sorry to interrupt your trip, but it's getting to be emergency conditions back here."

"Already? But I've only been away a day and a half. Things were bad, but not yet an emergency. So what's going on?"

"I'm scared, Aaron, and I need to talk to you immediately. Can we meet?"

"Well, we could, but can't we talk on comm? These lines are secure and use a private Sat-comm network. There's no chance in hell anyone can pick up our signal, much less be able to unscramble our encryption. Not even the mighty

Sister-President. Let's start with just a few details and see how it goes?"

Morrígan had to think that through. Any other reason, and she'd be all over it telling him everything. But this was a national emergency, top secret stuff. This information, if it became public, could start a worldwide rebellion. So she needed to be careful.

"I get that your Sat-comm is secure. But what I need to tell you is toxic—Armageddon-style toxicity. I need to be cryptic, so listen carefully. First, think of two words: lock-down and isolation. Next, add the component of tyranny with the foundation of insanity. Finally, put it in a blender and set a very short timer. That's for starters. Can you read that back to me so I know you are on the same track I am?"

"She's nuts and wants to take over the world," Aaron replied.

"Close enough. Wallyce didn't feel I was much support for her program, so I've been taken off the active player roster and told to take a vacation. The key players who are in support are ready to climb the hill with her. Cyto-47 has decimated the governmental structure, and the Pentagon stands close by to implement any orders given by their Commander in Chief. There hasn't been any talk about insurrection, but that'll happen by itself. With insurrection comes the potential for martial law. With martial law comes boots on the streets. Aaron, I've already gone way too far. We need to talk face-to-face. What should I do?"

"Get the hell out of there right now."

"I can't."

'Why not? You said you're no longer on the team."

"Oath of Office. I've sworn to uphold the Constitution

and defend the United States against all enemies. All enemies. All of them. Even the powerful ones."

"Think about what you just said. How can you defend these powerful ones against the most powerful person in the world?" Morrígan knew Aaron made sense.

"I have to figure that out. I'm hoping you can help me do that, Aaron."

"Okay. I'm in. But it starts with getting you to a safe place. There's a horse-riding club in the Headlands over Sausalito. After disconnecting this call, I'll send you the name and location. Memorize it, then delete it from your comm. Then go back to your home in Barca and grab only a few essentials. Anything else we need, we can grab on the way. Meet me at the riding club this time tomorrow. I have a place we can go where no one can find us as we work on a plan. I'll go home, grab some things, and go to the Headlands. Don't expect to stay there. We're heading out as soon as I get there."

"But shouldn't I stay and do what I can from Barca?" She didn't need to tell him she was familiar with the riding clubs in the headlands.

"If you stay, you're putting yourself at risk, and you won't be able to help anyone. You said the word insanity. The only way to be safe from her is to get as far away as possible and then work a plan from a distance. If she can't find you, she can't stop you."

"Okay, but I need another day to get everything in order from here."

"One more day can't be that important. You need to get out now."

"One more day, I promise. I'll be there in two days.

"If you're not there, I'm coming to get you."

Morrígan had never felt such fear in her life. She feared for herself, of course. But her overriding fear was for humanity. Her mind flashed images of nuclear clouds and jack-booted troopers killing innocents. The phrase World-War-Finale kept ringing in her mind. It was becoming clear that she might be the best one to protect the world. She had an inside point of view. This is my sister. Is my sister the next tyrant, the second coming of every murderous villain? She knew this madwoman and might know what it would take to stop her.

"Send me the riding club information. I love you, Aaron. I'll see you there." She tapped the comm button, and it went dark.

No sooner had she disconnected when her Blaid® came back to life. It was Agent Corey Gaiters, her Secret Service lead.

"Yes, Corey. What is it?"

"Do I have your permission to enter the office?"

"Of course, you do Corey." Morrígan was jolted by the odd request. As Secret Service lead to the Vice President, Gaiters had explicit permission to go anywhere the Vice President was without asking. So her senses were on alert as she waited for the agent to come in.

"Madam Vice President, I understand you requested to go outside the buildings for a brief walk in nature. Is that how you put the request?" He looked directly at Morrígan in a way she took to mean he wanted her to go along with the charade.

"Yes, Agent Gaiters. That's exactly what I need right now." She turned to the lift entrance and waited for the agent to follow. They traveled in silence as the transport took them directly to the Executive tunnel, where they could use the pedestrian walkway to the observation deck. Gaiters motioned for Morrígan to sit at the nearby bench, then he sat next to her. A bold seagull who had to be chased from the bench flew up to join the other gulls as they flew in random patterns above, creating a clamor of seagull symphony. Soon, sensing they weren't about to be fed, they moved on to bother other people taking pictures in front of the impressive Barca City main entrance.

"Madam, I want you to know, in addition to being your lead Secret Service agent, I am also the best friend you have in this God-forsaken place." He stopped talking and looked directly into her eyes.

"Corey, please, when we're not in public, call me Morrígan." She waited until he nodded, then added, "Now, make some sense. What are you saying? I know you're my friend and care for my well-being, but you're talking about something else, aren't you?"

"Yes, Morrígan. I am. I'll get to the point, hoping it isn't a mistake that puts me in federal prison." His hand shook a bit as he reached up to scratch an errant shock of hair from his forehead. Morrígan, I need to tell you that I know how difficult it must be for you to get away to have any time alone, or at least away from the prying eyes of the government. I also know several reasons you may need to do just that—get away. Follow me so far?"

Morrígan didn't know what to say. Had he guessed her plan? Did he overhear something? Was he a counter-spy for Wallyce? She caught her breath. I have no choice. I need to take the risk with him. "Get to the point, Corey."

"Yes, the point. I will. You may not like it, but the point is I have knowledge that you are in danger. Don't ask me how I know this, but believe that you are considered a serious problem in the way of the President's plans for Pandemic Abatement. I don't know what this problem is, but I know that the President has been meeting with certain people today, and the topic was how to get you out of the way. I overheard parts of the conversation, and I will tell you the president has conspired to have you be somehow killed and to make this look like an accident. One phrase I heard twice: 'No one can get in the way of this lockdown, not even my sister—not even the Vice President.'

Morrígan struggled to regain her senses. Her mind was a jumbled mess, trying to make sense of the unbelievable story this man was telling her. Morrígan wasn't aware that tears streamed down her face. But she clearly understood that her life was now in grave danger. One wrong step and she'd either be dead or be on trial for insurrection, plotting to overthrow the government. She could only do what her stepfather had done to her so many times when she was a child.

"Corey, turn to face me," she almost demanded. Put your hands on the palms of mine. That's right. Now, we'll close our hands around each other's. Good. Now, try to match my breathing." She paced her breaths, loud at first, so he could get the pacing. When his breathing and hers were in sync, she said, "Look into my eyes and try to find my spirit. I'll do the same to you." She felt them come closer in a spiritual sense.

"Corey, should I trust you with my life?"

The question was unexpected. Corey pulled back slightly, but Morrígan could sense that he forced himself to be present with her. She felt it must have seemed to him what a human lie detector might feel like.

"Morrígan, I place my life before yours. I'm sworn to die for you, which is the most sacred oath I have ever taken."

She knew it was true. In her thoughts, she thanked her stepfather for his wisdom, then she released Corey's hands.

Corey, I suspect you know what's happening. You know me, and you know I could never support what the government is putting together – isolation and lockdown. Forcing free people to be locked out and left to the devastation of Cyto-47 just to make the world slightly safer for those who will bow to your will. Those who refuse will be called enemies and treated like enemies—killed or locked away. When this happens, many Americans will do what Americans have always done, rebel against tyranny. This will ignite a global massacre. It's the strategy of an insane leader and will result in the death of most humans alive today. I don't have a better plan yet, but I will develop one. It's true. I'll probably need your help in the next few days. Are you ready for that?"

"Yes, more than ready."

"Then, don't hesitate for a second when I give the word. We need to move in a hurry."

"I'll stay on watch all day and night. We need a signal. If you think it's time to go, tell me you have a meeting right away. That'll be the signal to act. I'll follow you out of whatever room we're in. Otherwise, if you have advance notice of when you wish to get moving, simply tell me you have a meeting coming up, then give me a time for the meeting."

Morrígan waited for more, but Corey had paused, giving time to absorb what to her was very frightening. Then, he touched her shoulder and smiled. She saw in his eyes a sincerity she didn't expect. "Thank you, Corey," she said. I know the risk you are taking for me."

Corey spoke to her as a friend would. "I imagine you

might still have some fears. I can't take them away. But I swear to lay down my life for your cause and you."

Morrígan held her breath for a moment. Then, backing away, she smiled. "Corey, I'm so lucky to have you on my side. Please be ready when I call. It's not going to be long from now." She rose, and they walked back into the executive entrance to Barca City.

Chapter Eighteen

Wallyce jolted awake, having failed at meditation. It was getting to be more difficult by the day. Trying to run the country in a pandemic, she told herself, anything but peaceful. Nothing on Earth could make the life of a Pandemic President any less tense--not even her luxurious lifestyle. Her private home in Barca City was the beacon of technology. Lights raised or dimmed as needed, furniture arrangements would change to several different patterns, depending on the use—cocktail party, presentation, small discussion gathering, sizeable corporate meeting, or just about any need her imagination could conjure. The possibilities were endless, and all by voice command.

Regaining focus, she thought, I might as well see how I'm doing. "Goh, connect World News Update."

The presentation table flashed twice without a word, indicating a connection to the system that now presented World News Update in hologram mode. Another benefit of obscene wealth; being able to afford such a miracle.

The room lights dimmed to the best level for hologram viewing. A serving cart rolled into the room, stopping next to Wallyce's usual chair. She picked up the glass and sipped Brentwood Vineyards Red Tailed Pinot. She loved this wine so much; she bought the vineyard. About to snack on the crab cakes the chef had made for her, she was startled when the news jumped to life, sudden and loud, and in brilliant color—a feature that had been thus far missing from holograms. Most were still hollow, ghost-like vagaries. Another win for Barca, she thought.

"Welcome to World News Update, coming from the WNU headquarters in New York City. "I'm Ruger Fordyce, and I'll be your host for the next hour of world updates. Let's start right in with the current status of Cyto-47 . . . and I'm afraid it's not good news. Here in the United States, the pandemic is at a peak regarding new cases and mortality rates. We have the head of the CDC, Dr. Walters, to update us on the grim statistics. Dr. Walters?"

"Hello, Ruger. Thanks for having me."

Wallyce was drawn to the projection of her friend, Walters. As she approached, she circled around to get a view from all sides. Aside from a few stripes on his suit being slightly wavy, she was impressed by the image's clarity and how much it felt as if he were in the room with her.

"This technology has really come a long way, she thought.

"Of course, things are bad and getting worse," Dr. Walters continued. "As we've seen, the plague is on a rampage, infections are increasing by more than twenty percent per week, and the mortality rate hovers around 100%. Remember, what we think is a rare combination of bacteria and virus doesn't act like anything we've ever known. We are working around the clock to find the causes of this pandemic and hope to make some headway soon. But, in the meantime, Cyto-47 remains the most destructive disease ever faced by mankind. If you get it, you become very sick in a flash, and there's not much chance for survival."

"That's a pretty harsh description, Dr. Walters."

"I intended it to be harsh, Ruger. Every day, several times a day, we come on the news shows and tell people that this is a supremely deadly disease that will infect you if you're not careful to implement the precautions we've laid out in simple terms." By now, he was angry, nearly shouting. "Every day, I make no bones about what you need to do: Stay the hell home. If you must go out, cover your face and head with a full-head medical mask, wear surgical gloves, and scrub your hands when you remove the gloves. Change gloves every hour. If you have one, wear a full-body hazmat suit. Spray it down with sanitizer before you remove it. And mostly, stay the hell home. Don't go out. If you go out, it could easily be for the last time.

"Then, too, as if widespread apathy isn't bad enough, we see daily reports of massive protests; the people seem to blame the government for this pandemic. This isn't politics. It's real life. But the people don't seem to accept that. Some carry signs calling for the ouster of our President. Some demand her to step down immediately, calling her Tyrant Tilton. And what is the likely result? They'll get sick and die. President Tilton will be safe as she stays indoors in a bio-safe building. Do you really think the protests are going to save any lives? No," he shouted.

"I'm not kidding. Stay the hell home. Do this, or you will probably die soon. Now, Ruger, I'm sure you didn't expect me to be so harsh. For too many of these sicknesses over the decades, we have been soft, almost pleading with the public to isolate. Do most people listen? No. It's easier to blame the government and say that the plague isn't as bad as they make it sound. This time, it is worse than it sounds. I can't stress it enough. We can't afford to play games here. Millions are dying, and there's no end in sight."

"Thanks, Dr. I understand. Just so we're sure our viewers understand this Cyto-47, here is a scene from the Rapid Transport System in New York today."

The projection changed to a scene in midtown Manhattan. The hologram moved through the crowd of angry, would-be passengers as they learned the transport had been shut down for the foreseeable future. The plague was probably running rampant in the transport cars. People crowded into the train at one station, and most of them were infected when they reached the next station. Many were on the floor, unable to get up. Still, others were sick but headed home to unknowingly infect their family. You would have a tough time finding more than a handful of masks in use.

"To my viewers: I wish you would take this to heart. Please listen to medical professionals like Dr. Walters. There's a conspiracy theory that too many of you have bought into. The theory is that this is some plot to enslave us. The rumor is that the government is shifting from a democracy to a dictatorship, and you're determined to fight against this dictatorship by refusing to buy into what you think is the lie; a plague is trying to kill us, and only the government can save us. You are the reason this pandemic is racing out of control. You know me. I never tell my viewers what they should do. I report the stories, and I offer no opinion. This time, it's different. Keep this up, and we have no hope of survival. Please, listen to the people who know. Follow the lead of the scientists like Dr. Walters. We don't have much time. Stay the hell home until we have a vaccine or a cure for Cyto-47." Fordyce seemed at a loss for what to say next. After a beat, he spoke. "There will be no other stories tonight. I ask you to sit with your family and discuss what you heard and saw here tonight. Then, make the decision you need to make. Stay the hell home. I'm Ruger Fordyce. Hoping to see you tomorrow."

The screen flashed the Breaking News logo while an announcer broke over Ruger's voice.

"World News Update: Breaking News. This just into WNU headquarters in New York."

The hologram projected a chaotic scene in front of the California State Capitol Building. "A crowd of several thousand protestors descended on the State Capitol in Sacramento within the last half hour. The protest, loud and somewhat violent with rocks and a few tear gas canisters being thrown at Sacramento Police, started in response to the violent murder of three Bay Area mayors in San Francisco this week. Let's see if we can get more information from some protestors."

The hand of an unseen reporter pushed a microphone inches from the face of a young man who held a sign that proclaimed No to Tyranny. The off-camera reporter asked, "What's this protest all about?"

The young man spun to face the camera. "Are you fucking kidding me? What the hell kind of question is that? We're being herded like cattle into isolation camps. As we hear it, those who aren't sick will be put in long-term isolation, and anyone who refuses will either be slaughtered or maybe poisoned to make it look like Cyto-47 is real. What's this about? It's about a revolt. It's about taking back our country and our rights. Get in the way, and we'll roll right over you." He had barely finished when a police officer nailed him with some form of electric prod, sending him to the ground where they cuffed and dragged him away—no warning, no sympathy.

The UPN reporter continued." Reports are that similar protests are happening in Washington D.C., Chicago, Austin, San Francisco, and Los Angeles." As each city was named, scenes from each city flashed, showing that this revolt had gathered steam already and threatened to become a national revolt.

"In other parts of the world, the European Union government is in a shambles. Thousands of bodies have been buried in mass graves throughout the former territories of France, Germany, and the Slavic corridor. A no-fly zone has been enacted in the Chinese Empire, prohibiting non-Asian jets, drones, and other flying vehicles from fixing cameras over their empire. Satellite imagery, although sketchy due to the Asian Air Curtain's effectiveness at blocking video images from space, indicates bedlam all over the empire, with fires and bombings, mass suicides by self-immolation, and hopeless attacks on government buildings and transportation hubs. Emperor Tsien declared the Korean Sector an enemy stronghold. She has ordered nuclear and laser attacks on the cities of Seoul in the south and Pyongyang in the north. A complete lockdown has been declared, with anyone violating curfew at risk of immediate execution." The hologram faded to be replaced with the UPN logo. "This has been the UPN World Update. More news as it happens."

Wallyce commanded, "Close World News Update and disconnect presentation. Goh, tell our marketing division to set up a new program centered around the phrase, Stay the Hell Home. I want animated billboards, a jingle to be played continuously at all transportation hubs, and a message from me on every home projection screen telling people in my voice to Stay the Hell Home. I want this in sample form by tomorrow at 8 am.

Now, connect me to General McCann." A holographic image of the General appeared, but it wasn't him, just a statue-like representation of the General.

"I'm here, President Tilton. At your service. Sorry about the statue. I'm in the air now, so the signal might not be clear enough to translate on your end."

"Okay, now that makes sense. So, what's the latest from your POV?"

"Well, here is where I am and the mission details. I received a red alert from D.C. police that a crowd of angry protestors surrounded the Capitol building. Signs and chants indicate they are followers of the latest nut-job spouting some whacko conspiracy theory. This happens like clockwork about every dozen-or-so years. Though we had several drones in the air and visuals from our satellites, I wanted to see this for myself. It's not often you get to look in on a crowd of about fifty thousand bent on self-destruction. Imagine, they're here to protest the plague, probably by catching it."

"So, what's the next step?

"I just took it. We sent a handful of fire-control helicopters and a bunch of drones to swoop over the crowd and soak them with a strong sanitizer, hoping to kill whatever virus or bacteria might be floating around them. Probably won't work, but we gave it a try."

"General, I'm trying to wrap my brain around this. So,

you soaked the crowd of about fifty thousand with a chemical bath?

"Yes, Madam. That's one way to look at it."

"I have an uneasy feeling about this. The idea of the government dumping chemicals on a crowd of Americans exercising their First Amendment Rights in the early stage of a likely revolution will set off fireworks worldwide. I'm sure we're going to have to answer for this. Good intention, General—terrible solution. Keep me posted."

She disconnected before he could respond.

"Goh, assemble the team for an emergency meeting to begin right away. Don't include the Vice President. Add the Chief of Capitol Police in D.C. and have Brookfield send me the chart for the command structure of the California Guard. Don't share the chart with other members. Also, add the Governors of the surrounding states, Oregon, Nevada, and Arizona, as "captioned observers." Make sure they're only online until I disconnect them. Start now. I expect to be connected via hologram in my office within ten minutes."

"Yes, Madam."

Wallyce rushed through, changing her outfit from casual to official. No time for details, she thought as she skipped the makeup table and headed down to her office. Stepping in, she positioned her chair at the center of the video chamber. Wallyce could tell there were others without even looking up from her controller. It's odd, she thought, how potent the tension comes through in one of these sessions. It's as if they were here in the room with me. "Goh, please forward the members the most current version of the Pandemic Status Report. Please include the one-sheet summary so they can get up to speed immediately." She bit her lip when she realized she was using the "please" word with her Electronic

Assistant. It pissed her off that she couldn't break that habit. Goh indicated that he had complied. "Everyone," she spoke into the holocam videographer, "please review the summary as I talk to you. We have little time to waste. Now, welcome Governors Homah, Wyatt, and Babar. Your presence here today is an information-only participation. I want you to be clear on what's happening worldwide relative to Cyto-47 and our strategy as of today. I don't expect it, so please don't volunteer your opinions. Thanks.

"As we all know, Cyto-47 has reached pandemic status worldwide. The speed at which the damage is growing has been unimaginable. Hundreds of millions worldwide have already died. And there's no end in sight. CDC and counterparts around the globe have been unable to determine the cause of the plague, making vaccination impossible. We've had no success with any medication, so mortality rates are as bad as possible. Barca Corporation is only one of the many participants seeking a cure. Unfortunately, we've had no success yet.

This leads to the only hope for the foreseeable future: isolation and lockdown. Here in California, Governor Brookfield has agreed that the State of California will be on total lockdown until further notice. This means that all roads, waterways, airports, and border crossings will be closed to all people except military and specific government personnel. This exclusion includes those on business, personal travel, and even those residing here but outside the State when this lockdown was enacted. They will not be able to return home at this time. This lockdown will be enforced by California National Guard, under my command and under the direction of General McCann.

"In addition to lockdown, we've implemented a program

of isolation. Anyone who shows symptoms associated with Cyto-47 will be placed under observation in quarantine for three weeks. We feel this is long enough to determine if they are safe to rejoin the population. Details of our isolation program will be forwarded to you when they are final. To the governors: as President of the United States, I'm working with Congress to develop a plan that enables each State to develop its programs for combatting the plague. Be assured that you will not be permitted to ignore this problem by playing the hero role and just 'riding it out.' Any state that risks the security of other states or the country will be deemed to have given up its right to self-govern. Specifically, the federal government will evaluate your abatement and protection programs. If they're determined to be adequate, nothing will be done to interfere. If your programs are inadequate, we will impose a program like the one I've outlined today in your State after a brief but sincere effort to work with you. We can't, and we won't hesitate. Thank you for your time, and please contact my office immediately with any questions."

Wallyce disconnected the three governors. Then, she added, "Goh, package that message and distribute it to all of the remaining governors with a letter from my administration that leaves no doubt they are each under the same program."

Now, she turned to the assembled group, minus the three governors. "You've probably figured out that I selected those three governors based on proximity. They surround California. If they isolate and lockdown right away, it will add to our control, making this part of the country the most secure. But, on the other hand, if they hesitate or refuse, we will do what I warned we will;

immediate and total assumption of command over the states.

"Senate Leader Argen, what's the status of Congress?"

"Madam President, believe me when I tell you, there is no Congress in the usual sense. Senate members are dropping like flies, and the House members in place are primarily replacements. Many Representatives have died, and their Governors or state processes have replaced them with inexperienced people. Blind leading the blind there. Thanks to our system, Senate can still operate with a quorum available. Still, a majority vote is becoming less possible by the day. There's another major threat to our government brewing in D.C. in the form of an insurgency. This morning, an armed group of about fifty civilians began a loud and violent protest. Some gunfire has been directed at the buildings, but so far, no shots have hit any people. But it won't be much time before this turns fatal.

"Thanks, Bill. Is Capitol Police Chief online? Unfortunately, I don't see his hologram."

"Yes, Madam President. I'm here. Chief Reilly is ready for orders. I just don't have hologram equipment where I currently am."

"Okay, Chief. Pay close attention to what I'm about to say. I'm asking you to take control of the entire Capitol Building. Place it under strict lockdown—no one comes in or leaves until further notice. We've installed a closed ecological system. See to it you have guards on the controls 24/7. You're about to hear what many have speculated. First, you need to be under oath of confidential information. General McCann will administer the oath.

"Back to you, Leader Argen. What's the probability that you can get Congress to approve an emergency measures bill that'll support any Presidential call for a National State of Emergency, giving me the ability to declare martial law countrywide? And how quickly can that happen?"

"I've already started the process, President Tilton. When the first shots were fired, I had staff contact all Senators to ask if they felt this was enough to declare an Insurgency. The immediate answer was yes. Both houses have been in negotiations all morning. They report that they are close to agreement on enacting an Emergency Powers Act that will enable you to impose martial law countrywide."

"Bill, how did you know I'd be asking for this?"

"It's a logical next step, President Tilton. Hundreds of millions of people are dying all over the world. The cycle of death of this plague is mere days. No time to play politics. I knew we needed to be ready, so we're putting the key pieces in place right now."

"Excellent, Bill. Easy to see why you're the Senate Leader." She turned to the Chair of the Joint Chiefs. "Now, General McCann. As we've discussed, how soon can you distribute military forces throughout the country?"

"I can have it done by tomorrow evening."

"Good. Start the movement of troops now, but don't take any action yet. Try to make the troop movement low-key if possible. Don't want to raise any more alarms. Wait for my instructions."

"Governor Brookfield, are you ready?

"I am, Madam President."

"Prepare the channels to all media in California, including the EBS, Emergency Broadcast System. We'll send this out to all when we finish. Governor, you have my order to proceed," she said.

"Yes, Madam." He turned to the group. "Focus holocams

on me. I, Jake Brookfield, Governor of the State of California, declare complete lockdown over the State of California, effective immediately. Due to the rapid advances of the pandemic all over the world and here at home, there is no choice. In addition, I am sad to say, we are experiencing a growing number of violent protests in both Los Angeles downtown areas and Sacramento. Several have been shot in Sacramento, and buildings have been set ablaze in Los Angeles. In addition, the mayors of three Bay Area cities, San Francisco, Oakland, and San Jose, were murdered in an open assassination just yesterday. We haven't yet determined if this was an act of protest against the government, but this has triggered much chaos in the Bay Area. It's become clear that we must control the State tightly to prevent spiraling into a rebellion." Governor Brookfield paused for effect. Then he continued in a slow, official manner. "Reason dictates that in such a deadly world threatened by Cyto-47, any attempt to prevent the government from taking actions necessary to save as many lives as possible will be considered an insurrection against the government and a threat to the safety of the people. The California State Legislature, in a meeting this morning, determined that we have a clear responsibility to protect the citizens of the State from the Plague. Any attempts to block this, through violent protest, will constitute an insurrection, and any who form against the government in this war to defeat Cyto-47 will be guilty of treason."

As the Governor spoke, the other participants were shaken. None had heard any of this before.

"Due to these protests, I declare the State of California under Martial Law. Further, under the allowances and previous applications of the Insurrection Act, I place California under the control of the Federal Government of the

United States of America. Accordingly, I have signed this order as of this time and date, and I transfer statewide authority to the President of the United States, Wallyce Tilton."

The hologram slowly softened as the image of Governor Brookfield faded, to be replaced by the appearance of President Tilton.

"Thank you, Governor. To the people of California, lockdown is now enacted statewide. By tomorrow, you will have instructions on what the next stage of this plan entails. Please prepare to act as soon as instructions are made public. Again, I'm sorry for this necessary action, and I pray that we will soon defeat this terrible pandemic."

The hologram faded to flat, then out. Wallyce stood.

"Goh, edit the hologram from where Jake Brookfield begins speaking to the point where it fades to black. Then, clean it up and put it on all channels right away under the banner of Emergency Declaration." She turned to Jake Brookfield.

"Governor, I need a final list of lockdown and isolation locations statewide. Forward it to Goh before this evening at 10:00 pm. General, you will be responsible for staffing each lockdown location no later than tomorrow.

"Dr. Walters, you need to create a schedule and description chart of all necessary steps to be included in a comprehensive isolation program. Please have all stages, from identifying the person to be isolated and acquiring medical equipment, including an inventory of all clothing and hazmat suits and equipment that will be required, and a checklist for determining the type and length of patient isolation to be enacted. I want to see a formula. How do we determine who's to be isolated? How long before they no longer need medical support? If we're fortunate to discover some form of treatment, what are the requirements for survivors to be released from isolation? And provide a formal, stated guideline for how you'll handle the remains of the fatalities, and there will be many—nearly every person isolated will die. Put your best people on this. I expect a complete program on my desk by 8:00 am tomorrow.

"This leads to your part, Senator Argen." All side discussions stopped. Every head turned to Bill Argen. Argen, Leader of the Senate, was an ally for Wallyce from the beginning. In fact, he was once considered to be her running mate until she selected Morrígan. Everyone knew he'd be critical to the cause. "Bill, I have to count on you once again. If anyone can navigate the mess Congress has become, it's you. We need to be able to get things done in a Congress that's been crippled by the plague. I need you to pass some bills to allow us to make immediate decisions and act quickly to prevent mass chaos. Examples: We will seize control of all hospitals, stadiums, airport terminals, universities, and the like to turn them into isolation-capable facilities. There's no time to lose. Then, we must be able to declare some form of martial law across the country right now. Nothing less will work. Finally, we need the War Powers Act to grant me the authority to declare Cyto-47 as the enemy. Anyone who prevents us from doing what we need to defeat the enemy will be viewed and treated as an enemy combatant. When can you have this completed?"

Argen sighed involuntarily. "President Tilton, you might as well have asked me to reverse the Earth's orbit. How soon do you need these things?"

"By tomorrow at this time. At a minimum, I need the right to declare martial law by then. The rest can hold for a day. After that, people will be so shocked by the martial law that they won't notice if we write an Executive Order to give me interim powers to declare enemy combatants. After that, the courts, if we still have any, will drag their heels long enough for you to get the rest done. Can I count on you?"

"I'll get it done." Although Senator Argen was direct, he spoke softly. "If there are any issues, I'll let you know, but I commit that I will have what you need tomorrow."

Chapter Nineteen

Morrígan tried everything to calm herself. Nothing worked. Breathing, meditation, and even singing a soft song to herself made her more nervous. She tried logic. Okay, girl. So, here's what you know. Wallyce sees you as the enemy. She bounced you off her team, even though you're the duly elected Vice President to her President. She can't just do that—but she has. Then, according to Corey, who you don't trust much, she's plotting to somehow get rid of you, maybe even assassinate you. She takes her advice from an imaginary person. To top it all, she's begun the steps to take over this country in some autocratic way, maybe closing down the government and changing life as we know it.

On the other hand, Cyto-47 has already done that. You need time to think, and it doesn't look like there will be any time. So, what the hell are your options? Just as her instinct to scream took over, the door monitor chimed, causing her to jump out of her chair. "Viewer on," she commanded. It was Wallyce on the other side of the door. With some hesitation, she called for the door to open. Wallyce took charge right away.

"Morrígan, I didn't see you at dinner. Is everything alright?"

"Oh, yeah. I'm fine. Just not hungry. I thought you were in a meeting."

Wallyce was transparent in her manner. She saw Morrígan was tense, and Wallyce needed to defuse the situation and help Morrígan calm down. Her first mistake was to appeal to Morrígan's sympathies. Wallyce feigned a posture of defeat as if she couldn't devise any solution for a terrible problem. She moved closer to her sister with a look of candor, knowing full well that if Morrígan didn't know her better, she might think she was sincere. But, Wallyce understood, Morrígan knew her only too well.

"So, I'm still confused, Morrí." Using the familiar nickname, she said," I know you aren't a fan of the lockdown program. What's your objection? I can't come up with any other options, and I think this is the best way to save as many people as possible. But, you've fought me all the form on this. What's the reason, Morrí? More to the point, do you see any alternatives? I'm open to hearing what you might do in my place." She sat by the Bay-view wall, careful to look at Morrígan and not out the window. She put Morrígan on the spot. Morrígan had to answer either way.

Morrígan couldn't bring herself to look at her sister. She no longer saw Wallyce as family. Instead, she felt she was in the room with a dangerous lunatic bent on becoming the dictator over the country, if not the entire world. And, Morrígan thought, Wallyce is willing to allow millions of people to die in the process as long as she comes out on top.

But, Wallyce was waiting for an answer. Morrígan just didn't have one prepared for this encounter. She had to speak.

"Wallyce, I gave you my thoughts. I'm clear on that. You speak of locking down those willing to comply with your programs and holding those who refuse as enemies. You say you care deeply about your people, yet you seem perfectly willing to sacrifice any who go against you. Is that your program? What's your priority? Is it the people's obedience, or saving as many as possible while still giving them the freedoms they currently have?"

"Not sure I get that, Morrígan."

"Okay, then. Your plan offers only two options. People can swear allegiance to living and working inside your domain or earn the right to move into Barca City only after they isolate long enough to prove they won't infect anyone else. You haven't said what happens if they don't comply, but you've inferred they will die as a result–either from the plague or perhaps some other way. I'll fight you if you intend to be the one who orders their death."

"Why would I do such a thing? Morrígan, you've known me all your life. Am I someone you think would murder hundreds of thousands of people?

"I knew you. I'm not sure the Wallyce I grew up with and President Tilton are the same people. Do I think you're capable of such a heinous crime? No. But I also didn't expect you to seek counsel from your childhood imaginary friend. Truth is, Wallyce, you do so many things I would never expect–enough that I've stopped relying on my expectations. I'll give you this. You asked me what alternatives I can offer. I have none. I'm so glad it isn't me who has to solve this Armageddon puzzle. That said, I'd never give up looking for options. I'd keep trying to devise a plan up to the very end.

And I damn sure wouldn't surround myself with people like Brookfield and McCann. I'd bring in the best critical thinkers every day, all day, to help me see this from as many different perspectives as possible. Does that answer your questions?"

"That's fair." Wallyce had settled down a bit, somewhat calmed by Morrígan's honesty. It solved a problem for her. She no longer had any doubts about her sister's loyalty or lack of it. "Morrígan, I'm fine with our disagreement. I get it —you're not a supporter. However, I'm also clear that I can't tolerate any roadblocks. Take that for what it's worth. I love you, dear sister, but I will not allow anyone to get in the way of my plan to isolate and lockdown. Those who rebel will be considered enemy insurgents. I need to know what side you'll be on when it happens. We're about to enact martial law. Insurgents will be dealt with like enemy combatants. Will you be in that crowd, or will you take a back seat and sit there in silence as I do what we need to do?" She waited for Morrígan to absorb all that she had asked her.

Morrígan looked at her sister as if she'd never seen her. The sudden change in Wallyce's face frightened her. The eyes . . . that was it. She couldn't see Wallyce in these now darkened and fiery eyes. She could only see the woman about to make a decision that might doom most of the people alive today. She knew Wallyce believed she had to make a terrible choice—sacrifice many to save few. If Wallyce forced her to answer, she wouldn't know what to say. Morrígan knew it was time for rigorous honesty. Tell the truth and let it go where it goes. "Speaking to you as my sister, I'm just not sure. I always thought I'd follow you to the ends of the earth. But I never thought I'd really have to make this decision. Speaking to you as my President, I can't support your plan.

We'll have to wait and see if you come up with another plan."

Wallyce stood, turned, and left without a word.

* * *

"Aaron, I'm scared and don't think I have much time." Morrígan sat forward at the edge of the chair, her body shaking, almost vibrating. She forced her breathing to slow, allowing her to control her voice. It was all she could do to keep from crying into the comm.

"Honey, what's happening?"

Morrígan told him of her most recent encounter with Wallyce and the reality that the lockdown was imminent. She spoke so fast that Aaron had a tough time understanding everything.

"Wait. Slow down. Morrígan. Okay. Start over. What's going on?"

Morrígan forced herself to speak slower. "Aaron, Cyto-47 is on fire, growing so fast that there's no end. Wallyce has decided to impose a lockdown right away. Those who come to Barca City to sign on for long-term commitments will be placed in isolation for some weeks so they can be observed to make sure they don't have the plague. Pretty easy to tell, I hear. If infected, they'll be turned away, left on their own to die a horrible death. Those who aren't infected will be allowed in. There'll be a good number of people who will refuse the isolation order. They'll be traitors—insurgents. Wallyce says that if you are against the plan to lock down and isolate, you are the enemy and will be considered a traitor to the country."

"Are you sure? Is this what you heard her say?"

"There's more, Aaron. California has declared martial law, and the governor has turned control over to Wallyce. She doesn't know I'm aware of this. I suspect this was the easiest way for her to assume control over California. Looks like the entire country is next. She knows I'm opposed. Her plan sets up mass murder of any who oppose the lockdown."

"You need to get the hell out of there right now."

"Yeah. I know." Morrígan realized her knees were shaking. "Aaron, I think she wants to get rid of me. I don't mean she intends to make me leave. I mean, do away with me. You might want to be careful too. She knows where you are at all times."

"Do you have a way to get out?"

I think so. My lead agent, Corey Gaiters, is on my side. He's promised to help me escape when I give him the word. I think I can trust him."

Aaron was not ready to trust this person, Gaiters. "This guy is a career government cop. He's not likely to go against the President—not in a million years. Tell me why; make me believe I can trust him."

Morrígan gasped. "He made it sound simple. He pointed out he had sworn an oath to protect me, no matter what, even at the cost of his own life. He told me he'd die before he let anything happen to me."

"Yeah, maybe. But Gaiters has already lied. They don't take an oath to die for you. Their only oath is to discharge their duties faithfully and defend the Constitution. Sure, tradition and stories tell us they would take a bullet for you, but that's not what they swear to. No time to look it up. We don't have a real choice but to trust him, up to a point. Beyond that, we need to be ready. You need to be able to protect yourself until we're together. I'm heading south right now, and you need to head across the Bay to meet me where we agreed. Just get there any way you can. I'll get there as soon as I can. When do you think you can leave?"

"I'll leave soon. I just want to get some things."

"Forget the things, Morrígan. We can get what we need along the way. Just leave."

"I will. There's one thing I need to grab, then I can go."

Aaron seemed to get it. "Okay. Go ahead and get what you need, then have this Corey guy get you out of there.

* * *

Wallyce, still racing from the confrontation with Morrígan, went directly through her greeting room and continued across the penthouse to the observation deck overlooking the Bay Area. She sat on the lounge closest to the edge and looked over the water past Alcatraz Island and the hills above Berkeley. She needed a more peaceful mood, so she changed the experience levels. "View: the night sky, dense starscape, full moon. Audio: nature sounds, number 6." This soundscape removed all mechanical sounds, such as traffic and airplanes, and added in the sounds of waves lapping on the beach, seagulls crying in the distance, and the occasional splash of a whale as it broke the bay's surface. The change was effective. In a few minutes, she was beginning to feel less tense. She imagined she could smell the bay water softly splashing the tule reeds below her at the water's edge. Being so high above the water—more than 300 feet—allowed her imagination to create a new reality for life on the surface. She could only see things below on a macro level; the water, bridges, Alcatraz Island, and the sparkle of the lights in San Francisco. The rest was open to her imagination. When she was ready, she called for her adviser. "Goh, please connect to Dr. Sebastian in hologram."

"Yes, Madam." Though Goh was logically intelligent, he had no problem executing such a command. After all, the order didn't specify that Dr. Sebastian had to be authentic or alive. Wallyce had her technicians create a private channel just for such purposes. Once the media was ready, she could open this channel on the hologram platforms and comm-level face chats. The image of Sebastian, seated in an office chair next to a small drink table, came into view.

"Hello, Sebastian. I'm so glad you were available."

The Doctor gave a somewhat confused look, then gathered himself and replied. "I'm always available for you, Wallyce. What's up?"

"Armageddon is just around the corner, my friend. And it seems I'm the only person on earth who can stop it. Have you been keeping up with Cyto-47?"

"Yes, as much as I can. You likely have so much more information than I, so perhaps you won't mind giving me a closer look?"

Wallyce arranged herself in her chair. It was a habit she had when she was about to have a difficult conversation. "Dr. Sebastian, Cyto-47 has every indication it can be the Firestarter, the trigger for the end of days. Anyone who even comes close to it becomes infected. Those who are infected quickly die. There is no vaccine, no treatment, nothing to prevent the unimaginable mortality rate we are experiencing . . . probably 100 percent. I can bore you with details about how devastated our own government is and how much worse it is in the European Union, Asian Empire, and the rest of the world, but let's just say it's worse than here in America.

"Adding to the chaos, the usual gangs of conspiracy

theory crazies have fired up their protests, just as you might expect. Except, this time, it's worse than ever. I am pretty sure we are about as close to a revolution as we've ever been. The people have placed the blame for this pandemic on our shoulders. First, most think it's a fake story that we are reporting many millions of deaths to scare the population into compliance. On the other hand, those who believe it is a deadly threat also believe we haven't done enough. They feel we could easily find a cure or a vaccine, but we haven't done enough. And now, I've announced the start of isolation and lockdown. That seems to be the trigger for what will soon become a country-wide revolt. I have little choice but to isolate everyone until they are determined to be uninfected. When that happens, they need to quickly go into lockdown to prevent future infection. I've set up areas inside Barca City for isolation and long-term lockdown. I've also established isolation camps in every state, which will be controlled by the military. General McCann is in charge of isolation and has activated the National Guard in California to make it happen. My question to you is this; When the people refuse isolation, I declare them enemy combatants under the Insurrection Act. The full-scale revolt begins. How would you advise I move forward with isolation and lockdown?"

Sebastian was quiet for several minutes. Wallyce appreciated that he was deep in thought, so she waited for his plan to form. When he finally spoke, he was pointed and direct.

"Wallyce, you know damn well what to do. You just need me to tell you what you already know. Here it is. There's no way you can force people to comply. They'll just become a barricade that keeps you from saving those who will comply. In that case, we all lose. I agree with the need to isolate. The lockdown must be for the long term. The plague will still be there years from now, so you might consider that our entire human culture must change for a long time. Unless and until we have a vaccine, a cure, or both, people have to live in total lockdown, protected from the virus that will thrive outside the sealed environs you create. Those who comply with this will be protected. Those who refuse will sign permission for Cyto-47 to visit and kill them. This is sadly okay so far. It gets dicey with those who decide to tear control from the government and take over for themselves—in brief, a full-scale revolution. If they win, isolation and lockdown will never happen. Infections will never stop, and mankind will cease to exist. You can't let that happen. They must be stopped at all costs. Am I clear?"

"Yes, I believe you are. And I agree completely. Thank you, Sebastian. You've helped me clarify my plan. I wish you the best, and I'll see you in lockdown. Goh, close channel."

Dr. Sebastian's image faded, and the stars over the bay became slightly brighter. Wallyce had never felt more alone.

Chapter Twenty

Morrígan's knees shook, weakened by fear. She fought to keep from falling, replaying the sound of her sister's threats, lighting a fire of both anger and fear (aren't they the same thing?) in her gut. She hurried from the transport to her apartment, the anger/fear taking hold of her. Aware of the secret service cameras, she tried to mask her anxiety by smiling.

Once inside, she seemed to relax, knowing there were no cameras in her private chambers. It was time for action. She wore casual business clothes, trying to avoid looking like a politician. She packed a bag filled with sweats, comfortable shoes, and various layers of warm clothing. Knowing Aaron would be prepared with plenty of technology, she instantly charged her comm, grabbed the solar unit for additional power, and packed a small box of her favorite protein sticks and a few bags of water. Then, from whatever emotion drove her, she tacked the Vice-Presidential pin—the one she had worn every day since the inauguration—to the inside flap of her bag. She took the comm in hand. "Message to Corey

Gaiters. I have a meeting I need to attend in the morning, at 6:00 am. Please arrange transportation and security. Thank you, Agent Gaiters." As if he was waiting for this message, Gaiters replied.

"Message received and confirmed. CG"

Morrígan looked around the apartment. She knew this was likely her last time there. "Might as well make sure I don't leave anything important behind." But she knew she couldn't take anything with her, so she settled into a recliner near the viewing wall and took in the expansive San Francisco Bay. A glass of her favorite red from the wine cart nearby helped her stop chewing the inside of her cheeks. Then, with a soft soundscape playing throughout the residence, Morrígan soon drifted off to sleep.

The combination of the bay view and the music soon had her dreaming of better times—days when the Tilton family spent hours on the beach at Carmel. At the same time, the General and his political buddies played golf at Pebble Beach. In her dream, the girls waited for a call from the General to tell them how close to the beach his foursome was. Instead, they ran all the way down the coast, staying on the wet edge of the sand where they could run without their feet sinking into the soft sand, slowing them down. She felt excited, hoping to see their dad rolling down the fairway to the next tee box. As they came to the edge of the fairway, both nearly out of breath, Wallyce turned to face Morrígan. A grownup look fell over Wallyce's face.

"Morrí, you're a traitor. You can be executed for this crime," Wallyce accused her. Morrígan looked into her sister's face, trying to understand what she was saying. Finally, she screamed as Wallyce's face distorted, becoming a hideous devil-looking monster. "We'll find you." Jolted awake, Morrígan needed to gather her thoughts and understand where she was and what was happening to her. She shook out of control for some time.

No longer groggy, she jumped to her feet, looked round the apartment to ensure she was alone, then checked the clock: It was 4:30 am. There was a message on the comm. It was from Aaron.

"On my way. Can't believe the traffic on 101. Going to try another route. It's after midnight, and there are still protests everywhere. Thousands of people, body lights on. Looks like some kind of medieval lynch mob out to get the vampire. This is about to get deadlier. I can just feel it. So please, be super careful. Get to our place as soon as you can, no stopping. And I hope you have some way to protect yourself if needed. Love you. Aaron."

Maybe he meant to alarm her. It worked like a laser-guided missile. She walked to her office, reached her hand between the desk and the wall, and tapped the biometric lock. The wall right above the desktop opened to reveal a high-powered handgun—a relic handed down to her from the General. After checking the chamber for live rounds, she let the magazine slide out to be sure there was plenty of ammunition to fight off a single assassin. If there were more than one sent out to kill her, she knew she wouldn't be able to hold them off, so ammunition for a single assassin would be all she would take.

Satisfied, she took the holster and belt from her drawer, strapped on, put the gun in place, and covered it all with her sweater waistband. Her bag packed, protection in place, Morrígan sat in the armchair to wait.

"Goh, playback last night's Evening News from UPN." The screen came alive, and Ruger Fordyce was on the air.

"Welcome to UPN Evening News. I'm Ruger Fordyce. This is a special broadcast of the Evening News. Tonight's show will focus exclusively on the Cyto-47 pandemic and the horrific events it has spawned across the country and possibly worldwide."

Morrígan debated herself about turning it off. More bad news and anything that would add to the fear she was experiencing was too much, she thought. But she found it impossible to turn it off. So, she sat back while Fordyce continued.

"Debates in the Senate today introduced the country to the realities of martial law and how close we are to that happening in every state. In California, Governor Brookfield has declared a state of martial law. In doing so, he also turned all state control to President Wallyce Tilton. She, in turn, has announced mandatory isolation and lockdown. Isolation, to be clear, requires that anyone in the state must isolate, under government control, for several days until they are considered free from infection. Lockdown is, in effect, like wrapping California inside a fortress. All inside must lock down inside specified government facilities for an indeterminate timeframe. Food and supplies will be shipped in, courtesy of the federal government.

"Isolation will be under strict control. Anyone who isolates does so under the law; we expect most of these to pass through quickly as being free from infection. As we know, those already infected will typically pass away within a few days. Those who display signs of Cyto-47 will be further isolated, similar to solitary confinement.

"As we know, Americans are not the type of folks to stand for tyrannical mandates. The opposition has been swift and direct. Armed civilians have established reasonably organized militia groups with camps in rural and urban settings. In a speech this morning, Senator Bill Argen cast doubt over a militia's ability to overcome an opposing military such as the United States Combined Forces under the leadership of General McCann. As if to send Argen a direct response, the Northern Virginia arm of the Combined Forces was caught in an ambush as several hundred militia members hit them with automatic weapons, laser-guided grenades, and cluster bombs. Recent reports say there have been casualties from both sides in the hundreds.

"In a move that will turn into the next Civil War, President Tilton has asked the Congress to authorize special wartime powers enabling the administration to declare these insurrectionists as enemy insurgents. As such, any captured will be tried as war criminals and, if found guilty, will be punished accordingly, including possible executions.

"It's sad to say, this could be the shortest Civil War in the history of mankind. Army vs. militia will become a nonissue, as both have been violently attacked by the common enemy, Cyto. The apparent winner of this three-way war will certainly be the plague."

Ruger sets a darker tone by dropping his notepad and looking directly into the camera. "We have all heard the President's message; Stay the Hell Home. Unfortunately, it looks like we decided not to heed that message. The result will be that the government will force us to do just that. Lockdown and isolate. Now, let's look at our neighborhoods and cities."

The screen began to show scenes from various locations. Most locations were on the east coast, with many in large cities. Each scene was identified by a tag in the corner of the screen.

- CHICAGO – mass graves being filled by military dressed in full HazMat gear.
- WASH. D.C. – rebel unit firing laser cannons from within the WWII memorial, directly at the White House and Capitol Hill
- PHILADELPHIA – bodies are strewn in the streets, still smoldering from an explosion, and nobody is there to bag and haul the bodies off the streets
- NEW YORK- rebel camp in Central Park being destroyed by drone attacks. "And then there are the casualties of the Plague, our common enemy:"

Now the scenes were unnamed city fields, farms, and parks. Bodies piled high, waiting for identification and mass burial or cremation. Hospitals are protected by newly erected fences, and bodies are stacked on the sidewalks and parking lots. There is no hope they will be relocated or buried soon. There were no signs of refrigeration. The dead and dying were just left to rot out in the open. In some cases, rats had begun to take horrible advantage of the bodies, adding to the spread of the disease.

"It seems the common enemy is winning. We need to unite, folks, or we'll lose it all. Please, we must help the government do what it needs to save us."

Without warning, a shot rang out. The cameras kept rolling as Ruger Fordyce bled out on the studio floor. Finally, the screen went black as millions of viewers sat in stunned silence, wondering if what they saw was real and if Fordyce was dead. People struggled to understand why someone would kill an innocent reporter. One likely answer was in the belief by rebel forces that the government was lying to us, and these films were a part of the propaganda campaign they felt was being foisted on them.

Morrígan had a different reaction. For her, the murder answered her question: Is this the new norm? Answer: It is.

While she waited for agent Gaiters to arrive, Morrígan checked and rechecked that she had everything she needed to take with her. There wasn't much, just a couple changes of clothing and her comm. Instinct told her that taking much more would give people a reason to suspect she was going away, not just to an offsite meeting. She allowed one long last view of the bay area, wondering where this pandemic would take her.

"You have a visitor," came the announcement.

"Display." She saw it was Gaiters. "Allow entrance."

Chapter Twenty-One

Morrígan wasn't about to waste a second. Fear gripped her body and made it difficult to walk without tripping, speak without a stutter, and smile without breaking into uncontrollable sobs. Agent Cory Gaiter rushed to her side, scanning the area for unseen causes of her fear.

"What's up, Morrígan? Did something happen other than all Hell breaking loose?"

Morrígan understood his concern. "No, Cory. It's just all of this is happening so fast. I'm usually stronger than this, but none of us ever thought we might be facing the end of the world, at least for humans. The news last night, and the murder right on the screen of the news anchor . . . civil war has broken out back east. I'm scared, Cory."

"Morrígan, it's worse than that. I'm sorry to be the one to tell you, but the entire state of California is a war zone as of this morning. In the Bay Area, large groups of insurgents have started to appear, armed, loaded, and willing to kill anyone they think supports the President. The growing belief is that she has usurped complete power over the country, declaring Martial Law and forcing us all into isolation or imprisonment. The protest has morphed into rebellion. From what I've learned, we're in a civil war, and the battlegrounds cover the entire country."

Morrígan stopped breathing for a moment. Her entire focus was on the reality that the world had changed, a sudden and permanent change. Nothing would ever be the same for any of them. She thought about Wallyce and the horrifying monster her sister had become. Morrígan was even more frightened of what Wallyce's reliance on Sebastian meant. Had an imaginary childhood friend grown up to become an Imaginary Presidential adviser? Things had gone from bad to horrifying in a heartbeat. Had Wallyce gone insane? Morrígan needed to get out of Barca City as quickly as possible.

"So," she asked Cory. "What does this chaos in the streets mean to me? Can I get to where I need to be? Will we be attacked?"

"Yes. We will be attacked for certain if you're recognized. And, since the freeways are jammed with military vehicles and insurgent militias, we can't just hop in a car and drive there. I've anticipated this, and we have a new plan. I've arranged for a small Coast Guard craft to take us across the bay and into Sausalito. An old buddy of mine will take the helm, and since he's in uniform, we'll not have a problem with the military. Still, we have to worry about the insurgents who might have a mind to attack a small, defenseless military craft on the water. About that . . . I hope you can change into something less business-like."

"Morrígan headed toward her changing room. "No problem. I'll be right back." In a hurry to leave, Morrígan didn't waste any time. She returned wearing denim pants, a dark pullover shirt, rubber-soled shoes, and a brimmed cap. She carried a small tote in which she jammed a hooded sweatshirt and dark glasses in case the sun could burn through the morning fog. More cautious than before, she had tucked the handgun into a pocket holster, which she pressed down halfway into the waist of her pants. It had a full magazine, and one cartridge was loaded into the chamber. *Locked and loaded* was the old expression. "Okay, Cory. Let's go."

Cory led her to the launch area in the Seaport section of Barca City.

* * *

Wallyce Tilton had taken on a new role, that of Commander in Chief over the most powerful military force the world has ever seen, at the start of what might become the deadliest civil war in the history of mankind. The only thing that would keep the war casualties to a minimum would be that Cyto-47 would kill everyone first unless the government forces can act to stop the pandemic in the first place. She understood she was up against an inhuman deadly force. She was convinced she had no choice but to meet that challenge with an even more robust, brutal resistance. The United States Military wouldn't be enough. Wallyce had been developing a plan. In the Advance Robotics Design Lab, it was about to become real. She walked to the middle of the lab and surveyed the scene.

Even the sounds were inanimate; servo motors whirred as titanium feet clacked across the lab floor, a sign that robots were being tested for agility.

"Goh, what is the current status of the buildout?"

The environmental speakers came to life as much as AI can be called alive. "My reports indicate we are just a day away from your projected goal of 150,000 Warrior Intellibots, " Goh replied. "I am prepared to demonstrate the certified model if you wish."

Wallyce was excited, but she remained skeptical. This was, after all, the fastest project of its kind to make it from a design prototype to a certified working model. Finally, she tossed aside concerns that she was moving too fast. After all, Cyto-47 wasn't waiting for anything. "Proceed."

Goh assumed the demeanor of a military drill Sargent. "WarBot A 47. Front and center."

On command, the rear doors to the room flung open, and a robot the likes of which Wallyce had never seen ran at full speed into the room, directly toward her. She had no time to react, much less to get out of the way, so she braced for impact. At 10 feet away, the Intellibot stopped, crouched low, then performed a standing backflip in three seconds. It landed five feet from Wallyce, stuck the landing into full attention, and saluted its Commander in Chief. Wallyce gasped.

This wasn't what Wallyce had expected. There, feet away, was what most people would think was just another human, this one appearing male. He wore a black uniform, and his face showed little expression.

Goh snapped off a series of commands which the WarBot followed, ending with the order to *acquire and destroy target four*. It happened so fast, Wallyce almost felt she didn't see any movement. The WarBot located a wall target identified as number four, drew a laser gun, fired a perfect shot into the center of target four, and snapped to attention. The weapon returned to its holster.

Goh explained. "Madam, the Warbot has been programmed to seek, locate, and destroy enemy combatants on command. And it does so with great efficiency."

Wallyce struggled for the words to say. "This is a Bot? But I've never seen a functioning Bot appear so human-like."

The Bot faced President Tilton, Saluted, then spoke. "Madam President, I do hope that you approve. We have been designed to fit in any crowd for stealth purposes. Yet, we are superior to humans in strength and agility features. We can serve you well in cases of uprising and war."

Wallyce smiled. "Goh, you say we have 150,000 bots ready to go to war?"

"Yes, Madam President. As of tomorrow morning, they will be loaded into transport vehicles and ships, ready to go where you have ordered and standing by to perform at your command."

"Excellent, Goh," Wallyce was thrilled. "This will remain top secret, confidential. You will not discuss their existence except by my express authorization. Clear?"

"Yes, Madam. Clear."

"Now, what is my procedure for establishing command? How do I activate and command them?"

"Yes, Madam. First, I will outline the basic structure of your Intellibot Forces. They are logically assigned to ten different divisions, each assigned to a specific command under a Divisional Commander and a Warbot. These ten Divisional Commanders all report to one Warrior Commander, again another WarBot, programmed to superior intelligence. The Warrior Commander, called WarBot One, takes orders only from you or your assigned contact. Such is the programming of this Bot that you can give commands in your own words. The Commander will immediately interpret this into a specific list of orders to be given to the required Divisional Commanders. This list of commands will be given, often verbally, to you for final approval before being sent to the Divisions. Thus, you are ultimately in control."

"It's that simple?"

"Well, not quite, Madam President. That is an outline of the operational command chain. To relieve you of the massive tasks involved with daily activities, placements, maintenance, and espionage, we have programmed all command-level Bots with a general Performance Guide, which they will perform daily without human intervention. Any errors and mistakes will be noted, and repairs will be immediate. In short, this is a self-managed fighting force that acts on your orders. Even better, they are impervious to human diseases like Cyto-47."

"When do I meet my Warrior Commander, this WarBot One?

"Right now, Madam. I will now introduce WarBot One, Chief Warrior IntelliBot, whom you might address as Commander WarBot One, or simply WarBot One." The door opened wide. Wallyce anticipated a larger, frightening WarBot would stride directly through, slam to attention when it reached her, and salute smartly. But instead, she was surprised when a small, thin, and unimpressive older gentleman entered, stopped beside her, blinked red lights twice, and nodded.

"As you were, WarBot One," the Goh ordered. WarBot One quickly complied.

"Goh. Is this my Warrior Commander?" Wallyce was beginning to think this was a robotic joke.

"Yes, Madam. This is Commander WarBot One at your command."

"But, I expected something far more impressive."

WarBot One intervened. "Madam President," it said in a rather pleasant deep male human voice. "I understand your surprise. Based on human terms, size and strength are indicators of power. In the Bot realm, intelligence ranks much higher than brawn. Size and strength can be compensated by intelligent weaponry. But war demands intelligence to effectively use the size, strength, and weapons to our advantage. I hope this gives you some comfort. In addition, my job does not often put me in harm's way. I operate from a command center. Brains over brawn every day in command."

Wallyce was starting to feel good about this little roll-bot.

"Well, then, Commander WarBot. Assume, for example, we have declared a total lockdown over the City of San Francisco. Under the order, anyone found outside Barca City other than our troops, certain other specific personnel, and your Bots are to be considered enemy combatants. What would your orders be if I commanded you to secure the city of San Francisco?"

"A question. Is there a standing order to take enemy combatants into custody?"

Wallyce liked this question. "No, there is no order to take prisoners."

"Then, Madam President, my order, which I would put to you for agreement, would be to send in a Division to seek and destroy the enemy."

"Perfect, Commander. You passed the test. Please have your Division Commanders ready to meet me in this room, for introduction, at 0600 tomorrow. Understood?"

"Yes, Madam. Understood."

"Thank you, and Goh, well done." Wallyce turned and left the room.

Chapter Twenty-Two

Intense fear nearly paralyzed Morrígan. The bay crossing was scary yet uneventful. Given the heavy traffic on the bay, it was clear many people learned of the massive traffic jams on the surface roads and chose to take to the water in a desperate bid to escape the Bay Area before the lockdown took effect. Morrígan's fear nearly consumed her. If Cyto-47 didn't get her, maybe her sister would. Her life hung by a thread, depending on many things over the next few hours. Will Aaron break through the traffic? Will she be recognized, and will someone try to assassinate her? And if they do, where will it come from? From the anti-government or from the government? Fear after fear.

"C'mon, girl. Get it together. She told herself. You won't make it out of here alive unless you do. Control the situation." It's what General Tilton would have told her to do. "What the hell does it matter where the assassin comes from. An assassin is an assassin, no matter who they work for. The result's the same. Worrying about bullshit details only wastes time and energy. Focus on situational awareness. Everyone is a potential assassin. Look around. Notice anything out of place? What are your escape routes in the event someone does come for you? Is your gun accessible?

"Morrígan. Morrígan?" Corey's hand shook her shoulder. She looked up, forcing her mind to focus.

"Corey, what is it?"

"Are you okay, Morrígan? I spoke to you several times, but you seemed to be off in a dream somewhere."

"Oh, no. I'm fine. Just keep reviewing everything in my mind, hoping I haven't missed anything."

"Yeah. We're all on edge. It's a scary time. Hap here tells me there are too many boats in Sausalito for us to head right in. Probably best that we swing around behind the public docks and try to tie up with the fishing fleet. It's only for the few minutes it'll take to unload you and for you to head to your meeting place, wherever that is."

Okay, Corey. You know best." She looked down at her comm, trying to find the best route for walking from the fishing docks to the headlands above the City. "This is actually closer to my destination anyway."

Hap, the ex-Coast Guard Corey said to trust, was dressed in a tropical shirt with swim shorts, somewhat unusual for someone at the helm of a small Coast Guard lifeboat, but what did she know? Her background was all Army. Corey claims to have known Hap since childhood, and she should feel confident that he'll get them where they need to go. But she wasn't sure.

"Hap, how long have you been in the Coast Guard?" she asked.

"Me? Oh, I'm not in the Guard. I retired five years ago. So why do you ask? Am I driving this rig poorly?" He let out a gruff laugh that sounded to Morrígan to be forced, maybe fake.

She gave a light chuckle, equally false. "So that explains the uniform you selected for today?"

"Well, Corey here told me to dress down. Anything that'll keep you from standing out, he said."

Morrígan gave him a once-over. "Well, I'm pretty sure you'll keep me from standing out, and that's what I care about most." She felt she was sinking into a dark hole, surrounded by doubt and fear. Hap just didn't seem right to her. She knew something was out of place with him. She didn't know what it was, making her anxiety level race and her hands tremble. Just then, the bow of the boat bumped hard against the dock.

Hap jumped up, grabbed the mooring lines, leaned over the bow, and tied off to the cleat in record time. Then, with more agility than his oversized belly would indicate, he stepped aft, grabbed the other line, and tied the boat to that cleat. "Okay, now. He said. "Let's take care of business."

Morrígan assumed he was asking to be paid for his service. She turned to look at Corey just as the first of three bullets from Hap's handgun exploded the agent's head. Morrígan didn't stop to understand what had happened. Too many years of training by the greatest General the Army has ever seen sprang into action. Instinct took over, and before Hap had turned fully to bring the gun barrel to her face, Morrígan had drawn her own weapon and placed a single shot into the man's heart. He was dead before he slipped into the water.

Stifling the scream that nearly exploded from her, Morrígan looked around, trying to understand the danger that might still exist. She saw nothing. No one seemed to be in the area. She realized Hap selected this location as a place that would be private this time of day. This worked in her favor. Again, she wanted to scream when she turned to see Corey dead on the boat's deck—his face ripped apart by the impact of three high-caliber shots. She forced herself to remain in control of her emotions. A sudden burst of panic raced through her, shaking her to the core and filling her mind with rapid-fire questions. What just happened? Who was Hap, and how did he get his hands on a Coast Guard lifeboat? Was Corey the bad guy, and Hap tried to protect me? No, no. He was starting to aim at me. Assassin. But whose hired- killer was he? Probably Wallyce's, but how can I . . . is it possible? She's my sister. She now knew the basis for the panic. This could have been anyone. For the first time, she couldn't trust anyone. Maybe not even Aaron. She fought hard against that thought. Finally, she decided she had to trust someone or be alone. She had to trust Aaron.

More than anything else right now, she had to get moving. She grabbed her tote and jammed the gun into it. Quick thinking told her to grab both Cory's and the killer's guns. She might have to protect herself often on her way to the rendezvous place. She tapped the screen on the comm and selected the GPS, where the address of the place she was headed had been stored. In her mind, she thanked Aaron for suggesting she use his private satellite communications, knowing it couldn't easily be hacked by Wallyce's spies.

The walking directions were on the screen right away. Morrígan pulled the cap down over her eyes, hoping to look like any other person trying to hike up the hill to the place above the City, overlooking the Golden Gate Bridge and San

Francisco—two places she was in a hurry to get as far from as possible.

* * *

The alarm of the Bay Area Emergency Broadcast System screamed into life all over Northern California. "Reminder to all Bay Area inhabitants. The Executive Order for Isolation is now in full effect. You are ordered to report to the nearest Intake Center for immediate processing." The message was repeated throughout the San Francisco Bay Area. Freeway electronic signs, and video screens in all mass transit vehicles, including NorCal Maglev Transit, repeated the message in text, video, and voice announcements. Wallyce was clear in her order: Every citizen of Northern California will be aware of the order and what they must do within the requirements if they wish to stay alive to see the sunrise. The message was direct: "Lockdown is imminent. The consequence of disobedience is unequivocal. You will be left out where you can expect to die from Cyto-47. Those who disobey and then make any move toward rebellion will be dealt with accordingly. Execution will be swift. There will be no opportunity to plead for mercy, as there will be none" This was the final message for all to see and obey.

President Wallyce Tilton stood at the head of the war room conference table. She had called a final pre-lockdown meeting of her task force. The group was considerably smaller than the previous ones, as Wallyce would not tolerate discussions. Now was the time for decision and action. She selected Governor Jake Brookfield, General Peter McCann, Goh, and the leader of Barcan WarBot Forces, Commander WarBot One.

"The time has come," Wallyce said. "Cyto-47 has broken through our defenses which we hoped would buy us enough time to develop a vaccine, cure, or both. We have neither.

* * *

The sun forced Aaron's eyes to slam shut, which could be a real problem driving through the access tunnel to the Bridgeway. He hoped to make good time across the Golden Gate Bridge. Aaron reached over and mashed the windshield sunscreen button on the dash. In a flash, he could see the road ahead, just in time to stand on the brakes to avoid slamming into the miles-long line of cars that were backed up the entire length of the Golden Gate.

He figured things out in a heartbeat. "We aren't moving, and it had to take a long time for so many cars to get stuck in this mess. Damn, we're going to sit here for a long time." Panic wanted to settle in when he thought of Morrígan and how alone she must feel. He clicked off the e-drive and opened the door, stepping out to check with the other unfortunate bridge squatters. "Maybe they can shed some light on this mess," he thought.

The first group he saw was just a few cars ahead of his. He looked them over and decided to approach the closest person. The man turned toward him as he approached. He could see the man was in a panic.

"Hey. Some jam-up, huh?" Aaron asked.

"Yeah. Didn't expect any less. Did you?"

He looked at the stranger, trying to see anything in his expression that might hint at what he had just said. "My name's Aaron. I'm sorry, friend. I'm not sure I get what you're saying. Expect? Should I have expected something?"

"I'm Scott. You been sleeping for the last week?"

"Well, yeah, in a way. I've been on a hunting/camping trip. Do it every year. Just coming back from living off the land up in the Redwoods up north. Guess I missed something?" Now he was concerned. The man pulled a device from his pocket and shook his head slowly. He was measurably frightened.

The man didn't say another word; he just handed Aaron the device he held, pointing to the red button on the top corner. Aaron hesitated, wondering if this was some kind of setup. Then, looking at the massive traffic jam, he realized it was probably real and turned the device on. It was a hologram. As he held it, Aaron was fascinated by the technology and frightened by the message. A hologram of a Barcan Police Captain seemed to climb out of the center of the projector. Red lights flashed, and a deep alarm sounded.

"People of Northern California, we of Barca Corporation welcome you. We look forward to you joining us in Barca City. President Tilton has decreed that you must be present in Barca City on or before Monday, the first of the month, not later than 1600 hours. You will bring only the clothes you wear, your identification, and nothing more. Any who attempt to carry any weapon into the City will be dealt with severely. Any who decide they will not comply with this directive will be forewarned. You will be destroyed before the end of that day."

"Tons of these were dropped by drones all over the Bay Area," Scott added. "I'm not one to take these things lightly. Looks like I'm not the only one judging by the traffic. But the big problem is that we have less than a half hour to get there and are stuck on this bridge."

"Well, Scott, you're stuck, but I'm heading home. I live

not far from the bridge's other end in the old Presidio base. So I'll leave the car here and pay the towing fees later. Maybe I'll see you after this hoax is over."

Aaron returned to the car to retrieve his rifles and a bottle of water from the trunk. As he reached up to pull the trunk lid back down, he heard a strange whistling noise erupt from where he had just left Scott and his group. Then, over his shoulder, he spotted many of the small hologram devices hovering like tiny flying saucers, a fine spray pouring out from them, spreading over the crowds.

Many began to grab at their throats, some vomiting, others gurgling and grabbing at each other until most of them fell in a heap to the roadway. Some stopped moving. The same scene repeated as far as Aaron could see toward the San Francisco end of the bridge. Straining to look toward home, he was dazed to see what could only be fighter jets in formation, heading toward downtown San Francisco, where they unleashed a horrendous attack from the sky into the towering buildings with such power it was unlikely anyone would have survived. He grabbed his gas mask, which he had kept in the car since the terrorist attacks a few years before, and pulled it on as he ran away from the city back toward Marin.

Sensing he had no time, Aaron took a huge gamble. He jumped over the side of the bridge, diving almost directly across from the parking lot for the overlook. He got lucky. No longer over the bay waters, Aaron landed in a thick patch of bushes. Scraped and bruised, he froze in place—no noise or movement that might give him away.

Aaron imagined the Barcans wouldn't rely on the gas bombs to kill everyone on the Bridge. He was right. His spirit was rocked by the dead silence that followed the attack, a silence he had never heard on this bridge. All he could hear was the waves crashing against the headlands to the northwest. This did little to convince him the worst was over, so he waited motionless for an hour.

Slowly at first, then with ferocious violence, the sound became deafening. Aaron heard the terrifying noise that Hell must make as the gates opened to suck you in. For another hour, he listened and peeked out in heartbreak and disgust as soldiers, the likes of which he had never seen, inhuman, moved across the bridge. They were precise in their movement, so mechanical in their form, making their way the length of the bridge, firing directly into every human body in sight as if to make sure they were really dead. These Inhumans never looked over the railing to where he hung motionless. Aaron knew for sure; breathe too loud, you're finished.

As the night wrapped the now-dark Golden Gate Bridge, his mind spun in circles, hoping to figure out how he could ever get to Morrígan. He somehow drifted to sleep into a marathon of sickeningly frightening dreams he couldn't escape. His last conscious thought was to wonder what kind of world he would awaken to if he even opened his eyes again.

* * *

Morrígan forced herself to move; her baby steps grew into purposeful strides. She followed the GPS instructions with a careful eye ahead, needing to be sure there weren't any military or other government forces waiting to question her. She guessed she'd be spotted for who she was, triggering an interrogation in which Wallyce would learn her whereabouts.

She'd be grabbed and brought back to Barca to pay the price for disloyalty. She couldn't guess the reality would be much worse—she'd likely be murdered on the spot if any of the Inhumans spotted her. She didn't even know they existed. Even the thought of those seeming to be civilians threatened her. She couldn't get the images of Corey and Hap from her mind. "Trust no one," she said out loud.

She reached downtown Sausalito and stopped to get her bearings. Stepping inside a small coffee shop, she hoped to find someone who might tell her the best way to get up into the highlands, where the meeting place was.

As naïve humans, we're often caught off-guard when our expectations are met with a reality far beyond what would usually greet us when we enter an open door. In this case, Morrígan's spirit was so jarred she screamed before she even understood what she was looking at.

She realized she had tripped over a dead body, and the person had clearly suffered a recent and violent death. She scanned the small shop, trying to understand. Only some extreme violence could have caused this kind of devastation. Everything that could be destroyed was. She tried to imagine what could have caused this. But, all she could conjure up was a military attack on the town of Sausalito, changing this peaceful, oddly antique suburb into a war zone. Then, she saw them. She spotted three more bodies under the pile of rubble that must have once been the store's counter. She couldn't force herself to look closer. She could no longer deny that Wallyce, the President of the United States, had declared war on the country's citizens. Morrígan knew this might happen, though she tried to deny it. She just didn't know when or to what limit Wallyce would go to implement her plan. Seeing these people, the destruction that caused their deaths was only too apparent. There was no limit. Wallyce had declared Martial Law and was ready to launch a purge of anyone who thought they could ignore her commands. Lockdown and isolate . . . or be destroyed. "All this happened when I was out on the bay," she thought. She knew this was only the beginning.

Now the urgency was set. Morrígan must get out of sight and up to the Riding Club, where Aaron would meet her. She also had no idea how she would hike nearly 4 miles uphill without being spotted. She imagined herself rotting under some coffee shop counter. "There's no way I'm ready to let her win," she thought.

Just outside the war-zone-that-was-once-a-coffee-shop, Morrígan looked around for anything that might get her into the Marin Headlands. From the moment she entered the little shop to when she escaped the frightening scene, her denial system shut down, forcing her to see things as they were. Every vehicle was blasted full of holes, its occupants dead in their seats; some still gripping the wheel, others just a mass of destroyed humanity. Wallyce's trademark was emblazoned on several small drone-like devices that appeared to have sprayed something everywhere. Morrígan knew right away it was part of a chemical murder. She covered her face in case some slow-acting residue was still in the air.

Morrigan nearly tripped over a stack of electric bikes, usually rented to tourists who would use them for sightseeing. Looking at the nearby storefronts, she located the one with a sign that read; See the Bridge from the top of the headlands, a few minutes away on our rental cycles. "Okay, she thought. Let's find some keys." She was relieved there were no bodies in the store unless you count the woman on the sidewalk near the door. The color of the woman's skin and the foam still dripping from her mouth were signs she was a victim of the gas. Morrígan stepped over the woman to get into the store. Seeing the store untouched, compared to the coffee shop, gave her the chills. "Two murder scenes, so very different, but murder nonetheless," she thought. "Wallyce is committed to leaving no stone unturned, no human alive unless they follow her program." It was the first time Morrígan was convinced her sister must be stopped, and the only sure way to prevent such a tyrant was to assassinate her.

She filed that in the back of her mind. The immediate problem was finding keys to a bike. Morrígan finally found the metal box marked "Rental Bikes" in the back room, but it was locked. Morrígan had run out of patience by this time, and control had slipped away. Reaching under her shirt, she grabbed her gun, pulled it out, and fired once into the lock intended to keep the bike keys safe. The lid flew open, the box flew away, and slammed against the wall, spewing keys along the way. She grabbed a handful and ran outside to find a bike with the same number as a key tag. She made a match, started the cycle, saw it was fully charged, mounted it, and headed up the hill toward the Headlands and the Presidio Riding Club, where Aaron promised to meet her.

She was familiar with this place, having spent several summer camps learning to ride at this club as a child. At first, when Aaron suggested it, she wondered why he had selected this location to meet. In light of the murderous rampage, her instinct told her that the best way to travel now would be silent. Horses will be the best method. With government assassins hunting for what Wallyce called insurrectionists and enemy combatants, getting caught might mean immediate execution, even if you're the ex-Vice President. So back to the silent travel method. As if she suddenly awoke from a deep dream, Morrígan became aware of the near silence of the electric bike she was riding. She pressed the throttle forward to gain the most speed as she turned into the Bunker Road Tube, a single-lane tunnel. She slammed on her brake as soon as she entered the tube. The road was dotted with still-smoking cars, most with the bodies of their former inhabitants still in place. To call them dead was an understatement. These were demolished humans. She saw ahead that the bicycle lane was clear to the end, giving her a path out of this nightmare. She pressed the throttle forward again, riding as fast as possible through half-closed eyes. If she could have closed them all the way, she would have. Finally, she burst into the sunlight again.

Fear hit her hard, and she began to move her head like a swivel, trying to see in all directions. She knew there might be government killers everywhere, and only a portion of her ride would be hidden from view, especially from drones in the air. "No choice," she thought. "I hope to get close enough to ditch this bike and walk through the wooded areas." Farther uphill from Sausalito, she soon realized there were no more wooded areas, one of the results of drought-fueled wildfires that have scorched the state for decades. She headed up Bunker Rd., taking an occasional glance down toward the bridge, thankful she couldn't see it through the vegetation that had overgrown this time of year. She imagined the worst and couldn't bear to see it up close.

Chapter Twenty-Three

Unlike the Golden Gate/San Francisco purge, the rest of the Bay Area was under different instructions. Busses and trains were jammed with frightened, confused, and angry Americans, ordered to leave their homes and lives behind to be carted off to an isolation camp. The processing of citizens at one such station, Fremont Main Loading Zone, formerly Central Park, started out well-ordered. Families were asked to stay together as much as possible, a consideration designed to keep the fear from turning into rage. Unfortunately, too many similar situations ended badly, partly due to separating families during such great anxiety.

Soba Parkasian, the recent Daylight Project's annual award winner, stood alone. Panic gripped her soul. Just the day before, she was overjoyed to stand here and reconnect with her family. But, now, there was no place to hide, no path leading her from the nightmare of mass murder down to Fremont, where her parents had settled a year earlier. Her emotions, overloaded as they were, forced her to revisit the horror of yesterday, the worst day of her life.

It started as a blessed event. “Mom. Dad, over here.” Soba wept silently from the joy she felt, knowing they were there, safe and sound. Her mother turned abruptly toward Soba. Soba could see the fear on her mother’s face and read the words she mouthed soundlessly. Soba realized she was saying, “Run, Soba.” Her Dad pushed himself between his wife and a pair of heavily armed Bots, shouting at them as if he knew what was coming.

Instantly, he made his move, and the Bots opened fire. Her parents were dead before their bloody bodies slammed to the ground. Soba, too, crashed to the ground, unable to move. The bots must have seen her as dead, and they passed right by her to continue the slaughter.

She had no idea how long she lay there, unable to run when her fear returned, causing her to scream. No one noticed, as there was no one still alive. She leaped to her feet and ran—not toward anything, but away from the horror. When she stopped running, she crouched behind a large tree. She needed time to understand and maybe to think more clearly. She must have passed out from fright. She slept for a very long time.

When she awoke again, Soba knew she was changed forever, for the worse. She also knew she’d have to find a way to live alone and in fear. This morning was her first test. She began the day looking for a way to help others get through the hell the government had created. Soba knew from experience that helping others was the best way to help yourself. She found she was still at the Fremont Main Loading Zone. When her senses returned, she took a moment to get her bearings, try to understand how the system worked, and what she might do to help the people who were about to become prisoners for life or, worse than that, dead victims of Cyto-47, or even murder victims if the Bots returned.

Her instinct in such situations was to roll up her sleeves and act. Looking around, she noticed not far from where she stood was a small girl looking very scared and crying out for her momma. Scanning the area, Soba couldn't find anyone who might be the girl's mom. She didn't hesitate. She moved to the girl, dropped to her knees, and whispered comfort. "Hi, honey. I'll help you find your momma." The girl kept crying and calling out. Unaware the Bots had returned, Soba didn't listen to the announcements that went out over the speaker system.

"All citizens are to stay with their family groups. You must only be with those whose identification tag matches your own. This is not negotiable. Anyone breaking the rules may be subject to punishment, including arrest or termination."

Soba kept her focus on the girl. "What's your name, sweetie? What's your momma's name. Maybe the soldiers here can help us." She turned to a Bot Sergeant standing nearby, scanning the crowd, his eyes in constant motion, his hands rigid on the weapon he held across his midsection. "Sir, she called. "Sir, this girl lost her family. Where can I take her to get some help?"

The soldier, far enough away that he couldn't hear a word she said, glanced at the identification tags they wore. It was pretty straightforward. Soba had no tag. The little girl's tag was blue and identified her as a member of a family. His automatic reaction was swift. He raised the gun in case Soba was trying to grab the girl to masquerade as a family member to get preferential treatment. Singles were herded together into open cattle transports and then dumped into the empty warehouse buildings at the southwest corner of Fremont, a former toxic trash dump for manufacturing sludge. Families were taken to test sites. If they were found to be virus-free, they went on to the quarantine camps, where they still had a chance to earn isolation in Barca City. Instead, singles were treated like they had the Plague or soon would.

Soba reacted without thinking. She jumped and screamed at the soldier, thinking he might shoot her or the girl. "Shouting, "Noooo," she ran to press herself between the man and the girl. He fired without hesitation. Soba's face, the face of the Daylight Project's Annual Award winner, was gone in a second. Her forward motion caused her faceless body to slam into the soldier, knocking him to the ground.

Chapter Twenty-Four

When rights are taken away from free people, nothing else matters more than the return of those rights. Nothing. Not even life itself.

As ordered, Goh set the American Village Conference Center at Barca City for a moderate-to-large meeting. Wallyce arranged the attendance list to include all Senators, Representatives, Joint Chiefs of Staff, Cabinet Members, and the governors of every state who were not currently infected by the plague. The last group turned out to be a small list. She had initially expected several hundred participants, but the speed and voracious appetite of Cyto-47 had dramatically reduced the number of active participants. In addition, more than half of both houses of Congress were infected or had died from the plague. Most governors could not attend—either infected or in a desperate, violent struggle to contain massive protests that had turned violent.

The meeting was to be primarily remote, with no travel

to Barca City allowed. President Tilton would not tolerate any potential invasion of her sterile world by those still out and possibly infected. All guests were given an agenda that left no doubt they were only there to listen. This was not an open discussion. Wallyce would not only run the show, but she would also be the show.

The stage was set, the holograms were ready, and Wallyce Tilton, President of the United States of America, was about to usurp the country, restructure the government, and nullify most of the Bill of Rights in a sincere effort to save as many lives as would be saved. She had no misgivings. The plan was radical but necessary. It was win or lose humanity. She would never surrender.

The house lights all over the American Village dimmed slowly as Wallyce rose above the floor. Her projection dome glowed to focus all eyes on her. Wallyce appeared to be with the participants in whatever hologram room they were situated in. Of course, her image was somewhat larger than life, a tactic designed to intimidate. Without waiting for things to settle, she drove her message home.

"My fellow Americans, as you know, our country and the rest of the world have been attacked by the deadliest force we have ever come up against, Cyto 47 pandemic. To detail our defense plan, I will introduce some Anti-Cyto Task Force members who will brief you on situations they are dealing with. When they are finished, assuming they have done a good job of painting reality for you, I will outline my program to help us defeat this evil plague and possibly save humanity. You heard me right. If we cannot defeat this enemy, the future of humanity is in grave danger. First, I'll introduce our Congressional Representative, The Leader of the Senate, Senator Bill Argen."

Argen's hologram appeared next to Wallyce's. He acknowledged her as she faded into the background. He took a moment to express a somber mood, then he spoke. "Fellow Americans, I am tasked with updating you on the Washington government's status. In a word, things are dismal. We had strong hope that President Tilton's plan for securing the government centers, White House, Capitol Building, and Supreme Court by encasing them in bio-protective structures would buy us enough time to gain ground on the plague. The installation was completed in record time, thanks to the Barca engineers' and robotic fabricators' design and manufacturing prowess. But, sadly, record time is too slow for Cyto-47. We learned, too late, that during the construction, before any of the lawmakers and their staff were allowed back in, pockets of infection, possibly carried by the rodent population, took hold. As soon as we repopulated the Capitol, the plague spread like fire.

"Today, just a few days after repopulation, we've lost most of both houses of Congress to the plague. To be specific, we can no longer meet the requirements of a quorum for voting purposes. There are various processes to name replacements by the governors of the affected states. However, as you will hear, many governors fight their battles at home. The citizens have launched attacks against the governments of their states. Therefore, we can hardly count on these governors to quickly replace the dead lawmakers. In short, we have lost the ability, as a Congress, to fulfill our constitutional duties. Madam President, I am open to questions."

"Thank you, Leader Argen. Now, we will hear from General McCann."

"Thank you, Commander in Chief Tilton." The reference was intentional. "As you know, the Pentagon is secure. We've been bio-secure for several years. We went under lockdown a week ago, and I can safely say we can operate as usual without hesitation. I will also state that the United States Armed Forces, Army, Navy, Air Force, Space Command, Marines, and the newly installed WarBot Force have coalesced as a single command under my direct control."

At the mention of WarBot Force, a general grumbling sound rose from all participant sectors. Several signaled that they had questions, but General McCann brushed them aside. Now he spoke directly to the President.

"Since you, Madam, are the Commander in Chief, we are all under your direct command. We've repositioned all our human forces worldwide; however, most have been redeployed here at home. They are deployed as control agencies to ensure a smooth nationwide transition into a secure lockdown. Additionally, we've identified certain locations in every state to function as quarantine/testing sites and lockdown camps. Those who survive quarantine will be transitioned to long-term lockdown to ensure they can no longer become infected or contagious. Now, you might wonder who will fulfill the normal functions of the military. Please hold questions, and President Tilton will address those later. Thank you, Commander in Chief."

"Thank you, General," Wallyce said. Next, she introduced Dr. Emmanuel Walters for his frightening update on the plague. As expected, Walters painted a very dark, terrifying image of a world racing toward Armageddon—and there was no hope in sight.

Finally, Wallyce introduced Governor Brookfield for the

status of Martial Law in California and allowed for a few questions.

The first question was the one she hoped would never come. It was from Dr. Walters himself. "Madam President, if I might be so bold. We haven't seen the Vice President in any updates today. Is she safe and healthy?"

Without hesitation, Wallyce responded. "Thanks for asking, Doctor. The fact is, we have no idea where she is. All we know for sure is that she left early yesterday morning. Although I begged her to remain safe inside Barca City, she insisted that she would return only after she found her boyfriend, Aaron Rollins. He was out of touch on an annual camping trip and probably didn't hear any news about Cyto-47. She was afraid he wouldn't be prepared to protect himself. We've learned she took a small boat across the bay, but there is no evidence she landed where she was headed, Sausalito. This was around the same time that the insurgents attacked the City of San Francisco, forcing us to put down their minor revolt. I pray she wasn't caught up in the Golden Gate Bridge mess. My heart is broken. I have sent out Secret Service to find her. I'm sure they will.

"I know you've heard of the uprising on the Golden Gate Bridge. Here are the details. I alerted the population of the Bay Area that they would be welcome to come here, to Barca, to be tested for Plague, and to be relocated here as citizens of Barca City. I made it clear that this was a one-time offer. As you might imagine, thousands of cars flooded the freeways in hours, so many in fact that the Golden Gate Bridge was impassable. As the hour for entry to Barca drew close, panic set in, and infighting broke out on the bridge. We sent troops to prevent the bloodshed, but we were too late. When our troops arrived mid-span, many insurgents died in the fighting. Those who survived attacked our troops. As their orders instruct, they fired back. You will understand that there were no civilian survivors."

"But, Madam, we've heard of similar tragedies in Marin County and the entire Bay Area," Dr. Walters asked."

"Yes, Doctor. It's true. We have a full-scale uprising on our hands. Understand we can't send our human troops to every battle. They'd quickly succumb to the plague. So, now I'll tell you what we've done to protect all Americans. Goh, please send the Battle Bot here." In a flash, a large bot bounded into view, performing several human-like movements and some inhuman ones, such as running twenty feet straight up a steel girder, a trick afforded by magnetics in its foot pods. As the Bot returned to face Wallyce, it snapped to attention and saluted her. This robot was designed to look somewhat similar to a human in body, movement, and mannerisms. Its face couldn't be seen, as it wore a close, shiny black face covering. This robot was larger than the average human male and made quite an impression.

"Thank you, Bot 43. You may return to your station." As the Bot marched off, Wallyce gauged the shock level of her guests. She waited a moment for them to understand what they just saw. "Ladies and Gentlemen, you have been introduced to the Barcan Battle Bot Force. We deployed 150 thousand of them this morning. They'll be able to perform what our human forces can, with the added benefit of being immune to any virus or bacteria, and they offer the added advantage of superior thinking thanks to highly evolved Artificial Intelligence. In a world where the deadliest thing is the Plague, what better-armed force than one made up of these Bots?

"Now, I'll tell you how we'll use this technology to save

humanity. I am immediately placing the United States of America under Martial Law. The Armed Forces, under General McCann, and the Barcan Battle Bot Force reporting to me, will enforce total quarantine and lockdown across the country. All citizens who wish to be safe will report to the United States Quarantine and Lockdown Camps for processing. The military command will be stationed locally and guide citizens to the nearest Repurpose Centers, where our people will be placed under our care. Any who refuse will be left out in the unprotected atmosphere, eventually infected and dying. They will have one opportunity to submit. There will be no changing of the mind.

Further, any who interfere with our ability to protect our citizens will be enemy combatants and will be terminated on the spot. Interference includes actions so minor as launching a protest against the forces or attempting to prevent Quarantine/Isolation. We will not tolerate any attempt to subvert what we are doing to save lives. The troops will arbitrate what constitutes sedition, and there will be no trial. We can't afford the lost time." Wallyce turned to face the main camera and spoke directly to the citizens. "Attention all citizens—follow all instructions, or your future may be brief. Be advised this Martial Law is now in place and takes effect immediately. Each of you will report to your bases and begin the process of quarantine when this meeting closes. You will have this one day to gather your families and take them to the nearest camp. After that, you are on your own. That is all. There will be no questions." A nod to Goh and the system was disconnected.

"Goh, broadcast this entire meeting to every media access; video, online, building fronts that have broadcast screens established. Commander WarBot," she turned to the relatively small robot. "Command all sections across the country to set up projection vehicles in all rural sectors and anywhere else the citizens might miss the show. Then have them also broadcast this meeting to all. I need it done within the next half hour." The Bot flashed a salute, wheeled around, and left the area. No other response was needed.

This was the beginning of the end of Democracy in America.

Chapter Twenty-Five

Morrígan fought to remain focused as she rounded the final turn, where the Riding Club filled the view. She thought if the focus was all she needed, her heart wouldn't be pounding in her chest loud enough for any Barcan Troops in the area to hear. She pressed on. The nearer she came to the Club, the more she recalled her childhood summers and how she loved her horse, Major. That was his name, Major. She wanted a name that would honor her father, the General, yet wouldn't be thought of as being as vital to her as her dad. It was an almost military tradition. Treat everyone with respect, but how much is determined by the person's rank. So Major was a horse to be respected, but General Tilton was worthy of the highest esteem.

Her heart slowed to a reasonable speed, then skipped a beat when she was close enough to the stalls to see some of the horses. "Major? It can't be you," her thoughts erupted. Still closer, her hopes were dashed as she saw the horse, so like Major, it couldn't be him. This horse was a mare. But the resemblance was stunning. Same coloring, the same blaze, and the very same stance Major always took when he saw her come into view. This wasn't Major, but she was in love when she saw this beautiful girl. At the least, it took her mind off the fear she was fighting the entire trip up from Sausalito.

A look around the stables told her a lot. No one had been there to care for these horses for days. Feed bags and water troughs were empty. Morrígan didn't have to be asked. She fed and watered the four horses in the stalls, whispering to each as she did. Horses, like people, need love too. The thought reminded her of Aaron. Her fears returned. Did he make it? Was he on his way to her? Only time would answer these questions. Now, Morrígan was tired. She took a few saddle blankets to a corner of an empty stall and built a makeshift bed. She didn't have any trouble falling asleep. As she dropped into a peaceful sleep, her fears drifted into the background as pleasant dreams came alive. She was riding Major up into the headlands. Light fog and a cool ocean breeze repainted the view every few minutes. She wanted to look out over the ocean forever. But a voice invaded her thoughts. "Morrígan," it whispered. "Morrígan, I'm here." Realizing the voice wasn't part of the dream, she leaped to her feet, ready to run as fast as possible. Then, she saw him. Aaron. Was he real?

"Aaron," she cried out and grabbed for him. They stood there without words, holding each other as if to block out the real world. Then, finally, Morrígan allowed herself to melt into him. Her need to defend was gone for now. "You didn't answer my comm messages," she said.

"When I escaped on the bridge, I realized it was still in my car. I'm here, Morrí. Thank God you're alive." He stopped suddenly. "Morrí, things aren't good down there," he said, pointing toward the bridge. "I don't know what you saw if anything, but it's a massacre."

Morrígan's eyes widened as she recalled the bloodbath in Sausalito. Her impossible-to-unsee horror of Corey's head as Hap's bullets exploded from his gun's muzzle left little but an unrecognizable bloody mess. When her thoughts forced her to remember shooting Hap, she whimpered, her heart raced, and her muscles tightened. "I killed another human," she said out loud. It was too much to hold back the panic that ran through her. She couldn't forget the sound of the bullet as it left her gun, the slow-motion silent images of the missile as it tore through Hap's body at high-center chest. Her soul shook when she visualized the bullet ripping through his heart before exploding in exaggerated slow motion, leaving a fist-sized bloody pothole out from Hap's back. As she remembered, she relived it. She lost control. An unworldly scream that she knew must be coming from her soul filled the stables. The horses seemed to understand her agony as they bowed their heads toward her and nickered softly.

Aaron held her close. "I know, honey. I feel it too—helpless, desperate. But, right now, we have to survive. I know you, and I'm certain if you killed someone, there was no choice. The world flipped inside-out today. Everything's changed, and what we need forces us to do unthinkable things. You did what you had to. We need to get away from here, the massacre, and hide where no one can find us. She buried her face in his chest, knowing he was probably the only person alive who cared if she lived or died. She knew Wallyce didn't care. The thought that her sister would want her dead didn't make her sad. On the contrary, it gave her resolve—she resolved to live, no matter what it took, even if she had to kill Wallyce. "So, it's to be a battle to the death," she thought.

"Aaron, what can we do? I saw Sausalito turned into a slaughterhouse. Everyone's dead, killed where they stood. I know this was Wallyce. She warned us to submit to isolation and quarantine or be destroyed—but I didn't think she would murder them. I thought she meant Cyto-47 would do it for her." Her knees went weak. "Why'd she kill them all?" Morrígan broke down in heavy sobs. She backed away from Aaron, looking to him for answers.

"Morrí, there's no way to know what she thinks. I watched people the length of the Golden Gate Bridge as they were poisoned and gassed to death for not showing up at Barca City to surrender. Even after most of them were dead, several troops, maybe not even human; I think they were robotic, traveled the length of the bridge shooting every human in sight, whether already dead or clinging to life. Then, they left them there to rot. These murdered people were on their way to comply with quarantine orders. I talked to some right before they died. They were executed for the crime of being stuck in traffic. Suppose this is happening all over the Bay Area or even the country. In that case, it changes everything—all we think of as society has ceased to exist, replaced by a new order governed by tyranny. Do what the masters tell us, or be slaughtered by some robotic monster and left to decay, or be cast out to wait for the plague to find you and suck your life out.

"Morrí, I've prepared for the possibility of this type of massacre for a long time. From one election to another, our government has become increasingly tyrannical. Our leaders are more willing to sacrifice people for wealth and power. Wallyce may have seemed like the real thing for so many, maybe even you, but she had all the signs of a tyrant; maniacal drive for money, for power . . . Even more than others, she's willing to restructure our Democracy into her own form of Technocracy – government by technology. Those left in Congress have become whining puppies, ready to do whatever she commands. It didn't start with her. So many others have chipped away at our democracy for so long that we're left with an empty shell. Our Constitution is meaningless by now.

"I watched, and I prepared. I promise we'll be safe. I own a large forest up north where we can live under the cover of the trees. Food is stocked to feed a village for years, and I have a farm that will produce more than enough for us to live on. I also have a herd of sheep that roam the land to provide wool, meat, and hide. So, we can live simply for as long as it takes."

"But, Aaron. We need to fight her. We have to save as many as we can."

"Yeah. I was sure you'd want to stay here to "fix" the mess your sister created. Tell you what. We can load up a couple of the horses and ride across the headlands toward the ocean. You'll be able to see from here what's happening around us. Then we can make that decision. I promise I'll support whatever you decide. Agreed?"

Morrígan waited before answering. She saw the truth in his eyes. She knew he would let her make a choice and be with her all the way. "Okay. Let's go." She did her best to smile, but it wasn't there yet. "Aaron, how are we going to get there?"

"My horse is waiting in the next stable. I've loaded him with enough food and water to get us there, and my hunting gear, rifles, and bow are all set up and ready for when we might need them. I've been all over the riding trails between here and my forest retreat. I'm a survivor, Morrí. I know how to stay hidden and travel in darkness to avoid being seen, and I promise we'll get there. It's gonna take a few days—not like traveling by car—but we'll make it. Trust me, okay?"

The reality of the conversation brought Morrígan to a complete stop. "Aaron," she said, "it's never going to get better. Yesterday morning, life changed for me and everyone else. You tell me that some Barcan Robots are on a murdering spree, and Wallyce has likely slaughtered hundreds of thousands of the citizens. All this in one day?" Her speech was rushed, and her voice was louder. "It's only going to get worse," she shouted. The horses began to whinny and tug at their tether.

* * *

Riding the well-worn trails might have been pleasurable if it was daylight and one could see any danger before it hit. But this was the dead of night, and even the soft bath of moonlight breaking through the forest canopy couldn't make this ride less horrifying. Morrígan knew full well that this part of the Bay Area housed dangerous animals; mountain lions, coyotes, and even the occasional bear. She fought to comfort herself, knowing Aaron could protect her with his rifles. So that wasn't what made her shiver in her saddle. She believed her sister, Wally, would send her robot army to find her and Aaron. What better place to assassinate them than deep in the redwoods in the least populated part of Northern California?

"Aaron, she is going to try to kill me. Wally won't give up as long as she knows I'm alive."

"I suspect you're right, except for one thing. You're convinced Wallyce arranged to assassinate you in Sausalito, right?"

Morrígan pulled up on her horse. "I know it was her. Who else would have wanted to kill me? So it was her, alright."

"Okay," Aaron said. "So, who could have reported back to let her know you're still alive" The Secret Service Agent is dead. The assassin is dead. You know that for certain. Am I missing anyone?"

Morrígan tried to focus. "Yeah, unless she had eyes on me—like cameras or satellite scanners. So maybe she thinks I'm dead. Is that what you are saying?"

"Uh-huh." So now she can stop stressing about her little sister and focus on all the other murders she is probably committing or having her robots commit. This leaves you free to start over in our place up north."

Morrígan wanted to agree, but in her heart, she knew she might never be free to start over as long as Wallyce Tilton was alive on the Earth and free to perform her unique brand of mass murder. "We'll see, Aaron. You may be right. But for right now, we can only think about getting to a place where we are as free from Barca as anyone can be. I'm hoping your survivalist camp will make that possible. Tell me more about it."

Aaron spent much of the ride that night telling Morrígan about his private world above Duncans Mills in his Sawmill Camp. As he described it, he spent a few years acquiring as much forest land as he could that surrounded the former family sawmill. He had converted much of it to some called a survival encampment. Many of the original buildings were left as they were found, most in disrepair that people would think they were abandoned. Some, like the small worker's cabins, had fallen and were clearly uninhabited. He described how he left the visible buildings as they were, like a ghost town. But, he invested his time and money in creating well-hidden structures, some underground, some hidden within the trees, that would serve as a vast community for any who decided to live out of sight and be well protected. He was true to his survivalist spirit.

Morrígan listened to his description, waiting for him to reveal that some new buildings might be considered livable, if not luxurious. He told no such story. Instead, she formed a mental image of living in caves and fallout shelters. She began to think this wasn't such a great idea after all. Then, he gave a tiny bit of hope.

"You must wait until we get there to see it in real life. There's so much more to tell, but I'm gonna wait till you can see what I'll be talking about."

Okay then. Maybe there's hope after all," she thought.

* * *

The trip was long and, thankfully, uneventful. Much of their travel was by night, letting the horses and themselves rest during the bright daylight hours. Traveling at that slow pace, they arrived at Duncans Mills along the Russian River in the early morning of their third day.

Expecting so much more based on Aaron's description, Morrígan was only slightly impressed. The area identified by signs as Duncans Mills stood much as it must have a couple hundred years ago. It paused in time and space as an oddity for the thousands of tourists who flocked to the ancient-styled campgrounds each year. Morrígan delighted at the crude tilt-up buildings and simplistic hand-painted signs that called out a restaurant, general store, coffee shop, and more. She turned to Aaron to ask about the place. As her eyes swept the area, she lost her breath, realizing the cars, benches, parking lot, and picnic areas were filled with blood and bodies. Afraid to make a sound, she pointed as Aaron touched her arm to lower it. He turned his horse to the left and motioned for Morrígan to follow.

By now sensing death all around them, the horses needed to be coaxed into a sizeable commercial garage where, Aaron said, they might be safe for now. Inside, the old machinery that once was a repair shop had been tossed about like toys. Whatever did this must have incredible strength. Stay here," Aaron said, "and I'll give a quick look around the place to see if they're gone."

Morrígan tried to talk him out of that bad idea, but he was gone before she could say anything. Soon after she was alone, the enormity of what had happened cascaded over her. Her heart pounded when she imagined the Barcan killers might return any minute. The thought of it pushed her into a rush of panic. She envisioned what the horror must have looked like as Barcan Bots attacked anything that moved, shooting, burning, even ripping some apart as they screamed in terror. They must have known they would die soon, some wishing it would happen quicker to end their nightmarish pain.

Aaron came running back into the old mill just when she felt she might scream. Morrígan could see his face was drained of color, and he seemed unable to process what he saw. Gasping for breath, his words came in bursts.

"Bots slaughtered everyone. All blasted, some even run over by the Bot transports, many shot so many times they aren't recognizable. Everyone, Morrí. Old people, young men, women, babies . . . even their pets were killed." This was the first time Morrígan had seen him cry. "Babies . . ." He just sat there motionless for a few minutes. Then, he fought to regain control.

"I'm sure the Bots are gone. No reason to stay here since they ran out of people to murder. Plus, they left huge tire tracks in a bloody trail on the road leading out of there. We can head up the hill to my place to see what they left us." Morrígan remounted, and they headed up and across the river on the narrow car bridge. Less than two miles later, Aaron brought his horse to a stop in a thick pack of trees, dismounted, and signaled for Morrígan to wait there. He walked off to scout the buildings of his disguised survival camp. He returned soon, walking down the middle of his access road, a sign they would be safe there, at least for now. "It's clear up there, Morrígan. Let's head on up."

Avoiding the old road from the bridge, Aaron followed an almost hidden path through the forest, up the slight grade, then leveling off in front of what Morrigan guessed was the actual sawmill. This wasn't any modern computerized mill. That would have been overkill for the needs of the community and the few builders who used to rely on the mill for their lumber. Instead, this mill was intentionally small. The former owners were dedicated to reforestation, replanting what they cut and only cutting what was needed, never selling their logs to other mills.

The mill was somewhat small, as old mills can be. The logs were fed into the saws via flatbed rail cars that rode along a short track from the raw log piles to the saw beds. The logs were loaded manually, using a front loader to place them on the flatbed. The saw was once powered by solar energy, as was the entire camp. Aaron had repurposed the solar systems to feed the electrical needs of his buildings, including some dozen storage and living structures.

Morrígan was confused. She recalled that Aaron told her he had converted the place into a series of buildings and connecting tunnels that could potentially house an entire village, protected from all outside threats, including armed attacks, animal invasions, and even the familiar deadly threat to Californian lands, the deadly raging fires that happened every year all over the state. But, focus as hard as she could, this place seemed to be no more than an old, dilapidated, rusted-out mill, no longer any good to anyone and unsuitable for any purpose. And there were no signs of underground access points.

"Aaron, this place is supposed to have been converted into a community. Instead, all I can see is a falling-down bunch of machines. Are there other buildings?"

"Well," Aaron said, "now that you ask, let's see what we can find." Aaron took her by the hand and led her to the loader end of the sawmill. Morrígan's vision was starting to adjust to the darkness of the building. She scanned the area then, finding no doorways, she started knocking on the walls, thinking she might hear a hollow sound indicating a possible opening. After a bit, guessing she wouldn't find what she was looking for, she stopped. "Aaron, how about a hint?"

He smiled. "Okay. It helps to know this was a pretty small sawmill in its day, operated by a single family and producing a fairly small amount of high-quality wood products for a select group of builders and craftsmen. This helps you to understand why, when it was abandoned, the owners didn't leave all that much wood lying around. There was usually very little wood and scrap here, even when it was operating. What was left behind was pretty organized into two areas; the raw logs you see right here at the loading end and the first-cut scraps, the rounded edges of the logs, that were left after the saw squared the logs for cutting into boards. This is important as it explains the neatly stacked metal racks of round first cuts. Makes sense?" he asked. Morrígan nodded but rolled her eyes to indicate she didn't really get where he was headed with this. "Well, it means none of this looks out of place, right?" Another nod. "Okay, then. I'll just move this little rough-cut out of the way."

Aaron reached up to adjust a small rough first-cut scrap that looked like it might fall if it were bumped hard enough. He tapped the bark on the face of the rough cut with his knuckles. Then, as if an earthquake struck, the steel shelves at first shook, moved across the floor to reveal that the shelves were mounted on a rail track and powered silently, most likely by electricity. As the steel shelves separated, light from below showed a double-wide staircase that led somewhere below the sawmill.

Morrígan, stunned at first, soon understood what she saw. Aaron had built his Survival Community completely underground, and access was so well hidden that she didn't know it was there until he opened the staircase.

"Aaron, you could have warned me," she said. "Knowing you, I should have guessed right from the start that this wouldn't be a typical deep-woods campground. I can't wait to see this place." She wrapped her arms around him, kissed his cheek, and tugged at his elbow. "C'mon. Show me this new world. The old one scares the hell out of me."

"Not to worry, love. You're safe now. We can start over and make this world what the old one should have been all along." He took her hand and led her down the staircase.

Morrígan was just a bit comforted. She couldn't get past the thought of spending her life in the woods while the rest of the world dissolved through some evil form of reverse evolution driven by the survival of the most vicious. Nothing in her life prepared her for this. She suspected a small percent of humans may have had a hint of the looming Armageddon, folks like Aaron who prepared and practiced for life after society, but they were the minority. She saw herself as she was, a child of accidental privilege, highly educated, super successful in all facets of her life, except one; she had no idea how to start over in an unfamiliar world, with no concept of how to even stay alive in this shit storm.

These thoughts were front-of-mind as Aaron led her on a walking tour of the unexpected underground village he had created. At the bottom of the stairs, he placed his hand over a biometric scanner. With his print recognized, the entrance—a door similar to a bank vault—hummed and clicked. The door opened to allow access. "Impressive," Morrígan said. "Print scanners, although old style, are still effective."

"Yeah, I know," Aaron replied. Once we check the place, I'll help you set your prints into the system. I'm surprised you haven't asked me how I power all of this. Solar is a good baseline, but you must remember we are in the middle of California's fog belt, so solar isn't dependable enough. I've also added two other natural sources; wind and water flow. We have plenty of both here regularly. As the annual rains begin, they bring both water and wind. There are several wind-capture sources here. First, I've installed several windmills hidden above us and in the dark forest. They're disguised to simulate the trees around them. Then, I had paths cut through the woods to allow the typical wind patterns to directly pass through to these windmills. Very practical so far. As we are located at the lower half of some large hills, digging several trenches for water capture was also simple. The water we don't use for drinking, cleaning, and cooking is routed to our watermill at the river's edge, where we convert it to additional electricity. Do you follow?"

Morrígan was about to answer when the lights came on throughout the complex, showing what might be called an enormous corridor leading to quite a few side corridors. She could see that some of these led to substantial underground buildings. Each entrance was labeled with the purpose of each building: Food, Supplies, Medical, Social Gathering, Armory, and more. At the far end was a wide corridor labeled Entrance to Living Quarters. The size of the complex alone was enough to stun her senses, but what caused Morrígan to gasp was the beauty of it all.

Prepared to walk into open caves and dimly lit passageways, Morrígan never expected this—a place where its inhabitants wouldn't just tolerate life—they could actually enjoy it. Aaron's survival community would have been more accurately described as underground luxury living. A soft glow of filtered light exposed what appeared to be windows looking out over some of California's natural beauty. "Aaron, am I seeing Half Dome through that window?" Morrígan asked. "But that can't be. Yosemite is a couple hundred miles from here." She leaned in for a closer look through the window but couldn't figure out how this could happen.

Aaron smiled. "You're right. It is over 200 miles from here. You're looking at it through photographic magic provided by one of the startups I founded. This is actually called "Fourth-Dimension Photography, or FDP. They developed a printing method, layering different aspects, allowing the viewer to see different parts of the photograph from different angles. I'm not smart enough to tell you how it happens, but you can see the result. It looks like you see Half Dome through a window, right? I've placed several such pieces of art throughout the complex. As you can see, it makes you forget you're underground. After many months underground, I figured there's a tendency to feel closed in; some might call it "buried alive syndrome," so these kinds of things will become more important as time passes."

The need to stay underground for the long term hadn't occurred to Morrígan. From then on, she viewed everything Aaron showed her through the lens of "buried alive." There was so much to take in. The food storage was simple yet efficient. Both freshness dates and their corresponding "Use-or-Destroy-By" dates were labeled. At the top of each storage section was a digital countdown clock alternating between the calendar date and the number of calories available to each inhabitant for that particular day. Morrígan was curious. "What does that calorie number mean?"

"Well, since we can never tell how many will eventually live here, I needed to devise a way to tell how many months we had left on current food supplies. I'll show you the farm in a few days, and you'll see the livestock roaming freely as we wander the complex above ground. But our future success will depend on just how nutrition-smart we remain. So, this is a simple app that calculates our food needs based on population versus our supplies."

The tour was brief and included only the closest facilities to the entrance. Any more would have been too much for Morrígan to take in so soon. "I just realized you had all the walls covered in traditional surfaces like we would expect in an above-ground building. I can't see any rocks or natural surfaces except these tree trunks growing from the floor and through the roof. What's up with that?"

"Great question," Aaron said. "Imagine right above the roof is the ground. Leaving the ground bare in the shape of our Survival Village would be a red flag telling the enemy where to drop the bombs. Think of this; military craft and drones are programmed to notice certain things–one of these is patterned bare ground in an otherwise lush landscape, such as the middle of a forest. In the case of these trees, nature has gifted us with the perfect canopy, many ancient and large trees that blend in with the rest of the forest. This area looks like more trees from above, and there is no reason to suspect anything else. So do you want to see more?"

Morrígan didn't have to answer. Aaron led her into a corridor labeled "Private Residence." As they approached, the door slid open, having recognized Aaron's face. Lights slowly came up to a comfortable level, letting Morrígan have her first look at what was about to become her home for the next however many days, months, and years…? "But," she thought, "this apartment is beautiful."

As they walked into the center of the main living room, soft music played, almost imperceptibly, one of Morrígan's favorite songs. "Man, this guy doesn't miss a trick," she chuckled.

Aaron put his arm around her waist and guided her toward the bedroom. "Now, I'm about to crawl out of my skin after three days on the trail. What do you say we hop in the shower and get some clean clothes on?"

She looked around the room. It was easy to see that Aaron was careful to avoid décor that might feel too much like the rugged outdoorsman he is or says he is. After seeing the amount of work and thought he must have had to come up with to create this underground world he calls Survival Village. She couldn't imagine him doing much hiking, hunting, or camping—things Aaron claimed took up his time and attention on these trips. She knew he didn't do any of the building himself. He would have hired the best designers and builders to create such a masterpiece. Still, she was sure he wasn't the type to sign checks and leave the builders to do the work while he trotted out into the forest. The thought of it made her laugh.

"What's funny?" he asked.

"Oh, I was just thinking that you must have been too busy with this huge project to spend much of your famous time-alone-in-the-wilderness trips alone in the wilderness."

"Okay, caught me. This has been my goal for more than ten years. The people who did the design work are long gone, and the builders have already moved into their neighborhood a half mile from here. I gave it to them as a thank you, letting them know they're part of the community. In short, I can trust them. Now, how about that shower?"

She didn't answer. Taking Aaron by the hand, she walked toward what she thought might be the bathroom. She guessed right, as she found herself in the middle of a large room, half of which was an open shower. There were no faucets or any other way to cause water to rain down on them, so it initially confused her. Aaron took the lead. He gently removed her clothes, one piece at a time, tossing them into a heap in the far corner of the room. Then he stepped out of his own clothes, all while they were kissing and caressing each other.

When it looked like they might never shower, she whispered to him, "How do you turn the water on?"

He burst out laughing. "Oh, yeah. I forgot that." Then, he simply said, "Shower on all outlets." Warm at first, then just a touch hotter, the water seemed to rain on them from every angle, washing it all away—first the trail dust, then the novelty of the Village and her concern that it might have been just an elaborate campground, far from the complicated underground world he had built for their future. But, as she was cleansed by the water and softened by his touch, the enormity of life slammed down and overwhelmed her. Leaning her wet body against his, she began to sob into him, hoping he could absorb some of her agony. He must have sensed it as he held her and kept her from falling to the shower floor, a helpless, empty shell.

They stood there long, but it seemed only a few minutes. Then, when Morrígan's sobs finally settled to a soft whimper, he took the chance. "Are you okay?"

Biting her lip helped her not break down in sobs again. Finally, after another minute, Morrígan was able to use her voice. "The world's over, Aaron. It's over." She still had a few more sobs; her anger spilled out. Her mind played an endless stream of horror; murdered bodies in the streets of Sausalito and the little village of Duncan's Mill, the assassination of three city mayors probably ordered by her sister, her friend agent Corey's head blown off three feet from her own. She replayed time and time again the instant she pulled back on the trigger and took another human's life and the final horrific step into Armageddon. Cyto-47.

She felt Aaron pick her up and carry her to the bed. Grabbing a towel from the chair next to the nightstand, he dried her and pulled the covers over her. She could tell he sensed no words could be spoken between them, which could soften the horror of her feelings. She didn't need words. She needed the world to be as it was only a few months ago, but that could never be. Reaching up to touch his face, her feelings overflowed. Was she feeling love, or was it desperation built from the reality that he was all she had left to rely on? He was her future and her savior. And, the truth was, she felt them all; love and fear, and she was desperate to feel human again. So, she pulled him down to her, holding him with all her strength. She made love to him, her lover, her future, and the only human she could now trust. And she loved him with desperation.

After, she drifted off to sleep, her dreams shifting from happy thoughts of her love for Aaron to the abject horror of what her sister was doing to the rest of the world. Somewhere in between, Morrígan found some peace, and she slept.

* * *

She awoke softly to birds chirping and the too-welcome smell of bread baking in an oven somewhere. She opened her eyes and took a few moments to remember where she was and what horror brought her there. She suddenly needed to see Aaron near her, ready to protect her no matter what evil came. "Stop it, Morrígan," she told herself. "Stand tall, and no more trying to hide from this evil world. You're better than this." She was never one to need a protector, and she wasn't about to let that happen to her now.

Chapter Twenty-Six

The drone hovered silently and unseen above the San Francisco Bay. Its super-mirror cameras scanned the expanse of Barca City, streaming video back to its operator. It was apparent from the piles of rotting corpses, dumped or perhaps fallen at every possible entrance, the attack had already happened, and the attackers clearly didn't win. One thing is for sure; Cyto-47 and the rest of the world had come to California. These corpses were both evidence and carriers of the most deadly plague ever known to humanity.

Besides the macabre vision of bloated corpses, the place was decked in elegant military fashion. From the rooftops, gigantic statues had been modified from stunning artwork to sinister battle stations. Motion-triggered floodlights flashed over the edge of the buildings, lighting the battleship-style cannon batteries and dozens of what appeared to be super-sized Bots, standing ready to blast anything within their impressive range. Below, the seaport and airport were buzzing with activity. Military ships paraded back and forth across the entire front of the City. Drones were launched in several directions to scan the Bay Area for signs of life. But, of course, finding any living humans wasn't expected. And none were found. Cyto-47 had taken care of that. Those who survived the plague were massacred by marauding groups of Barcan WarBots.

As if advertising billboards hawking products, random floating 3-D images and video streams passed across the front of Barca City, some relatively minor and others spanning dozens of stories. Their message emblazoned on every blank space: "Those who now wish to join us in the safety of Barca City must first apply for quarantine at one of the Repurpose Centers. The closest Repurpose Center to this location is the former San Francisco Airport. Enter through the International Terminal Main Entrance."

Woven in between messages was a brief video of President Wallyce Tilton. She wore a military-style jacket with gold buttons, the Barcan logo on each lapel, and a bright red throat scarf. Her message was clear: "We look forward to our friends joining us through the Repurpose Center. All who attempt to enter Barca City without passing through the Centers will be repelled, possibly executed, to prevent any Plague infiltration into Barca."

The floating, rotting corpses were probably left in place to prove her deadly point. In real-time, Wallyce was enjoying Barcan's daily life, directing her senior staff on the ways of a corporate Master. The holographic cameras captured her precisely as she wanted to appear, as a God, holding dominion over her reluctant populations.

Wallyce held her most recent anti-sedition trial at the main entrance to the city. Today's lesson was intended to define, without any doubt, who were the Masters and servants. She taught her team exactly how she wanted them to perform the same processes.

"Goh, bring the refuser to the front," she said. Any citizen of Barca, whether there by choice or by force, who disobeyed rules, performed their job poorly, or was a general disturbance in the strict calm of Barca City, was called a refuser. Refusers would either conform immediately if allowed, or the punishment was swift and irreversible. This was the case of a refuser caught protesting or speaking to others about the need to revolt. Goh, ever-faithful (if that was a word that might apply to an AI robot), summoned the refuser forward. The poor guy didn't have a chance to refuse this command. He was strapped onto a chair that was fastened to a moving platform. As he neared President Tilton, his platform rose three feet off the floor. It was turned to face the crowd assembled there and the hologram cameras that would send this event all over Barca City, even out to the East Bay farms and the nearby silica mines. This was a lesson to be studied by every citizen of Barca City. It was one they would never forget.

"Citizens of our fair city," Wallyce Tilton began. "I am deeply sorry that I must ask you all to watch the following. This happens to anyone who promotes or attempts sedition against our great country."

That introduction held very little truth. First, Barca was anything but a "fair city." Second, Wallyce wasn't the least bit sorry. In fact, she loved this. Third, there was no "ask" about what was happening. Everyone was required to watch. The punishment for refusing to watch was to receive the same sentence. The only truth, then, was the threat that this would happen to anyone who is the least bit seditious.

"Citizen P3457," she demanded. "You have been found

guilty of sedition. Do you have anything to say before we apply the punishment?

Citizen P3457 pissed his pants and shook. There being no reason to wait, Wallyce proceeded. "Citizens of Barca City. The criminal before you, former Citizen P3457, has been found guilty of sedition against our country and has been duly sentenced to banishment and infection. No details were offered. Every citizen of Barca was too aware of what the sentence meant.

Wallyce, President of Barca, and the remaining United States nodded toward her electronic assistant, Goh. "Proceed." Absolute silence from the crowd underlined the electronic hum as the prisoner's chair rotated back toward President Wallyce Tilton. As the young man's eyes met hers, in a desperate look of pleading for mercy, the President gave him what might be taken as a smile. "Goodbye," was all she said.

The chair suddenly moved toward the main southern exit from the city. Massive doors groaned open to allow the chair to enter an airlock that led to the outside of Barca City. Hologram streams followed the chair as it was sealed into the airlock chamber. A massive hissing sound indicated that the outside air had entered the section. P3457 was now in the horrible chasm between life and death—between the safe, comforting clean air of Barca City and the deadly "Out," a world controlled by Cyto-47, where every living human soon becomes a tic mark on the "List of the Dead." He would soon be released in the middle of the building labeled "Contaminated. Entering this place will kill you." No explanation was given, but everyone in Barca City knew it was true. They had seen holograms inside the building, and they were convinced.

Wallyce called for attention. "People of Barca and of America, we are your life, safety, and home. So don't fuck it up." She turned off her hologram stream, knowing that was the most dramatic way to end the show.

"Goh, send Sebastian to my office." This was a new command for her. How would Goh send an imaginary character anywhere? A few days ago, Barca's robotics experts finished a critical project, creating an Artificial Intelligent form based on a living person. In this case, the Bot was named for Dr. Sebastian, Wallyce's lifelong friend, and adviser; the same Sebastian that Morrígan claimed was a figment of Wallyce's imagination, her childhood imaginary friend, now all grown up into an imaginary Presidential Adviser. Although she denied this claim, Wallyce was not willing to give the team direct access to Sebastian's brain so they could neuro-map it to the AI version called Sebastian. Instead, Wallyce stood in as the source of Sebastian's brain and personality. And from what she had seen so far, it worked. Her memories of Sebastian and his thoughts were copied from Wallyce's images of him as he lived in her mind. Sebastian, the AI version, was given a quasi-life form.

But, as things go, she knew there would be possible glitches and probable nuances that outsiders must overlook. So, she decided to keep Sebastian a secret until she could feel confident the world would be able to forgive his flaws, whatever they may be, and see him as human. "I'll put him through the paces myself, have the nuances fine-tuned, then allow him to face the ultimate test—live among us as a human. As this robot was given human-like features, it was easier to imagine him as alive.

As her anticipation grew, the door to the storage room adjacent to her office opened, and a man, perhaps in his mid-fifties, entered her office. "It's been a busy day for you, Wallyce," he said. Executions are rarely easy, right?

"Well, we have to send these little reminders to the masses occasionally," she said. It keeps them humble. But. Let's talk about you, Sebastian. How are things going for you?" The vague nature of the question was intentional. She wanted to see how he would handle it.

"Well, Madam President, you know the answer to that question better than anyone else. As you were the direct source for my personality in this form, you have an innate sense of my thoughts and feelings. True?"

"Yes, true." She smiled, knowing this was a well-played answer based on straightforward logic. One test passed. Now, Sebastian, what do you think of how I presented our latest casualty—former citizen 13457."

"On a dramatic level, I give you a seven. Perhaps a bit more discussion of the reason for the verdict and the support for 13457's execution might have added to the intrigue. As it was, your drama level was just okay. On a successful impact level, I give it a nine. None of them will doubt he was eventually killed by Cyto-47. The message was understood, for sure. To the question of your own power image, you get a ten. The little smirk you gave him as he was headed out to his death was brilliant. You have risen to the level of a living evil being. There will be no doubt you are in total control. Good thing you got rid of that pesky, annoying do-gooder Morrígan."

Wallyce smiled. "Yes. I'll admit there was a time when I feared she wasn't dead. I had nightmares every night. It was a terrible time trying to sleep. In my dreams, I see her. She's walking on water, crossing the Bay, coming for me. She says she'll come soon to end my dynasty. Dynasty? What the hell dynasty does she mean?

"I know what I was afraid of. I expected to hear from my Secret Service that she and her agent were killed in the uprising in Sausalito. Stupid. She never knew we tracked her halfway across the bay. We did find the body of Agent Gaiters in the Coast Guard skiff, but we never found Morrígan nor the assassin we employed to finish her. I waited a long time. It just got to the point where I can't imagine she could outlast the Cyto-47 plague that's killed every Californian who hasn't joined us inside Barca City or the Repurpose Centers. Even if she survived, I'm sure the WarBots will have terminated her by now. So, here we are. I've decided once and for all that she's gone, killed by my assassin, the plague, or the Bots. But either way, I'm finished with her."

Wallyce felt the familiar anxiety come over her whenever she thought of Morrígan. She hated the feeling. "Sebastian, I have things to do. Return to your storage locker. I will call for you soon."

"Of course, Madam." The AI Bot returned to the storage, and the door was sealed shut.

"Goh, dinner, please." Her anxiety refused to leave her. Instead, she decided on a nice bottle of Livermore Sirrah to accompany her meal. Soon the elegant feast, usual fare for a President, was placed on her table. As she sipped from the Sirrah, she saw the message signal flash on her wall screen. Turning so she could read the message, Wallyce let out a loud scream. "WARBOT ONE! COME HERE RIGHT NOW!" She screamed it repeatedly until the Commander of Bot Forces appeared in her quarters.

"Madam?"

As if unable to speak, Wallyce's shaky hand pointed her finger at the screen above them. The message was unmistakable. It was labeled with Morrígan's access code.

"My Dear Sister. I want you to know that this is not finished. See you soon, M."

Wallyce's agony became blood-curdling as she threw her glass against the screen.

Chapter Twenty-Seven

The activity at the Fremont BART station soon became a disaster. Put tens of thousands of normally free people with a centuries-long history of loud and successful protest against several artificially intelligent WarBots who exist only to follow orders no matter what, and you have a horror formula.

This station's empty parking lot was assigned as a local intake station, where those who wished to obey Wallyce's Lockdown and Isolation order would go to be given one of only three options: The first option was Barca City's own Isolation Intake, where those with no symptoms would first spend a week under strict isolation. Any who survived could join Barca City as new citizens, probably for life. Of course, those who didn't make it through would not live through the testing period. They would be determined to be infected and either wrapped in a body bag or, if infected but still alive, given a quick injection and then wrapped in a body bag. No need to wait was the order.

The next option was that they would be determined to

be US-NS, the acronym meaning Unknown Status – No Symptoms. WarBots would load them into transports after giving them full-head masks to reduce transmissibility. If infected, their breath would be contained to minimize the chance they could infect others. Once delivered to the US-NS isolation centers, they were placed in total individual isolation, awaiting their results a week later. Infected? Injected. Not infected? Taken to Barca City. The real difference between the first and second groups was that the second group members might have a slim chance of survival. The first group was more or less walking dead.

The final group was simply called the refusers. At first, the WarBots would round these refusers up and march them into the hastily built enclosure at the east end of the parking lot. They were summarily executed under the rules of martial law and Wallyce Tilton's command. They were branded as insurgents, gassed then loaded into freight cars for transport to the incineration station at the southern end of the reclaimed bay lands in the former Alviso.

This was designed to operate smoothly, with little warning to the unlucky citizens. But, as these things are, rumors spread at the speed of light. Soon, chaos erupted as all were led to believe they were about to be killed. Their panic turned into a desperate riot to overturn the WarBots. . . a mistake from the start. Before long, the order came down from Barca City: "Execute all immediately. This can't happen again."

The efficiency of the WarBots was astounding. Nobody escaped.

* * *

Morrígan threw on some clothes and went to look for the source of the smell of bread, fresh from the oven. Aaron continued to find ways, often simple things, to help her heal from the horror she and so many others had to face, a result of the WarBot attacks on American citizens—a murderous purge of all people whose only crime was to ignore a command from her sister, President Wallyce Tilton. However basic it was, bread healed her in a way she could never have expected.

The security door slid back into place as she headed toward where she remembered the community dining hall. It was an easy decision, as the aroma filled the air down the first major hallway she came to. A few steps on, she stopped in her tracks, hearing an unexpected sound jolted her. "People?" she asked herself. "This sounds like a crowd of people." She became concerned. She knew no other people were in the compound when she arrived, "was that last night?" But the sound was unmistakable. And there were sounds of a meal being eaten; plates tinking, forks scraping the plates, liquid filling glasses. . . She hesitated only momentarily when Aaron called her from the hallway behind her.

"Good morning, sweetie. I was beginning to wonder how long you were going to sleep." I went in to wake you. There's so much I need to tell you."

Morrígan turned to find him right there. "Well, I might have guessed, hearing the noise from the dining hall. It sounds like a pretty big crowd is having breakfast." She was at a loss for words, so she stopped talking.

"Well, that's what we need to discuss—that and more." He walked her over to the nearest tree, where they sat on a bench around the base of the trunk. Aaron took her hand

and looked into her eyes. She immediately understood that what he would say next would be life-altering. She was right.

"Morrígan, I haven't been completely open with you," he began. "I haven't lied, but I sure left a whole bunch of details out when we talked about my trips up here. And the purpose of this compound is so much more than I've let on. I'm so sorry I didn't give you the whole story, but I was afraid I would scare you away." He paused, then said, "Please believe me, I love you with everything I am. And, from here on, I'll never leave you out of any part of my life."

Morrígan held his hand as if to say, "Don't be afraid. I'm not going to be angry. Just open up to me."

This gave Aaron the gentle push he needed. "Okay, but wait till I finish before you judge." He looked to the floor, wondering where to start, "Morrí, I'm a survivalist. Do you know what that is?" She nodded. "I didn't set out to be one, but sometimes reality offers little choice. Over time, I realized that people will never understand the damage we've done to the world. And once I started to question that, it became clear that people just flat-out don't care. It's an attitude that says that as long as I have what I need, the rest of you can go to hell. Once I opened my mind to this, the more wealth I accumulated, the more I was forced to see that people with all the money, including myself, have all the power. And many of those with all the power just don't give a damn about anyone else's problems. But I couldn't buy into that. It goes against humanity. So, I saw myself as a crusader —someone who believes that each one of us deserves the same rights and protections as all others. Now came the question; "what will you do about it?"

"I watched in disgust while governments, wealthy individuals, and power-hungry ego-maniacs trampled over the rights of anyone who wasn't wealthy or self-focused enough to become one of the privileged few. It wouldn't be long before we became a society of masters and slaves again. I couldn't become a part of such a world, so I invested much of my wealth in building another reality. I have been working with so many others over the past few years to create a community where everyone can live in peace, with no fear that someone with all the power, such as your sister, can force them into servitude—force them to live under some super-rich's commands or be relegated to the ranks of the disenfranchised poor. Are you following me?"

Morrígan nodded. "I think so," she said. "But what will happen to your community now that Cyto-47 kills everyone it touches? Won't the people who aren't under Wallyce's lockdown protection be at risk of getting the plague? Then, what? And," she asked, "where will these community members come from? What type of government will you have? There must be rules and some form of societal structure, no?" She felt a sudden sob that fought to come out. It was all too much to absorb. "Aaron, how will this new society ever survive with all the forces of Barca aimed at destroying any who don't submit to Wallyce's evil power?" She paused momentarily, then asked, "How will you prevent a similar power grab in this new society?"

Aaron was prepared for these questions. They formed the very base of his mission in life going forward. "Morrí, the people you will meet when we enter the dining hall should be more than enough to answer these questions. They have been brought together not based on what they have or the strength of their power but for who they are. They'll tell you in their own words, but you will easily identify with many people who put the good of others before their own." He took her hand and stood, looking at her to gauge her readiness for what she was about to learn. "I think it's time you start to meet some of them. He gently coaxed her to her feet and led her across to the room with a sign that read "Dining Hall."

As they approached the doorway to the hall, an eerie silence threw a dark shadow over the room, as if those inside could tell Aaron and Morrígan were about to join them. Morrígan looked to Aaron for reassurance. She felt insecure. She'd never been on the edge of a new society before, and about to meet the originators of this bold undertaking—the rebels—it gave a feeling that was a mixture of fear and solidarity. She wanted to be a part of this, as scary as it might be. She looked to Aaron for strength.

"Follow me," he said. "Let's go meet your friends, both old and new." He opened the door and led Morrígan into the room, not waiting for her to ask any more questions. They would be answered as soon as she walked in. There wasn't enough time to take in the whole room when a young lady came running up to her with arms outstretched, a smile as wide as possible. Morrígan was confused, then stunned.

"Manda?" she called out. "Manda Watson? But, I never. . . you. . . oh, Manda," she mumbled as she hugged the girl. Morrígan looked at Manda's face, smiling in recognition. "But, how are you involved? I don't get it."

Manda, the past winner of the Tilton Award from Project Daylight, smiled knowingly. She gently moved Morrígan so she faced the room full of people. "Look around, Vice President. So many of us came here through the Daylight Project. Aaron gave a talk once about the need to redesign society. A "societal reboot," he called it. Aaron described a society in which every person put all others before themselves. He said that the power of many must come before the power of self. When Aaron speculated we would rather have everyone caring for everyone else instead of each one fighting the world alone, well, it just made sense. Then, he asked us if we knew anyone who was a great example of being focused on others instead of self. We each thought of you, the most selfless person we knew."

Morrígan teared up. She asked, "But how did you come to be here? What did he say that made you think about joining this new society?"

"He just offered each of us to join in helping the country become what we need it to be—a benevolent society—one in which we all commit to helping each other. That was an easy decision for me and for all of us. Now, Vice President, we all would be so happy if you would join us."

Morrígan realized the entire room was staring at them and likely listening. She looked to Aaron, who smiled like a brand-new lover. She turned to the crowd again, smiled, and then spoke.

"Before I say anything, I need to tell you this. You would be wrong to call me Vice President. I left Barca City quickly so I wouldn't be forced to work with Wallyce and her evil plan for America. She tried to have me assassinated, but I made it out alive. I have no reason nor desire to ever return to serving a country that would allow her to murder its own citizens. As a result, I renounce my oath of office, stating that I cannot and will not uphold a Constitution that has enabled a dictator to so easily rise to power, all the while murdering her own people."

The room stood in unison, heads bowed, as they all said, "We welcome you into our community, where the good of all is more important than the desires of the few. Please join us as we build a new world." Morrígan smiled, sobbing, and nodded, hugging as many as possible.

Next, she walked over to Aaron, held him for a long moment, and then said to no one in particular, "Well, I am one of you, so give me a job to do."

After the laughter died down, Aaron gave her an answer. "There'll be many jobs, and we'll all do them. For now, maybe you can help us understand how best to avoid the criminals from Barca."

Steady applause and a loud cheer broke out.

Chapter Twenty-Eight

Wallyce sat at the head of the new Barca City Government dais, quickly scanning over the day's tallies:

· Thirteen infections, each terminated then cremated.
· Four insurgency trials, each was found guilty. Executed.
· Nine deaths by suicide
· Seventeen murders

She read the footnotes. The murders mostly resulted from attempted thefts of food. Her decision to keep them hungry was taking a toll. She made a note to consult with Sebastian.

"Goh," she called. "Give me access to General McCann, Sebastian, and Governor Brookfield. Set it up on this hologram display."

Goh, ever quick to comply, was also a stickler for details. "Certainly, Madam. When do you wish the meeting to begin?"

"Immediately, if not sooner," she said. Goh did as ordered.

"General, Governor, Sebastian, thank you for your promptness," she said as if they had any choice. "Forget the formalities. Let's get started. General, update me on the progress in locating any humans still alive outside our facilities."

McCann was to the point. "Madam, we have located more than seventeen thousand bodies. They have been dead for some time, based on the level of decay. We have not yet found any living humans anywhere. We continue as ordered, especially on the lookout for the head insurgent, your former Vice President."

"Not good enough, General," Wallyce snarled.

"Governor Brookfield. I placed you in charge of the area of WarBots to search for remaining insurgents. What have they found?"

Jake Brookfield felt his hands shake. He knew his answer wouldn't place him in a good light. But he knew better than to lie to her. "Madam, the Bots have reported that after close grid-searching of Northern California, there is not a single living human outside Barca City and your Repurpose camps."

Wallyce showed her displeasure. "Jake, also not good enough. You and I know they are out there. Would you like it if I sent you to ride with the Bots? No, of course not. You would be dead in a few days. One more week, Jake. After that, you'll be assigned to a workstation."

"Sebastian?"

"Yes, madam. What would you like to know first?"

The AI Bot called Sebastian was a perfect example of Barcan technology. He looked lifelike, and his speech patterns would fool most. Wallyce counted on his superior intellect to keep the others on edge. He managed the entire country and Barca's remote cities, all biologically pure and secure.

"Sebastian, I want a country, then a government update."

"Yes, Madam," the ManBot replied. "All of your remote state-by-state bio-secure facilities are up and running, except for New York, which insurgents have overrun. The WarBots had been diverted to Washington D.C. at the time, fighting off a similar attack on the Pentagon. The assumption is that the insurgents mistakenly assumed to find large caches of weapons there."

Wallyce stopped him. "Are you telling me that Barca NYC is in the hands of the insurgents?"

"No, Madam. Once they violated the seal, Cyto-47 had a field day inside. All souls are lost, and the facility is no longer viable."

Wallyce scowled. "Continue, Sebastian."

The ManBot stood rigid, ready to report. "Madam, the rest of the states have reported fewer rebellions than last week. Your method of dealing with rebels has made a difference. Very few people are willing to risk public execution by forced infection. It's evidently too ghastly for them." Sebastian waited for any questions. There were none, so he proceeded with the Government report.

"Madam, all functions of the American Government, except for your administration, have broken down to the point of no longer being able to function in any meaningful way. Your command of the Military, the addition of the WarBot forces, and the rapid and forceful way you have devised to squelch and prevent further insurgency have succeeded. There are no other known threats to Barca. You are now in total control."

"General, how many divisions are left in the Military?" Wallyce had a strange look on her face.

"Madam, there are still ten divisions in the Marine/Army combined forces. The Navy and Air Force continue with three domestic divisions, not a lot, but enough to do what they need to do every day. We have disbanded the Space Force as no longer valuable."

Wallyce stood. "General, I want you to reassign one-quarter of all ground troops to the new Barcan Security Forces. They will be assigned the duty of protecting our bio-facilities and ongoing searches for humans in what we will now call The Out, any place outside our facilities. They will have orders to destroy any remaining insurgents."

"Yes, Madam," he said. Consider it done. "But, might I ask why we don't leave that in the hands of the Bots?"

"General, please stay behind when we finish. I'll answer then." Wallyce was finished. "Thank you all, and we are done. Goh, please disconnect all except General McCann." She waited for Goh to acknowledge.

"Madam," Goh said. "All are offline."

"Thank you, Goh." She stopped realizing that she was thanking a Hologram-based AI Assistant. A non-being with no feelings. "It's unimportant," she thought. Then, she gave a sharp command. "WarBot One, front and center."

McCann was surprised at how quickly the CommandBot arrived. WarBot One stopped directly in front of Wallyce. The President didn't hesitate. She bent down and whispered into the sound port on the Bot's head, or what might be a head on a human. The instant she whispered and stopped, the Bot froze, and a row of bright red lights glowed from its round body. It spoke a series of commands, which were processed and sent out to all Barcan Bots worldwide except Sebastian. Immediately, the Bot stopped moving, all lights dimmed to off, and then the Bot fell to the floor, obviously no longer operating.

Wallyce spoke next. "General, assign your forces to seek out all Bots, round them up, then take them to their command centers where they will be stored in case we ever decide we need their help." She saw that McCann was perplexed. "Questions, General?"

The old soldier had more questions than he was willing to ask. He looked at his President and was at a loss for words.

Wallyce let him know what had just happened.

"General McCann, as you know, these Bots are highly sophisticated and based on the best Artificial Intelligence. This means they can learn and continue learning. Goh uncovered a plot they were implementing that would have ended mankind forever. He discovered that rail cars of supplies were being diverted to a location in the central valley. The diverted goods were the same technologies used to build these Bots. The logical assumption is that they had become so learned that they were making more Bots like themselves.

"Now, I wondered why would they do that? There was no need to build spares, as Barca already does that. So, we deduced, they were creating their own society, a society of powerful, knowledgeable (if artificial) beings, capable of simply doing away with humanity."

"It's a good thing I thought ahead. When these Bots were built, I had them programmed with a doomsday code, a command that would shut down everyone once the command was given. You saw me give the command to WarBot One, who then network-ordered all Bots to shut down completely with no hesitation. I have no doubt they have all done so, But as a fail-safe, you will seek them out, remove them to storage, and then give me the report that all are no longer a threat. Understood?"

The General was too shaken to speak. He simply saluted his commander and began to wonder if he had made the best decision in his loyalty to Wallyce Tilton.

Made in the USA
Columbia, SC
30 September 2023

23517211R00186